Books by Clara McKenna

MURDER AT MORRINGTON HALL

MURDER AT BLACKWATER BEND

MURDER AT KEYHAVEN CASTLE

MURDER AT THE MAJESTIC HOTEL

Published by Kensington Publishing Corp.

MURDER AT KEYHAVEN CASTLE

CLARA McKENNA

KENSINGTON
PUBLISHING CORP.

www.kensingtonbooks.com

KENSINGTON BOOKS are published by

Kensington Publishing Corp.
119 West 40th Street
New York, NY 10018

All Kensington titles, imprints, and distributed lines are available at special quantity discounts for bulk purchases for sales promotion, premiums, fundraising, educational, or institutional use.

Special book excerpts or customized printings can also be created to fit specific needs. For details, write or phone the office of the Kensington Sales Manager: Attn.: Sales Department. Kensington Publishing Corp., 119 West 40th Street, New York, NY 10018. Phone: 1-800-221-2647.

The K with book logo Reg US Pat. & TM Off.

First Kensington Hardcover Edition: July 2021

ISBN: 978-1-4967-1782-5 (ebook)

ISBN: 978-1-4967-3835-6

First Kensington Trade Paperback Edition: October 2022

10 9 8 7 6 5 4 3 2 1

Printed in the United States of America

To the man who married me twenty-five years ago

MURDER AT KEYHAVEN CASTLE

CHAPTER 1

~❧~

September 1905
Hampshire, England

Unable to bear the stench of bananas, horse dung, smoke, and salty air, Jesse James Prescott pulled the red bandanna up over his nose. He stretched his shoulder blades, sore from leaning so long against the clapboards, and shot a glare up at the bunches of yellow fruit dangling above his head. Nasty things. Made him choke the one time he'd tried one. What had he been thinking, suggesting Snook's as the rendezvous point? Sure, in the chaos and bustle of the ship's arrival, the fruit merchant nearest the wharf, with its flashy displays of exotic produce enveloping the entire storefront, was an eye-catching landmark no one could mistake. But the god-awful smell . . .

Jesse raised the flap of the bandanna and spit into the street. Wagons rumbled by, and Jesse barely missed the polished hoof of a nice-looking sorrel Belgian draft. He'd seen some fine horses since he'd been here, enough to make him think about staying. But that would complicate everything. Best stick to the plan.

Jesse stretched his back again as a wagon driver spurred his team safely across the path of a passing tram only to collide into a stack of weathered rum barrels. Jesse snorted in laughter.

"Excuse me, son, got a light?"

Jesse's head whipped around, his hand reaching for the thirty-eight tucked into his coat's inside pocket. The fella was a few feet away, on the curb. Jesse never saw him coming.

"Sorry, I didn't mean to startle ya," the bearded stranger said in an accent that made Jesse homesick. With a crooked grin, the middle-aged man raised his five-cent cigar. "Just needing a light."

Jesse eased his hand away from the hidden revolver, chuckling nervously. How could he have been so stupid? He could've given himself away.

"Sure, I got me some matches hereabouts."

He patted his pants pockets and retrieved the matchbox with a lion on it he'd picked up somewhere. As he handed it over, he noticed a boy of about ten, with dirty blond hair partly crossing one eye, tug the hand of a freckle-faced girl half his age through the crowd. The girl, her wide eyes darting from the stacks of cargo and luggage to her fellow passengers scattered along the wharf, stumbled along behind. The fella lit his cigar and took a couple of quick puffs, letting the smoke stream out from between his lips.

"Thank ya, cowboy." The fella's broad smile revealed a small chip in his front tooth. He dropped the canvas knapsack he'd had flung over his shoulder and handed Jesse back the matchbox. Jesse, who usually didn't mind being compared to his namesake, suddenly felt foolish and self-consciously yanked the bandanna off his face.

"It's the bananas, you know. The god-awful smell." Jesse pointed above their heads.

"Never seen so many in one place, that's for sure," the fella commented before shouting and waving to the children above the heads of passersby. "Over here!"

"You from the States?" Jesse asked.

"Kentucky. We just arrived. These here are my children." The children huddled around him. The man put his arm around the little girl, inspecting a smear on the worn, frilly yoke of the girl's dress, and then ruffled the boy's uncovered head. "Lost your cap again, Sammy?"

The boy glanced at his feet and muttered something. Jesse, embarrassed for the boy, whose tousled, unevenly cut hair probably hadn't been covered for days, scoured the sea of hats for the man he was waiting for.

"You sound like a Kentucky man too. Am I right?"

"I might've said so once," Jesse muttered, scratching an itch on the back of his neck. He wished these folks would move on. Feeling cornered, he stepped away from the wall.

"Now, now." Jesse cringed when the fella slapped him friendly-like on the sore muscle in his shoulder. "Once a Kentuckian, always a Kentuckian, I say."

Jesse didn't agree but said nothing. It wasn't that he couldn't give this fella a piece of his mind on the subject, but any argument on his part would only invite the stranger and his kids to stick around. And he needed to get rid of them and fast.

"Fixin' to catch a train?" Jesse said.

"Sure are, but seeing you're not from these parts, you probably can't tell me which one takes us closest to Morrington Hall, can you?"

Morrington Hall? A flash of anger exploded through Jesse's chest.

"I sure in hell can!" Jesse spit out the words and instinctively reached for his gun again. The stranger squinted sideways at him, smoothing down his long mustache.

Before the fella started asking questions, Jesse added, "Trains are over there," and pointed up the street toward the train depot. "You'll be wanting the Rosehurst station. The big mansion is just outside town."

"You know it? What luck," the fella said, squeezing his arm around his little girl.

"I know it all right," Jesse muttered, his anger seething beneath the surface.

Why'd the fella have to mention Morrington Hall? Couldn't he have just lit his cigar and moved on? Why'd the boss have to make me wait so long? The usual alarms rang in Jesse's head, warning him he was about to do something stupid. And as usual, he ignored them.

"Who knows. Might be seeing you there myself."

"You going to Stella's big wedding too?" the boy asked.

"No, boy. I don't care nothing about that wedding. I've got me a score to settle."

It slipped out before Jesse grasped what he'd said. Damn it all to tarnation. Why did he have to go and say that for?

Jesse stared at the fella's face, gauging his reaction, his hand drifting slowly toward his hidden revolver. The fella lifted an eyebrow, the straggly graying brown hairs on the ends curling around, almost poking the man in the eye. But instead of saying or doing something they'd both regret, the fella held out his hand.

"Well, thank ya, kindly," he said. Jesse, relieved to be rid of him, shook it.

The fella snatched his knapsack up from the ground and touched the brim of his hat. When he moved off, he shooed his children ahead of him. They dashed away. Jesse watched the fella go.

What else could he do, shoot the fella right here? *Now that would be really stupid.* He seemed like a smart fella. Maybe he'd keep his mouth shut. But would it make a difference if he didn't? No, sir. Jesse hadn't crossed an ocean just to get cold feet.

Brushing aside the encounter, Jesse reached over into the nearest fruit bin and, with the grocer's back turned, plucked out a crisp green apple. Propping himself against the wall with his foot, he crunched into the apple. *Now this here is a real fruit.* Jesse wiped the juice from his chin with the bandanna around his neck and turned his attention back to the steady stream of passengers spilling down the pier, hoping he didn't have to wait much longer.

Three more days.

Perched on a tapestry-covered footstool in the middle of the drawing room, Stella Kendrick could hardly believe it. She twisted one way and then another, examining herself in the free-standing full-length mirror. Miss Naplock sighed in frustration, attempting to pin the hem. The loose topknot on the seamstress's head bobbed as she worked.

"If you would stay still for one moment, miss."

But Stella couldn't help herself. Caught in the bright morning sun streaming through the French windows, the bursts of orange blossoms of pearl embellishing the bodice and train of her dress shimmered when she moved. The sweeping gown of white silk muslin overlaid with cascades of silky, delicate Chantilly lace caressed her figure like a glove. It was the most beautiful dress Stella had ever seen.

What a stark contrast to the man who spared no expense in acquiring it for her.

It wasn't that Stella wasn't grateful. She was, despite his lack of affection, his finding fault with all she did, his occasional burst of temper. Truly. He'd given her everything: this dress, a lovely home, a beloved horse, a vast fortune, and a secure future. He was her father, after all. She owed him her very existence. Yet as her wedding day approached, and with it a promise of a new start, Stella was counting the days her father went back to Kentucky.

Was it possible to love someone and still wish they would go away?

As if in answer, the door flew open, and the strong scent of his aftershave proceeded Stella's father before he stomped into the room. "Why aren't you upstairs getting ready?"

Startled, Miss Naplock shoved a pin through the hem, piercing Stella's ankle. Stella yelped at the sting and jerked her leg away. The seamstress, her cheeks red with embarrassment, muttered a horrified apology. With a dismissive wave, Stella reassured Miss Naplock and encouraged her to go back to what she was doing.

"Come on, girl. Don't want to be late," Daddy said. Stella still didn't know why she had to go with him. He could meet the boat without her or bring Aunt Rachel instead. "And what are you doing wearing the dress again? You might ruin it."

Stella instinctually glanced down. Miss Naplock had raised the silk muslin underskirt, examining it for bloodstains from the pinprick. Had they damaged it? After a brief pause, the seamstress released the underskirt and returned her attention to the hem. Stella blew out her pent-up breath.

"It's the final fitting," Stella explained, swishing her hips to show him the seamstress's handiwork. The light danced off every pearl. "When we're done, it will be perfect."

"For what it cost me, it darn well should've been perfect in the first place," he said, drifting toward the long, narrow oak table set up to receive wedding gifts.

With his back turned to them, Miss Naplock offered Stella a sympathetic frown. Conscious of the pins running down the length of her sleeves, Stella added an exaggerated eye roll to her modified shrug, to convey her meaning of, "See what I have to put up with?"

But she couldn't stay exasperated for long. How could she with such a gorgeous gown on? Besides, the gesture had made her chuckle. How often had Lady Atherly done the same? Usually aimed at her. Too many to count. At least Stella could laugh about it.

"What are you looking for, Daddy?" Stella asked, absorbed in watching the seamstress deftly pluck pin after pin from between her pinched lips and slip it into place.

"Tims said a new package had arrived," he said, picking up one box after another. "I want to know what it was and who sent it."

He sorted through all the presents, some still in their boxes, others set out for display. Stella could barely find a hint of the white damask tablecloth beneath them; there were so many spread out across the table. Like the pearls on her dress, the silver trays and tea sets, the porcelain dishes, the crystal bowls, the necklaces and earrings of diamonds and jewels, all sparkled like a dragon's treasure in the morning sunshine.

And like a hoarding dragon, her father hovered over it. The arrival of a new package was a highlight of his day. Either the gift was one of extravagance, like a jewel-encrusted tiara, which gave him cause to brag, or it was one of inconsequence, which gave him the excuse to deride the gift-giver to whoever would listen. Stella had stopped listening weeks ago. She'd also stopped looking forward to their arrival. The well-meaning presents brought out the worst in her father.

"Is this it?" He held up a long rectangular package that fit neatly in his hand. "It's addressed to you." That was unusual. Most were addressed in care of him.

His face lit up. "The return address is from a jeweler in London." Without further hesitation, he ripped off the brown packing paper and lifted the lid.

Miss Naplock, pins still poking out between her lips, held the dress's hem absentmindedly, her attention on Daddy and the package. What did the seamstress imagine was in the box: a string of pearls, an engraved silver cake knife, a diamond-encrusted pair of scissors? Stella had received one of each.

"No card inside," he grumbled, replacing the lid and chucking the gold-colored box onto the table. Its contents clattered when the box caught the edge and dropped upside down on the floor.

"What did you do that for?" Stella asked.

"If you ever think to give such a good-for-nothing wedding gift," he advised the wide-eyed seamstress, "you should have the decency to own up to it." He was annoyed. The anonymous sender had robbed him of the pleasure of poking fun at them.

"Who sends such a worthless trinket, anyway?" He didn't wait for an answer before adding, "Like I said, we leave on the hour. Go get ready."

The door closed behind him before Stella tried to hop off the stool. She had one stocking foot on the swirl of lacy train puddling on the carpet when Miss Naplock tugged at the hem.

"Please, miss. I'm not finished."

"Would you mind getting the box, then?"

The seamstress nodded, plucked the last two pins from her mouth, and tossed them into the shallow glass dish on the floor beside her. Crouching over, she picked the crushed box up off the floor.

"What is it?" Stella asked. "Is it broken?"

The woman lifted the bent painted cardboard lid. Even before she held it out toward Stella, a glitter of reflecting light hinted at its contents. Laying secured by two tiny pieces of wire against the green velvet cushion was a spoon. A souvenir spoon like the ones Stella had collected her whole life, the collection gathering dust back home in Kentucky. She had one from every place she'd visited and many from places she'd never seen. She had gold-plated ones, sterling silver ones, ones made from nickel, steel, and even wood. Some had portraits of famous people, like George Washington, in the bowl, others were carved into the shapes of plants or animals. She had several from two different World's Fairs. But by her bedside upstairs was the only spoon she had in her possession, the one she bought in a little shop near the Southampton port the day they arrived in England. The day she met Lyndy.

Stella's breath caught when Miss Naplock placed the box in her outreached hand.

This spoon was one of the finest she'd ever held. Surely her father should've recognized its monetary worth, even if he had no appreciation for the thoughtfulness behind the gift. But then again, compared to a tiara, it was a modest present. To Stella, it was priceless.

Its handle, of two interwoven vines, was topped by a carving of two connected hearts framing the likenesses of Queen Victoria and Prince Albert set on a bouquet of ribbons and flowers topped by a crown. Its meaning wasn't lost on Stella. Theirs was a great love story. The sender of this spoon wished the same for Stella and Lyndy. But who had sent it? Who knew of her fondness for souvenir spoons? Certainly, no one in England.

"Isn't it beautiful," Stella said.

Miss Naplock nodded, kneeling back down to finish her work. "I hope it wasn't damaged."

"Me too." Stella lifted the spoon (luckily, without a scratch on it) and its attached cushion from the box and found a piece of unadorned white stationery folded beneath it. The handwritten message inside read:

May this complete your collection. May you find love that completes you.

A quiver shot through Stella's shoulders and back, and she involuntarily shook. The seamstress peered up from her work. "Are you all right, miss?"

Stella nodded, cradling the spoon in her palm. The tender sentiment, such a rarity in Stella's life, brought a wistful smile to her lips. But there was no signature on the note. Like her father, though for different reasons, Stella felt robbed of the pleasure of knowing who gave her the spoon.

But then why send it?

CHAPTER 2

Viscount Lyndhurst, or "Lyndy," led the others confidently down the long aisle of the stables. All was as it should be. Every brass finial reflected the morning sunshine. The mahogany stalls had been freshly stained, not a stray piece of straw or clump of horse dung littered the recently scrubbed cobblestone floor. A half dozen horses whinnied and snorted in greeting when he passed. And soon, there would be more.

"This is Tully," Lyndy said, stopping in front of the horse's box stall.

The dappled gray mare approached the door and nudged Lyndy's hand with her muzzle, knowing what was hiding in his fist. She eagerly snapped off the end of the peppermint stick he held out to her. She was a sweet, magnificent creature, much like her owner. His thoughts straying to her owner, Lyndy scratched the white blaze on the animal's forehead.

In three days, Stella would finally be his. Three interminably long days.

After offering the last of the peppermint stick to Tully, Lyndy reached into his pocket for more peppermint and moved on to Tupper's stall. The sleek chestnut filly wasn't as friendly as her neighbor and had to be coaxed to approach. But what was that to him? The horse could demand an orchard of apples or her weight in peppermint candy for all he cared.

"Tupper, as you know, won the Princess of Wales's Stakes this year," Lyndy said, patting her soundly on the neck. "And placed in the St. Leger Stakes last week."

Such a welcomed triumph for the family, though the filly technically belonged to Stella's father until after the wedding. The Searlwyns hadn't had a champion since Grandpapa retired Augustine years ago. Lyndy hoped, with Tupper, they would do so again. Even Mother recognized the filly's potential. Had they owned Tupper already, their share of the purse would've allowed his mother to hire a proper second footman (giving Lyndy back his valet), and a live-in gardener (instead of relying on the unpredictable local man she had to suffer with). Lyndy already had plans to enter the filly in the Trial Stakes at Ascot next year.

"Yes, yes. These are all lovely, Lyndy, but where's the stallion?"

Lyndy glanced over his shoulder at his companions: Sir Alfred Goodkin, his round-faced, bespectacled old chum from Eton, and Sir Owen Rountree, Lyndy's younger, but much taller, cousin. They were but two of the cadre of his family's friends and relatives hovering about Morrington Hall in anticipation of the wedding. Some, like Owen, were guests up at the house, while others, like Alfred, lived close enough to pop around unannounced to join in the festivities. Lyndy had little use for most of the visitors, but these two, like him, were enthusiasts of the turf. And they were keen to see the champion thoroughbreds.

It was Owen's impatient voice that drew Lyndy's attention. Owen, having arrived too late last night for a trip to the stables, had insisted Lyndy show him Orson, the Kendricks' world-famous champion stud, right after breakfast. Owen had no patience with fillies and mares. Alfred, fortuitously having dropped by for a chat, decided to tag along.

"He's over here." Lyndy pointed across the aisle to the box stall marred by a gnawed and splintered wood casing. Gates, the stablemaster, still struggled to find an exercise regimen or a daily routine that would keep the ornery stallion from chewing on the door.

Owen stepped across the aisle and peered in. "He must be black as pitch." Owen shielded his eyes from the light streaming through the stable windows with his hands. "It's too dark in there. All I see is his outline."

The horse peered out from the darkness. Without warning, the stallion poked his head through the door's opening, seized the brim of Owen's fedora between his teeth, and flung it. The hat sailed down the aisle before dropping through the open doorway of an empty stall. Orson, peeling back his lips as if in laughter, nibbled at the door frame.

"Bloody hell." Owen touched the crown of his head where his hat once sat.

Alfred burst out laughing. Lyndy riffled his younger cousin's hair, remarking on its similarity in color to Tupper's coat, before motioning for the stable boy to fetch Owen's hat.

"I say. That stallion better be first-rate, for he's as irascible as his reputation says." Owen brushed the front of his tweed jacket. When the boy offered Owen back his fedora, Owen waved it away, laughing. "Be a good lad and burn it." Shimmering with horse saliva, it smelled foul.

Lyndy had forgotten what a good sport Owen could be. Before he'd been sent off to Eton, Lyndy had relished the carefree weeks spent every summer at Hubberholme Park, Owen's family estate in Yorkshire. Free of all restraints, the pair would venture out into the countryside, fencing with sticks atop stone walls, fishing ankle-deep in the clear bracing streams, racing their ponies across the moors. And when inevitably Owen would trip on a raised root or stumble on a stone allowing Lyndy to win a foot race, Owen would laugh it off and be ready to race again.

"Oh, he's first-rate, all right," Lyndy said. "Perhaps the most valuable stud in the country."

"That's what I heard said about Challacombe when he won at Doncaster," Owen said.

Bam! The feisty stallion slammed his hoof against the door in a kick, sending all three men scuttling to a safe distance.

"I think he disagrees," Alfred chuckled as Leonard, the head groom, came running to calm the stallion down.

"As do I," Lyndy said. "May I remind you Orson won half of all his starts, still holds the American record for seven furlongs and has already produced a Derby winner?"

"Hear, hear!" Alfred cheered in appreciation. "Besides, Baron Branson-Hill isn't known for breeding his horses, now is he? Challacombe might languish from too many oats before he ever covers a mare."

"Baron Branson-Hill?" Owen asked when the men retreated toward the stable yard. "Did Singer sell him Challacombe?"

"Supposedly, the baron purchased the stallion yesterday, or the day before. Not long."

"How did we not hear of this?" Lyndy said.

"What I can't fathom is why?" Owen asked. "Singer seemed too enamored with his winner to sell so quickly."

Alfred shrugged. "I hadn't heard a hint of it either, until this morning. Lady Atherly was discussing it with someone while I waited for you two."

His mother, talking about a racehorse? Lyndy wished he'd witnessed such an extraordinary conversation. Clearly, staying out of Mother's way came with a downside. What could she possibly be up to now?

"Seems the baron plans to bring Challacombe to Morrington tonight," Alfred was saying.

Owen scrunched his nose. "From the Island? Whatever for? I'd be willing to hop the ferry to see that horse."

Alfred stopped to pet the stray pup that had turned up in the stable yard one day a few weeks ago, brown, scruffy, and friendly. Gates had made the case it was a good watchdog. No one had dissuaded him from keeping the new mongrel; after the events of last May, the stables required a canine sentinel. Secretly Lyndy was delighted. Once Grandpapa's hounds had died, neither Mother nor Papa saw the need to keep a pet.

"Something about a dinner party?" Alfred said, rubbing behind the dog's ears.

"Mother's planned one for tonight to introduce Stella to Owen and a few others who've yet to have the pleasure," Lyndy said, encouraging Mack, as the dog had come to be called, to jump up and put his feet on Lyndy's chest.

Lyndy had been eagerly anticipating dinner. He hadn't seen Stella in two days. To get to size up Challacombe up close was an unexpected treat. But why was the baron bringing the champion stallion around? Mother couldn't have suggested it. Whom had she been talking to? Before he could ask, Leonard approached to receive his instructions.

"I'll ride Beau," Lyndy told the groom when the dog shoved off his chest and bounded over to greet Leonard. "Sir Alfred will ride his horse, but I believe Sir Owen would like to take Tupper out." Owen nodded enthusiastically. "And he will need something for his head."

When the groom strode off to prepare the horses, Mack dutifully following, Owen said, "Well, I certainly hope your filly treats me with more respect than your stallion did, old chap."

Lyndy laughed. "I can assure you Tupper is much more amiable."

Owen shook his head. "I wasn't talking about that filly. I was talking about this American you've foolishly gotten yourself attached to."

Lyndy frowned. "If you're speaking of Miss Kendrick, I am indeed attached to her, and you would do well to remember that."

"No need to be cross," Owen chuckled, noting he'd touched a nerve. "At least, from what I've heard, she's easy on the eyes and comes with the much-needed infusion of cash."

"Yes," Lyndy said, tight-lipped. He didn't appreciate Owen bringing the topic up. His family's financial difficulties were the reason Stella and he were marrying in the first place. It was only by providence Lyndy found in her his perfect mate. "There is that."

"Miss Kendrick is far more than an attractive heiress," Alfred said, unexpectedly coming to Stella's defense. "She's quite charming, nothing like Lady Philippa. Not to mention an excellent horsewoman." Lyndy winced at Alfred's comparison to Philippa, having hoped never to hear that woman's name again, but sensed his friend's good-natured appreciation for his bride-to-be. And if he were trying to win Owen's good opinion, Lyndy couldn't have found better words. Owen couldn't resist admiring a good horsewoman.

"Beautiful yet nothing like Lady Philippa and a good horsewoman?" Owen teased. "Maybe I'll try to woo her away from you, old chap. If she's sensible, she'll prefer a good-natured Yorkshire squire than the dour viscount she's been shackled to. Is it true she's from the wilds of the American West?"

"Kentucky, actually. It is not the lawless, wild place you imagine."

Lyndy had pictured Stella's home as Owen did before he'd

heard the Kendricks describe the manicured ranches, the elegant racetracks, the cultured high societies of Lexington and Louisville. He planned to attend the Kentucky Derby one day. "You won't find gunslingers or unruly cowboys there."

"Doesn't mean she won't be a bit wild and unruly on her wedding night," Owen said, winking at Alfred.

"Ahem." Alfred coughed nervously in surprise, which sent his spectacles sliding down the bridge of his nose.

"Don't say you've never thought of it," Owen said.

Alfred, still sputtering his denial, took his spectacles off, pulled a handkerchief from his breast pocket, and proceeded to wipe them clean.

"I'm certain the bridegroom has," Owen said. "Eh, Lyndy?"

Lyndy tugged on the lapels of his riding coat. What did Owen expect him to say? He'd be a fool to deny he hadn't imagined his wedding night. He'd caressed the silky strands of Stella's hair, felt the curves of her body against him, tasted the sweetness of her lips, shivered at her breath in his ear, hadn't he? But that was between him and her, not a topic of casual conversation in the stable yard.

"You will refrain from speaking of my future wife in any manner less than is befitting the future Countess of Atherly and the future mother of my children. Else I will have to pummel you with my fists."

Owen laughed, lifting his fists to his face. He danced playfully back and forth on the balls of his feet before jabbing Lyndy lightly in the ribs. Lyndy didn't crack a smile.

"Oh," Owen said, halting in place, his arms still held up before him. "You weren't joking." Lyndy shook his head. "Heaven help us. My rakish cousin, who once considered courting a sport, is besotted." Owen winked at Alfred. "After Lady Philippa, who could've dreamed Lord Lyndhurst would lose his head again?"

"Oh, I think he's lost his heart to this one as well, Sir Owen," Alfred said, happily adding to the jest as he resettled his spectacles on his face.

Lyndy clenched his jaw. It was true. He had wantonly pursued many women, like foxes during a hunt, careless of their hearts. He blamed Philippa. After her rejection, he'd sworn never to be vulnerable to a woman's whims again. Yet here he was.

All three turned at the *clip-clop* of horse hooves on the cobblestones.

"Shall we?" Lyndy said. The other two heartily agreed as their chosen rides approached.

As the groom held Beau's reins, Lyndy slipped his Irish Hunter a piece of peppermint and then checked that the girth and billet straps weren't too tight.

With Lyndy's horse between them, Owen lowered his voice and, without a hint of jest, said, "I do hope this one's as worthy as you say, Alfred. I'm not certain what he'll do if she proves otherwise."

"That's not what worries me," Alfred whispered back. "It's what will happen if this wedding doesn't come off."

"Why wouldn't it?"

"Because it's happened before."

"But wasn't that because a man was murdered?"

"True, but, Owen, you haven't met all the players yet. After you've met old man Kendrick, then tell me you're not worried."

Lyndy hoisted himself into the saddle, which afforded a better view of the two men gossiping across Tupper's back like washing women at a clothesline.

"I'm not worried," Lyndy said, "and neither should you be." The two men had the decency to avert their eyes in shame at being caught out. "Now, shall we ride?"

"You're absolutely correct, old chap," Owen said, swinging up onto Tupper's back. He shot a worried glance at Alfred before forcing a smile on his face. "The wedding's in three days. What could happen between now and then to stop you from wedded bliss?"

CHAPTER 3

⁓

The wharf was a sea of people. Passengers poured down gangways, hurrying to set their feet on land after their long journey. Porters pushed carts of stacked suitcases and trunks before them, parting the crowd as they went. Dockworkers stabbed bales, barrels, and sacks with large wooden-handled hooks as they unloaded the cargo. Spectators, come to share in the excitement, gawked and waved to strangers on board a departing ocean liner when a tug, its steam and smoke billowing into the bright sky, pushed it back. Above them all, the large chimney stacks of the ocean liners cast their shadows. Stella's carriage, braving the chaotic throng, made slow progress down the longest pier. But Stella was glad she'd come.

"Look, Daddy."

Stella pointed out the window when a dun-colored Quarter Horse, blindfolded and dangling from a sling, was hoisted through the air and into the hold of a nearby ship. She'd heard of horses transported this way, and the danger associated with it. When they'd brought Tully, Tupper, and Orson to England, her father had paid whatever it took to have them secured safely in a custom-built padded box on deck, large enough for the horses to walk around. When they'd docked, the thoroughbreds had disembarked down the third-class passenger gangway.

"Barbarians," Daddy said. "They'll be lucky if the horse survives the trip." He craned his neck, searching the crowd. "Do you see the Swensons?"

It didn't surprise Stella that her father, who hadn't invited his brother to the wedding, had insisted the Swensons be on the guest list. The Swensons were old family friends from Kentucky. Mr. Swenson, Theo, was both her father's rival as a racehorse breeder and his closest friend. The two families' horse farms were less than a few miles apart. But the Swensons weren't fond enough of Stella to cross the ocean to attend her wedding. And yet they'd agreed to come.

Unfortunately.

"I don't know how you expect to find one face out of all—" Stella paused midsentence when a woman in a bright red straw hat passed by Stella's window. Hers was a face Stella recognized, one she never thought she'd see again.

"Mama?"

Stella unlatched the door and shoved it open. But when she prepared to jump out, she was yanked backward by a firm grip on her traveling coat collar. Her head snapped forward, the brim of her hat bending against the door frame when the force of her father's tug propelled her back into the carriage seat. He reached across her and drew the door shut as a wagon, laden with piles of bags labeled "Royal Mail," rumbled past.

"What do you think you're doing?" Daddy growled. "You could've been trampled."

He was right. What was Stella thinking? So focused on the woman with an uncanny resemblance to Katherine Kendrick, she hadn't noticed the oncoming mail wagon. Would she ever stop seeing her mother?

Stella's hands trembled from the close encounter, and yet she followed the strange woman's progress until her red hat was swallowed up by the crowd. It was a trick of the eye, Stella reminded herself, a wishful thought. Stella's mother was dead.

Her mother had died of influenza visiting friends out West. Hoping to spare her, Stella's father attended the funeral without her. For years after, Stella spotted her mother everywhere. But when Stella confronted her mother's double, it would only be in the curve of the jaw, the stance of the shoulders, or the shape of her nose in profile that had reminded the girl of her much-missed parent. This woman was no different. From the moment Stella had decided to marry Lyndy, she'd lamented the absence of her mother. Mama would never meet Lyndy, would never see Stella in her gorgeous gown, would never cry with pride when Stella became a wife.

"There they are!" Daddy announced, pounding on the roof to tell the coachman to stop. "I can't wait to see the expression on 'ole Theo's face when he spots us getting out of a carriage that once belonged to Queen Victoria. And you practically that royal's kin."

Stella sighed. So that's why he wanted to meet the Swensons in Southampton. He wanted to show off the carriage he'd bought on impulse last month and its passenger, the soon-to-be Viscountess Lyndhurst.

"And how about that? They've brought their darling daughter with them," he added. "That should make you happy."

Stella leaned forward, searching where her father pointed until she'd spotted Penny Swenson, one of Stella's few childhood companions. Penny, crinkling her upturned nose in distaste, raised a lavender nosegay to her face to ward off the warring scents of smoke, horse dung, tar, and wet wood. She lifted the hem of her skirt as she skittered around a cluster of men, their caps worn, their shirtsleeves rolled up as they hauled and stacked cargo. Once past the workers, Penny smoothed the thick auburn curls softly swirling around her forehead.

Stella sank back into the padded wall of the carriage and blew at the wisp of hair framing her forehead. *Darling Penny Swenson.* Now there was a wedding guest Stella could do without.

So many easy pickings. The man skirted a stack of wooden crates, fiddling the contents of his deep, bulging pockets. A coat two sizes too big had its uses. His fingers flipped through and caressed leather wallets, watch fobs, a small gold watch, three pocketknives, a silver cigar case, and a gold-filigree fountain pen. He hadn't done this well since the World's Fair. He chuckled. *Heaven bless the ruckus.* With the distracting crush of passengers, porters, wagons, and horses, he could dip into pockets and bags, freeing unsuspecting marks of their valuables, as easy as collecting eggs in a henhouse.

He ducked into the darkened doorway of a nondescript warehouse, crushed the nub of his cigar under his toe, and, dropping his sack, squatted down to one knee as if in need of retying his bootlaces. Instead, he unwound the string cinching the mouth of his bag. Alert and focused, he deftly emptied his pockets. In the span of five heartbeats, the pocketknives, the wallets, and watch fobs disappeared into the folds of laundry in his bag. With one quick downward glance to assure the sack blocked any view of his leg, he shimmed his trouser leg up over a gun, a pearl-handled thirty-eight revolver, shoved into the top of his woolen stocking. A shiny bit of the nickel-plated barrel shone through a frayed hole. He waited until a passing team of horses shielded him from view before slipping it out.

His heart raced at his luck. Just the touch of the cold metal of the thirty-eight in his hand made him feel like a gunslinger. He had his share of shotguns back home, come by honestly, for the most part. But this was a first. He'd never lifted a gun off a mark before. His target had figured himself somewhat of a cowboy, bandanna around his neck and all, but who knew, here on the Southampton wharf, the fella would be packing a valuable revolver?

They say God will provide.

Until now, he hadn't believed it. But here now was this revolver, its handle glowing in the sun like the pearly gates themselves. But he wasn't pawning this, no siree, Bob! Money was nothing compared with how this beauty was going to get him his due.

He ran his hand down the revolver's barrel before setting it reverently into his sack and securing the ties. He straightened up, swung the bag over his shoulder, and eased back into the passing traffic, whistling "Hello! Ma Baby." He'd been swindled out of what was rightfully his and had come over, thinking it was high time he did something about it. It had been a long shot. But he sensed the odds just shifted in his favor. His bet just might pay off.

"Theo, over here!" Stella's father leaned out of the window, waving his arm frantically.

Mrs. Sarah Swenson, a blue feathery hat perched high on her head, spied them first. She placed her hand on her husband's arm and directed his attention toward the Kendricks' carriage. Set into a chiseled face accentuated by a neatly trimmed beard, Theo Swenson's eyes widened in alarm.

Stella stuck her head out the carriage window, curious. Surrounding the carriage and beyond were men with sacks strung across their backs, ladies in traveling suits stepping into coaches, awestruck children clutching their mother's hands. Nothing worthy of rattling a man like Mr. Theo Swenson.

Stella returned her attention to the couple. Both Mr. and Mrs. Swenson were waving and smiling as the family approached. Unlike his wife, whose etched forehead gave her a maternal air, the crinkling wrinkles Mr. Swenson bore gave him an impish, ageless charm. Had Stella imagined his distress? She certainly wasn't imagining the condescension on Penny's face as she and Mr. Swenson laced arms. With deep dimples defining her pouting lips, and curves tightly defined by her tan and black traveling suit, Penny hadn't changed a bit.

"You made it," Daddy said, bounding from the carriage like a man half his age. Stella reluctantly followed. "How was the journey? My, you're pretty as ever, Sarah."

"Why, thank you, Elijah." Mrs. Swenson tilted her head, offering him her upturned cheek. With hat in hand, he obliged her with a peck. "The food was tolerable, and the sailing was as smooth as we could ask for."

"And you, Theo," Daddy said, shoving out his hand. "Aren't you a sight for sore eyes."

"We sure are glad to be here," Mr. Swenson said, enthusiastically returning his handshake. "But there was no need for y'all to meet us. We expected to take the train."

"Anyone can take the train. I wanted you to ride in style." Daddy stepped back and, with outstretched arms, gestured toward the carriage. "Not every day you get to ride in a coach once owned by Queen Victoria."

Although the body of the carriage had been repainted, Stella's father had insisted he could still detect the outline of the royal crest on the door. Either way, it was a stately landau with bright red wheels that would seat all five of them comfortably. He'd had to buy two gray Irish Draught horses to pull it.

"Oh, my, Elijah," Mrs. Swenson twittered in appreciation, tapping her fingertips together. "I don't know what to say. May we ride with the top down?"

Daddy rubbed his hands together, pleased with her reaction. "Of course." He gestured to the coachman to fold back the top.

"I want one of these," Penny cooed, lovingly stroking the carriage's gold lacquered curves.

"We have to find you one of those noble husbands first, Penelope, darling," Mr. Swenson joked.

Now it all made sense. The Swenson family weren't here to oblige Stella's father or to help her celebrate the joyous occasion. With Stella able to make the necessary introductions at the wedding, they were hoping to find an aristocrat to marry Penny.

Good luck!

Though Penny's inheritance was almost as much as Stella's, Penny's disposition would be the stumbling block. Stella pitied the unsuspecting nobleman Penny set her sights on.

"Which reminds me," Mr. Swenson added. "I've been so rude. Congratulations, Stella, darling, on your upcoming nuptials."

"Thank you, Mr. Swenson."

"Yes, indeed," his wife echoed. "And my, how you have changed. For a poor motherless child, Stella, you're so . . ."

"Freckled and scrawny?" Penny offered.

Leave it to Penny to say something so ridiculous. No one gets freckles under a cloudy, rainy English sky. But Penny had picked on Stella since they were children, even if it meant pulling insults from thin air.

"I was going to say radiant and sophisticated," Mrs. Swenson said, plucking a thread from around one of Penny's jacket buttons. "You should take note, Penny." Penny glowered at Stella. "It seems this new life agrees with our little Stella."

"Thank you," Stella said, out of politeness.

Despite Mrs. Swenson's perceptiveness that Stella was flourishing here, Stella didn't care much for the lady's comments. When they were children, Penny's mother had a way of using compliments to compare the two girls, with Penny always coming up short. If left unprovoked, Penny could be friendly and generous. But one "compliment" from Mrs. Swenson to Stella and Penny would vent her frustrations by teasing Stella or pulling her hair. Luckily, Mrs. Swenson was rarely around. Desperate for a friend her age after her mother died, Stella had endured the occasional taunts, until Penny, particularly out-raged one day at Mrs. Swenson's fawning over the "poor mother-less girl," threw rocks at Stella. Stella had barely managed to be civil to either of them ever since.

"When are we going to meet this viscount of yours?" Penny sneered.

"Excellent question, Penny," Daddy said, jabbing his finger into the air. "And the answer is tonight! I've arranged for us to all dine at Morrington Hall. What do you think of that!"

"I don't know, Elijah. We've just stepped off the boat. I don't think . . ." Mr. Swenson, stroking his beard, surveyed the crowd. "Where are those trunks, anyway?"

"Watch out, Theo!" Mrs. Swenson warned just as a small black and white dog with a studded collar darted between Mr. Swenson's legs and across Stella's father's feet, leaving muddy paw prints on his boots.

It bolted down the pier toward town. A harried footman, spouting apologizes as he dashed past, scurried after the loose pet. Stella followed the escapee and his would-be captor's progress, curious how far the dog would get. She turned her at-tention back to their guests at the sound of Mr. Swenson's sigh.

"I'm sorry, Elijah. I don't think any of us are up to a formal dinner engagement."

"Speak for yourself, Dad." Penny, using her handbag's hid-den beveled mirror, dabbed stray red lip rouge from the corners of her mouth with a handkerchief. "I'm dying to have a proper meal that doesn't involve a view of the endless ocean."

"Especially if it is of a table teeming with eligible aristocratic bachelors," Mrs. Swenson added, without a hint of sarcasm.

"But we still have to collect our bags, travel to Rosehurst, rest up, unpack. . . ." Mr. Swenson complained, craning his neck to see around a group of black-haired women wearing loose, billowy skirts and colorful scarfs draped around their necks. Stella had met a few women like them once while riding on the Forest. They'd been cooking over a campfire next to a colorful patchwork tent.

"I won't take no for an answer," Daddy said, "since I've also arranged a surprise for you." A surprise? Stella's stomach fluttered. What was he up to? "Since you couldn't make it for the St. Leger Stakes . . . I still don't understand why you didn't come."

"Neither do I, Elijah," Mrs. Swenson pouted, mimicking her daughter. "I so wanted to, but Theo insisted he had business to attend to."

"It was unavoidable, darling," Mr. Swenson said, still preoccupied with finding his luggage in the crowd. "I've already explained it to you."

"And I still don't understand," Mrs. Swenson said, seizing on what must have been a point of contention. "Why couldn't we have come sooner? What difference does a few days make when we could've attended the oldest of England's classic races?"

"Not to mention the countless men I would've met," Penny lamented.

Penny was right. St. Leger's was one of the highlights of the Season. As Lady Atherly would say, everyone who was anyone was there. For Stella, it had been a riveting event, and her first trek into the rolling, stone-fence-covered hills of Yorkshire. She'd enjoyed every minute.

"You should've been there, Mr. Swenson," Stella said. "Tupper was magnificent."

Mr. Swenson abandoned his searching to focus on Stella. "Did you say Tupper won? I thought—"

"No, Challacombe won. I was talking about—"

"You remember my filly Tupper, don't you, Theo?" Daddy interrupted. "Did you ever think she'd place?"

Mr. Swenson smiled warmly. "Of course. I remember Tupper. And you're right, Stella, darling. I do wish I could've been there." He returned to searching the crowd. "Now, if I could spot that porter who took off with our trunks."

"Speaking of the race," Daddy said, "that's my surprise. The winner, Challacombe, will be at Morrington Hall for your inspection after dinner tonight."

"Hold on. What?" Mr. Swenson said incredulously, whipping his head around as if expecting the horse to emerge from the crowd.

"Incredible, isn't it? I have so many connections over here, now that my name is attached to that of the local earl. You'll see. Marry Penny to one of these impoverished lords, and the world is your oyster, Theo. Mrs. Astor be damned!" Daddy laughed.

Penny, who had been silently admiring her reflection, snapped her handbag shut, unamused. Penny was more than willing to trade her inheritance for a title. What was it Stella's father said that made it less appealing?

"That may be, Elijah, but Challacombe?" Mrs. Swenson said. "How did you manage it?"

"There's a local buffoon who collects horses like souvenir spoons and is close friends of the earl. He purchased the stallion, and I've convinced him to bring the champion racehorse around to Morrington Hall tonight."

Her father's mention of souvenir spoons aside, Stella was unnerved that Baron Branson-Hill, the "horse collector" her father referred to, was carting Challacombe over from the Isle of Wight. A rough crossing on the ferry could spell disaster.

"What do you say, Theo?" Daddy said. "Aren't my temptations worth leaving your napping and unpacking until tomorrow?"

Mr. Swenson stroked his beard but said nothing.

"If the racehorse isn't enough to convince you, Theo, do it

for Penny's sake," Mrs. Swenson said. "Elijah has gone out of his way to accommodate and amuse us."

"Please, Dad." Penny laid her hand on her father's arm, pouting, and batted her lashes at him. Stella knew that plea well. Penny had employed it effectively their whole lives.

Mr. Swenson patted his daughter's hand. "Of course we'll go, Penelope, darling. How can I say no? But first, I have to go see where those trunks are."

CHAPTER 4

Jesse tossed the apple core onto the street and watched it land in the path of a chestnut Morgan lashed to a nearby post. The horse plucked it up, dirt and all.

What in the Sam Hill is taking the boss so long?

Jesse continued combing the faces of the passersby, panic building in the pit of his stomach. What would he do if the boss didn't show up? How would Jesse get paid? What if the boss planned to cheat him, or worse, turn him in? No, sir. Jesse wasn't going to let that happen again. *Besides, a gun's got more than one bullet.* As Jesse's hand strayed toward his hidden revolver, he spotted a face in the crowd and froze, midmotion.

Well, I'll be a son of a bucktoothed goat. Who knew that bastard would be here?

The scoundrel, sporting a spiffy suit with a gold watch chain dangling from his pocket, leaned against a carriage like the fanciest Wells Fargo stagecoach Jesse had ever seen. Jesse self-consciously noticed the muck on his boots and stomped his feet to loosen the dried manure; he agitated a fat black fly instead. It buzzed about his head and face before settling on the top button of Jesse's dusty, rumpled jacket. Jesse swatted at it, with the impatience of a man incensed by having to do it at all. Easily avoiding Jesse's hand, it flew toward the bunch of bananas dangling above Jesse's head. Jesse, curling his lip, brushed off other nonexistent offenders.

It wasn't fair.

How come the scoundrel, who couldn't keep his mouth shut, had everything, and Jesse, who'd done what he'd been told, had nothing? Well, Jesse did have one thing that bastard didn't, and it was going to shut him up for good.

The thrill of revenge ran hot in his blood. Pins and needles tingled his arms, face, and feet just thinking about what he was about to do.

In one concentrated motion, Jesse kicked off away from the wall, stepped off the curb, and reached for his gun. When his boot squished into a pile of fresh horse dung, he stopped in his tracks. It wasn't there. His revolver wasn't there.

He desperately patted the length of his jacket, thinking the gun might've slipped. He checked his vest pockets, his pants pockets. Nothing. He whirled around, searching the sidewalk, the doorway, the wheel-treads crisscrossing the hard-packed gravel road. A man stepped out of the fruit market and into his path, and Jesse shoved him aside.

"Oi! What's the big idea?" the grocer complained when Jesse rummaged frantically through the fruit stand nearest to where he'd waited, apples, oranges, and pears dropping onto the dirty pavement. Jesse kicked one out of his way. He threw another at the grocer when the man approached to intervene.

Where is it? Where could it be?

"Police! Police!" the grocer yelled; his shrill voice like a screech owl rang in Jesse's ears.

Jesse clumsily swung at the grocer to shut him up and caught a glimpse of the rich scoundrel and his party moving away, disappearing into the crowd. Jesse couldn't lose his chance. He didn't have a weapon, but his hands, despite his small stature, were big and strong. If Jesse had to, he could choke the bastard to death, and search for his gun after.

Jesse shoved his way across the street, knocking into a lady carrying a straw basket, dodging several horse and buggies, and tripping over an apple that had rolled onto the road. Whistles blared, and a hand grabbed him, slowing his progress. He whirled around, blinded by rage, and the futility that finally caught up with him, and punched the face belonging to the hand. Only after blood started streaming from the man's hawkish nose did Jesse notice the man's brass buttons and the distinctive domed cap. *Dang it!*

Struggling against the policeman's hold, Jesse hollered, "I'm gonna kill the bastard!"

Perhaps it was the pain of the policeman's broken nose or the shock of Jesse's words that got to him, but either way, the policeman's hold slipped. At that moment, Jesse yanked free, dodged the policeman's attempts to reapprehend him, and ran headfirst into the scattering crowd.

"Now, Elijah, tell me more about—" Shouts, muffled curses, and a policeman's whistle cut Mrs. Swenson off midsentence. "What's going on?"

The source of the commotion, shielded from Stella's view by an increasingly growing knot of onlookers, was centered near the front of a colorful fruit market. Below the market's dangling banana bunches were an ocean of hats. When the distinctive hard dome of a policeman's helmet waded through the expansive gathering, Stella speculated about what had happened. Had someone tried to rob the fruit market? Had the pickpockets she'd heard frequent busy ports struck an unsuspecting passenger? Had someone been injured? Had they captured a stowaway?

"Whatever it is, it doesn't sound good," Penny said when the shouting continued.

"Don't worry," Stella's father assured them. "They make a lot of fuss about nothing over here."

Stella wasn't so sure. With multiple police whistles now blaring, she hoisted up the hem of her skirt and took a step forward.

"Where do you think you're going?" her father asked.

"To find out what the ruckus is all about."

"Remember, a future viscountess doesn't rush toward trouble."

"But—"

Her father gripped the stiff fabric of her jacket sleeve and tugged her closer. Ensuring the Swensons' attention was still captivated by the disturbance near the fruit stand, he leaned in and lowered his voice. "You will not embarrass me in front of my friends."

Stella bristled at his insinuation and jerked her arm away.

He should talk. He'd embarrassed everyone at the engagement party. But saying so wouldn't do Stella any good. She held her tongue.

"I think I'll go see what's going on," Mr. Swenson said, stepping forward.

Stella willed her face not to betray her satisfaction. Had Mr. Swenson overheard the confrontation between father and daughter? Or was his comment a coincidence? Not being able to catch his eye, Stella couldn't tell. Either way, she'd been vindicated; she wasn't the only one bursting with curiosity.

"Don't, Theo," Mrs. Swenson said, laying her hand on his sleeve. "You'll only be getting in the way."

"Nonsense. I have to go check on the luggage anyway." Without a backward glance, Mr. Swenson joined those still making their way down the wharf.

Mrs. Swenson pinched her lips in disapproval, deepening the creases around her mouth and sagging chin line. Stella always thought of her as youthful. When had she aged so much?

"See, it's already dying down," Daddy said when the whistles quieted. "I say we meet Theo with the carriage. I'll have my coachman wait for your luggage."

"Excellent idea, Elijah. Thank you."

Mrs. Swenson, offering Stella's father her hand for his assistance, stepped lightly into the carriage, followed by Penny, who forcefully shouldered her way in front of Stella to enter the carriage next. When she was a child, Stella would've been miffed at Penny's behavior. Now Stella was untouched by whatever petty advantages the other woman sought. Besides, Stella didn't want to get into the carriage at all. She squinted in the direction of the fruit stand, straining to spy Mr. Swenson in the crowd that was already thinning out. Mr. Swenson wasn't there, but a disgruntled policeman was, shouting curses as he held a handkerchief to his nose and waving onlookers to move on.

"Get in the carriage." Daddy's stern order startled Stella, and she clambered in.

He banged on the carriage door to spur the coachman on, but they made little headway. Joining the hansom cabs, buckboard wagons, and passenger coaches squeezed together on the pier, they inched along in their effort to reach the broader city streets. Pedestrian stragglers outpaced them—it was exasperating! Stella wanted to leap over the side. But remembering her earlier lucky escape, she stayed put. To avoid Penny's smug stare, she commiserated with a New Forest pony pulling a dogcart a few yards behind them; neither of them was as free to roam as they'd like.

"What the hell?"

Her father's curse alerted Stella to the hard, frantic rumbling of hoofbeats as a team of horses tore into the crowded street. Screams followed. Men and women, dropping suitcases and snatching up wailing children, scrambled out of the path of the runaway wagon. Still trapped on the pier, Stella's father's carriage was well out of harm's way, but Stella witnessed everything. One abandoned travel trunk, with destination labels from Shanghai, Paris, and New York, lay where it had dropped in the middle of the road. A policeman again blared his whistle. The driver of the wagon, his feet pressed against the footboard, shouted for the team to stop. He tugged back on the reins with all his strength, but to no avail. Barreling into the trunk, the driver barely managed to keep his seat. The team careened forward, leaving the travel chest crushed and forgotten behind it.

"Watch out!"

Stella bolted to her feet and shouted when a hansom cab, unaware of the approaching danger, rounded the corner. With others adding to her warning, they alerted the cab driver to the impending danger. He yanked on the reins, steering his horse to the side, hoping to avoid a collision. And it worked. The runaway horses of the wagon veered away. Then suddenly, a man stumbled into their path.

"Get out of the way!" Stella screamed.

The man never had a chance.

Within seconds, the frightened horses enveloped him, the wooden bar between them smashing the man in the chest. A spray of bright red blood spurted from the man's mouth and clung to the sweaty froth on the horses' shoulders. Struggling to breathe, he flailed his arms, grasping, clutching for any part of the wagon or harness, as the force of the horses' speed lifted him off the ground. Unable to catch hold, his head snapped back, a red bandanna around his neck evoking a bloody gash. In the next instant, his body was swept beneath the hooves of the horses. Shrieks punctuated the horror of it.

"Dear God!" someone gasped when the cab, having rattled over the man's trampled body, tipped and crashed, hurtling the driver into the street. He lay crumpled and unmoving while his wagon, smashed into shards from bouncing behind the bolting horses, lay scattered across a field of debris dozens of yards long. Spent from their exertions, the runaway horses finally halted when they reached the walls of the train depot at the far end of the street. It took less than a minute, and among the ruins of the wagon lie two broken bodies.

"Let's go!" Stella's father called to their coachman.

"But—" Stella began, her hand on the door handle, enthralled by the wreckage. "Shouldn't we offer to help?"

"We need to meet up with Theo," Mrs. Swenson said, nervously searching the crowd.

"Besides, this doesn't have anything to do with us," Daddy said when their carriage jerked forward, sending Stella backward into her seat. "And for once, you're going to have to mind your own business."

CHAPTER 5

~⚡~

Lyndy glanced up from his racing paper at the sound of Mother's scissors. *Snip. Snip. Snip.* Green tips littered the table-top as she clipped the stems of her Michaelmas daisies. Why must she insist on doing this while he was there? Wasn't it enough she'd sent Owen and Alfred out into the garden to collect dahlias? Must she disturb the only peace he'd hope to find until tonight? Lyndy tossed the paper to one side in defeat. He'd admired the zeal with which Mother had taken up the mantel of flower arranging when their situation demanded economy; she was surprisingly good at it. Every room burst with the fragrance and color of her bouquets. But given her proclivity for doing it in his presence, Mother wouldn't be the only one gladdened to hire a proper gardener again.

"Now that we're alone, there is a matter I've been meaning to speak to you about," she said, eyeing the arrangement carefully before sticking the lavender daisy among the others in the vase. Lyndy tugged at the end of his sleeve. He didn't like the sound of that. He should've joined Owen and Alfred while he had the chance. "I think it's time we—"

With his impeccable timing, the butler arrived, ending all chances of an intimate conversation. Lyndy popped up out of his armchair, hoping to escape while he could.

"What is it, Fulton?" Mother said. To Lyndy, she added, "You, stay put."

"I regret interrupting, milady," the butler said when Lyndy plopped down into the nearest chair, crossing his arms and stretching his legs out before him, "but there is a somewhat scruffy 'gentleman' with two young children at the door."

"What could they possibly want?" Lyndy wondered out loud. "Are they selling something? Has their horse gone lame?" His questioning surprised him and brought Stella to mind. He allowed himself an inward smile.

"What does it matter?" Mother said curtly. "Send them away, Fulton."

"I tried, milady, but—"

"Try harder, Fulton." Mother's tone as she snipped the leaves off another daisy should've dismissed the butler, but Fulton held his ground.

"I beg your pardon, milady, but he claims to be a guest of this house, that he was 'invited to stay at Morrington Hall by Her Grand Ladyship.' His words, not mine."

"Who on earth? I would never . . ." Mother sputtered, annoyed to be imposed upon in such a way.

"He gave his name as Mr. Jedidiah Kendrick, milady."

Mother dropped the flower to the floor.

Lyndy snorted in disbelief. "Are you certain this man called himself Kendrick?"

The butler nodded. "I am, my lord."

Mother's cold stare shifted from her flowers to Lyndy to the butler. She was not amused.

"You may let them into the hall, Fulton, and have them wait. Someone will arrive shortly to deal with them. And get this cleaned up, will you?" She motioned toward the colorful jumble of stems, leaves, and petals on the table and floor. The moment Fulton left the room, Mother glared at Lyndy. "Do you know anything about this?"

"Me? I've never heard of the man."

Stella had never mentioned having any other living relatives. Though, to be honest, Lyndy had never asked.

"Nevertheless, since he claims to be a relation of your fiancée," Mother said, her voice strained, "you will sort it all out."

Lyndy, curious to meet this uninvited mystery relative, was all too happy to "sort it all out." But when he strolled into the hall, he wasn't prepared for the scene before him. Sitting on the ladderback chair was a man unquestionably related to Elijah Kendrick, albeit with a scruffy beard, an amiable crooked smile, and considerably less around the middle. A heavily worn knapsack and small travel trunk with tattered edges lay on the floor at his feet. On the trunk sat two modestly but well-groomed children, their hands folded in their laps. The fair-haired, cherub-faced boy bent his head toward his younger sister, whispering something as she kicked her legs mindlessly against the trunk.

"Mr. Kendrick?" Lyndy called.

The three faces snapped up at him, and Lyndy's breath caught in his throat. The little girl, despite the shy, frightened expression on her sweet face, was how Lyndy imagined Stella as a child. The boy's green eyes held the same eager curiosity and kindness evident every day in Lyndy's future bride. There was no mistaking the close kinship.

"I'm Lord Lyndhurst. You must be relatives of Miss Kendrick's?"

"She's our cousin," the boy said, puffing out his little chest in pride. The girl's face gleamed as she grasped her brother's hand, but she said nothing. She might resemble her cousin, but she lacked Stella's vitality and courage. Perhaps Stella was once like this shy little girl too. Lyndy chuckled to himself.

I doubt that.

"I'll answer His Lordship, Sammy," Mr. Kendrick said. It was a rebuke but laced with a warmth seldom heard on his brother's tongue. Mr. Kendrick rose and held out his hand. "I'm pleased to meet ya, Lord Lyndhurst. Jedidiah Kendrick, at your service. As the young'un said, Stella is my brother's girl. So, may I add my hearty congratulations to the many I reckon you've already gotten."

Lyndy took the man's hand without hesitation. This Kendrick's manner was so unlike his brother, Lyndy took an instant liking to the man. "Thank you, Mr. Kendrick."

"Please, call me Jed. Everyone does."

"And since we are soon to be family, please call me Lyndy."

Jed glanced down at his children and grinned in surprised triumph, revealing a chipped front tooth. "Well, how do ya like that. I haven't been in this country twelve hours, and already I'm on a first name basis with an English lord." He poked the boy playfully in the shoulder with his elbow. "Oh, I forget my manners. This here is Sammy, who's ten."

"Please to meet you, Sammy," Lyndy said.

Without hesitation, the boy stood, wiped his hand on his trouser leg, and offered Lyndy his hand. Lyndy, who'd spent so little time in the company of children, managed not to laugh at the earnest expression on the boy's face when he deliberately shook Lyndy's hand up and down twice before letting go.

"I'm ten and a half," Sammy said, correcting his father.

"And this is my little sweet pea, Gertie."

Gertrude leaped down from the trunk, dropped into a curtsy, and quickly bobbed back up. The awkward, sweet action recalled the day Lyndy had met Stella and the deep curtsy she'd so carefully practiced. While Mother had been put off by the awkward gesture, Lyndy had been as captivated as he was now with this little creature.

"I'm six," she declared. Lyndy chuckled. "Why'd the man

laugh, Daddy? Didn't I do what you're supposed to do?" The little girl's high-pitched voice rang out, offended.

"Ya did very well, Gertie," Jed reassured his daughter. "Now, Lyndy, where should we drop our bags?" He picked up his knapsack and threw it over his shoulder.

Lyndy stiffened at the reminder of the problem at hand. "As to that, Mr. Kendrick," Lyndy said, a note of regret in his voice. He'd have no problem housing these charming creatures, but Mother would never allow it. "There has been a misunderstanding."

"Jed, remember? And what is this about a misunderstanding? We were invited to stay with Stella, so here we are." He dropped his bag again, squatted down, and began rummaging through it. "I've got the invitation in here, somewhere."

How odd. Stella's father hadn't included his brother on the guest list. If Lyndy recalled right, Mr. Kendrick hadn't invited any of his family besides Miss Luckett, Stella's great aunt. Stella must've sent the invitation. Whom else had she invited? What other relations might they expect?

"It's not that," Lyndy said, motioning for Jed to quit searching. "The thing is, Miss Kendrick doesn't live here. She, your brother, and your Aunt Rachel are currently residing in town at the dowager house."

Jed's face twisted tighter in confusion with every word. "Are ya trying to tell me we've come to the wrong house?"

"Essentially, yes. But don't worry. I'll arrange to have your luggage transported to Pilley Manor and word sent to Miss Kendrick that you are here."

"Thank you, kindly, Lyndy. It was heavy work carrying the trunk from the train station."

"Indeed."

They walked?

Lyndy took in the condition of the assemblage with new insight. In places, the trunk's leather straps had thinned and lost all color. Several of the steel studs had popped off. The blue ribbon on Gertrude's little hat frayed along the edge, Sammy didn't have a cap at all, and Mr. Kendrick's beard could benefit from a trim. But instead of squirming under his scrutiny, the trio waited patiently, with open, friendly faces.

Poor relations, then. Is that why Stella never mentioned them? *More likely, it's why her father didn't invite them.*

"Would you like to meet my mother and a few of the other wedding guests while you rest a bit? And if you're hungry, I'll see something's brought up."

Lyndy knew very well the invitation wouldn't meet with Mother's approval. But her displeasure would be but a bonus. In showing this family a little kindness, and getting to know them better, perhaps he'd discern how the woman he loved came to have such a gentle nature. She plainly hadn't taken after her father.

"Well, thank ya, kindly," Jed said. "That is if ya don't think we'd be imposing?"

"Absolutely not," Lyndy said, pushing the button summoning Fulton. "My mother will be delighted."

What a mess! Inspector Archibald Brown could see the extent of the wreckage from here. Brown didn't envy those assigned to its cleanup. Whatever Clark meant by "unusual circumstances" didn't bode well for the investigation into the accident either. Happily, for him, all this was a job for the Southampton County Borough Police. He was simply here to help an old mate. Matilda, the police horse, nickered, declaring her readiness to head home now.

Constable Waterman, the brown bag of apples cradled in the crook of his arm, offered one to the mare. Matilda greedily gobbled it up while Brown handed tuppence to the grocer.

"Right!" Brown said, stuffing the banana he'd bought to bring home to the Mrs. into his waistcoat pocket.

Brown patted the mare on the neck and stepped away from the police wagon. Ignoring the press of onlookers in the street, he approached the nearest local policeman keeping them at bay. Brown flashed his warrant card and, without waiting for a response, motioned to Constable Waterman to dispense with the apples and follow him. Brown located Sergeant Clark, a competent fellow he'd known from his uniform days, and headed for him, straddling splintered planks and sidestepping broken wagon wheels as he went. Behind him, Waterman did the same.

"Archie," Clark said, acknowledging him with a solemn nod. "I appreciate you coming so promptly."

"What's all this about?" Brown said. When he'd telephoned, the sergeant had expressed the urgency of the situation but little else. "I've seen nothing you Southampton lads can't handle."

"Oh, we can handle it all right," Clark said.

"So why ask for me?"

"Over here." The sergeant led Brown, with Waterman in tow, down a stretch of debris-covered street to where a gray woolen blanket covered the prone figure of a body. Three bloodied fingers poked out from underneath. "As I told you over the telephone, we have two casualties. The wagon driver sustained several serious injuries and is lucky to be breathing. We've already sent him to hospital. This chap, however"— Clark indicated the body at their feet—"wasn't so fortunate."

Clark knelt, with apparent difficulty, the old horse injury still plaguing him no doubt, and pulled back the blanket. Lying beneath was the mangled, broken body of a man, his limbs flailed out and twisted in unnatural ways. His nose was crushed to one side. One cheek, scraped and bruised, bore the muddy imprint of a horse hoof. Blood was everywhere. Thick mats of it caked his hair and eyebrows. It pooled beneath his head and in the unnatural recesses around his battered eyes. It had dried in streaks down his face. Instinctively, Brown shied away for an instant. Brown had viewed more than his share of damaged dead bodies. Yet he couldn't remember anything worse than this.

"Is that . . . ?" He trained the tip of his boot on a bloody lump of something lying near the man's head. Behind him, his constable retched.

Clark shook his head. "It was a bandanna or necktie of a sort. Someone tried to use the cloth to stem the bleeding. I'm guessing it was red to start with."

Brown nodded, relieved not to have been pointing at bits of the man's brain. "What happened? He wouldn't have gotten all that from falling from a wagon."

Clark replaced the blanket over the victim's face and struggled to his feet, shrugging off all offers of aid. "He wasn't in any of the vehicles. He was a pedestrian, the poor sod. Got tramped by a team of bolting horses and then ran over by the wagon."

Brown knew of one other case where horses had trampled a man, and that poor chap survived, though he never walked right again. "So, who is he?"

"We don't know. When we searched the body, we found no wallet, no money, no identification whatsoever."

Brown glanced over his shoulder at the curious crowd straining to see past the barriers being set up by Southampton's uniformed lads. Then he peered out toward the docks. Smoke-stacks, from no less than three ocean liners, towered above the city. "He could be anyone. With several newly arrived ships, he might not even be local." The sergeant nodded.

"Which is why it's imperative we put a name to this man, posthaste."

"Why the rush?"

"Because before he died, multiple witnesses overheard our victim threatening to kill someone, and we have but one clue to this man's identity. Here, Inspector, is where you come in."

"How's that?"

Clark held out a creased, soiled newspaper clipping that had been torn out by hand. Brown took the fragment and read it. He hesitated a moment before passing it to his constable to read. Constable Waterman whistled his surprise.

"I'll need photographs taken immediately," Brown said, hoping the trauma hadn't made the man's face unrecognizable.

"I thought you'd say that. The police photographer is already on his way." Clark rubbed his injured sore knee. "Now you see why you're here."

Brown, pinching the bridge of his nose, closed his eyes and nodded. The circumstances Clark had calmly described as unusual, Brown silently dubbed a *potential powder keg*.

"I suspected you'd want to be the one to handle this aspect of the case, Archie," Clark said, his voice dropping to a whisper, "seeing Morrington Hall is on your patch."

CHAPTER 6

～❧～

Squashed between Penny Swenson and the wall of the carriage, Stella concentrated on the landscape they rumbled past, trying to shake the tragic accident they'd left behind. She hoped the changing scenery would divert her attention in a way the inane chitchat between her father and the Swensons about the quality of the meals, the cabins in first class, and the company on the ocean liner had not. The brick and stone three-story buildings lining the city streets of Southampton gave way to vistas of meadows and farmhouses on one side, mudflats and the broad channel of the River Test on the other. They rattled across the iron expansion bridge, through the modest village of Totten, and finally under the overhanging branches of a New Forest woodland. She remembered the journey from the day she arrived in England, though at a less puttering, jolting pace. She'd been driving her father's Daimler and fluttering with excitement and anticipation, unaware of what was to come: betrayal, ridicule, tragedy, love. Had she known what had awaited her, she might've turned back. Yet now, when the carriage emerged from the shelter of the shaded grove onto the sprawling heath land, checkered with green grazing lawns, shallow seasonal ponds, and fading purple heather, a soothing calm rippled through her, much like that of returning home.

When the carriage creaked to the pace of spilled molasses, Mrs. Swenson interrupted the men's talk of Saratoga and the Travers Stakes to ask, "Why are we moving so slowly?" where a quick peek out the window would have told her why.

Up ahead, four shaggy donkeys, one white and three of varying shades of brown, loitered in the middle of the gravel road. When the animals showed no signs of moving on, the carriage came to a halt. Stella's father poked his head out the window, shouting for the coachman to do something. Before the coachman could clamber down from his perch in the front of the carriage, Stella opened the door, ducked through, and hopped out.

"What are you doing?" Penny Swenson said as if Stella had stepped off into a lava field.

"I'll just be a minute," Stella said, leaving the door ajar.

She approached the animals cautiously, shooing them away, her gloves like white flags waving in a brisk wind. Although one donkey, the white one, squinted at her with disdain, the others were more skittish and scampered to the safety of a tall gorse bush on the other side of the road. A few yellow flowers still clung to its prickly branches. After a few clicks of Stella's tongue, the last donkey sauntered away to join the others.

After Stella settled herself back in the cramped space of the coach, Mr. Swenson, across from her, leaned out their shared window. He held the crown of his hat tightly against his head.

"I'll be darned. Folks let their livestock run wild here? It's akin to what the West was like before barbed wire."

"Crazy people even allow the animals in town," Daddy said. The carriage jerked forward again.

"It's true," Stella said, to the expressions of disbelief on the Swensons' faces. "And wait until you see the pigs." Stella laughed when Penny's expression flashed from doubt to disgust.

The pannage season, as the locals call it, had just begun. When the oaks dropped their acorns, pigs were allowed free range on the Forest, to forage for the nuts poisonous to cattle and ponies. The lumbering animals snorted and squealed as they rooted through fallen leaves across village greens, along wooded roadsides, and between gravestones in churchyards. The first time Stella had encountered one, she'd slammed on the breaks, leaped from the car, and pursued it across the grassy triangle between the crossroads. She'd crept closer and closer until she realized the pig didn't have a mouthful of acorns, as she suspected, but was dragging the carcass of a rat in its mouth.

"But aren't they dangerous?" Penny asked as they approached the outskirts of Rosehurst and its famous watersplash.

"They can be," Stella said. "I'd stay clear if I were you."

When the carriage waded into the stream flowing across the road, Penny peered out the window, her forehead wrinkled in worry. As if the landau might be swept away by sudden rapids or rabid animals might leap through the window at any moment. Stella had forgotten how Penny didn't have an adventurous bone in her body.

She's in the wrong place to find a husband.

"Wait a minute," Penny said, in surprise. "Is that Miss Ivy?" Penny's voice rang with both hope and disappointment as she dismissed the vision before her. "It couldn't be. Could it?"

No, it couldn't be.

"Where?" Stella scoured the street but saw no sign of the woman Penny had spotted. Rosehurst lacked the commotion of the Southampton wharf, but it still teemed with bustling traffic.

Penny pointed toward the corner hotel, the White Hart Inn, a redbrick building with half-timbering on its many gables. Skipping down the wooden steps was a petite dark-haired woman dressed in a smart wine and gold walking suit. The woman glanced up at the corner street sign, and Stella's breath caught. Hers was another face that resembled Stella's mother. This must be who she'd seen at the wharf.

"Stop the carriage!"

Catching a glance of the woman who'd turn at the sound of Stella's shout, Daddy swore under his breath. "For God's sake, what the hell is she doing here?"

Mrs. Robertson stepped into the kitchen again. And she was right to.

Why was there still a sack of unpeeled potatoes at the foot of the table? Didn't Mrs. Downie need to put them to boil? The wee lad would be so disappointed if they didn't serve neeps and tatties. Yet Mrs. Downie was rolling out pastry. And why did the room smell of gingerbread when they'd agreed on Dundee cake?

Could the cook not have started yet? How can that be? Twenty minutes ago, Mrs. Downie had insisted supper would be ready on time. Ten minutes ago, Mrs. Downie had assured the housekeeper she had everything in hand.

Mrs. Robertson strode from one end of the kitchen to the other, peeking under tea towels, sniffing over steaming pots of savory broth, lifting pot lids. The smells wafting from the dishes of roast pheasant, plum jelly, fig compote made her mouth water. She bent to retrieve a wooden stirring spoon from the floor.

"Might I remind you, Mrs. Downie," Mrs. Robertson said, "that we have a guest coming for our servants' supper?"

"As you have reminded me six times in the past hour."

"And to what end? From the state of things, we'll never be ready on time."

"When have I ever failed in my duties, Mrs. Robertson?" The housekeeper flinched at the cook's injured tone. Mrs. Downie was right. She, in all the years they had worked together at Pilley Manor, had never found Mrs. Downie's cooking or her punctuality wanting. Granted, the cook gossiped a wee bit much, but that was beside the point. "But this might be a first," the cook continued, "if you don't stop traipsing through my kitchen and bothering me."

"Aye, you're right, of course. I should leave you to it."

"Yes, please." Mrs. Downie, a strain in her usual congenial voice, nodded appreciatively as the housekeeper swept from the room. But then Mrs. Robertson remembered something else, swiveled on her heels, and returned to the kitchen again.

"Lordy, Mrs. Robertson," Mrs. Downie complained. "What is it now?"

"Is the table in the servants' hall set?"

Mrs. Downie, laying her crust across a pie tin, blew frizzy wisps of hair from her face. "I should think so. Ethel walked by with the Battenburg lace tablecloth, the one used at Christmastime, draped over her arm an hour ago." Mrs. Robertson, inspecting the potted herbs growing in the window, was barely listening. She pinched off a sprig of rosemary and held it to her nose. At that moment, the herb's fragrance overpowered every other in the kitchen. "I should think she would've had time to lay the table for supper as well as the master's tea."

Of course, Mrs. Downie would prepare the afternoon tea first. Having arranged everything for the arrival of Mr. Kendrick's guests, the housekeeper had allowed herself to be distracted by the imminent arrival of her visitor.

"How silly of me." Mrs. Robertson brushed the herbs onto the counter. In one fluid motion, Mrs. Downie placed the pie tin in the oven, snapped shut the door, and swept the sprigs of rosemary into her uplifted apron with the flat of her hand.

"Are you well, Mrs. Robertson? It's not like you to fuss."

"Aye, you're right. I'm being ridiculous. He's only my sister's boy, after all." She lifted the small watch dangling from her chatelaine. "But why isn't he here yet? His ship must've landed hours ago. It doesn't take more than an hour from Southampton." *What will I tell my sister if something has happened to him? Or worse yet, what if he's too high and mighty now to want to visit his auntie?*

"And here I thought you were worried about having more Americans in the house," Mrs. Downie said, deftly chopping carrots.

Mrs. Robertson bristled at the accusation. She held nothing against all Americans—just one. Besides, didn't her nephew now hail from America? The old aunt, Miss Luckett, was harmless enough. And wasn't Miss Kendrick a lovely girl? Granted, she'd proven to be the most unconventional mistress the housekeeper had ever worked for: young, brash, a bit too familiar, prone to odd requests. It was off-putting at first. Yet once Mrs. Robertson understood it was what the girl was used to, that she meant no offense by it, the housekeeper learned not to mind. *The young woman's father, on the other hand . . .* And what was to become of them once Miss Kendrick married? Would the master stay on at Pilley Manor, alone? Mrs. Robertson rechecked her watch, refusing to indulge in further worry on the subject.

"From what Willie, the greengrocer's boy, said when he dropped our order off earlier, they might all be late."

"And why would that be?" Mrs. Robertson thought little of the gossip gleaned from hall boys and nursemaids. But if it had any bearing on the arrival of their expected guests, the housekeeper should be aware of it.

"There was a carriage accident near the Southampton docks. From what he said, it caused a great commotion."

"And how would the greengrocer's boy from Rosehurst," Mrs. Robertson asked, already dismissing the gossip as the hearsay it was, "know anything about what happened this morning near the Southampton docks?"

Mrs. Downie, having moved on to the celery, paused with the chopping knife in the air between them. "Willie got it from a delivery man who'd been to Snook's fruit market this morning. You know the one. They have the dangling bunches of bananas in the front?" Mrs. Robertson nodded, regretting, with the cook's every word, that she'd encouraged Mrs. Downie to repeat such idle nonsense. She glanced at her watch again. The lad was quite late.

"Well, that delivery man," Mrs. Downie continued, "said the traffic was backed up all along the town quay. Said a team of horses bolted and that they'd found a man trampled to death among the wreckage. Said blood was splattered everywhere."

"That will be quite enough, Mrs. Downie," Mrs. Robertson snapped, releasing the watch chain. It thumped against her leg. She raised her chin, straining to fill her lungs properly, a bitter taste clinging to her mouth. "I'll hear no more of this monstrous chatter."

Unaware of the suffocating dread the housekeeper grappled with, Mrs. Downie, abandoning the knife and chopped celery at one end of the table, upturned a ball of dough onto the other end and began kneading it with a heavy hand.

"No need to bite me head off. Mind, you're the one who asked. And seeing as your nephew arrived from America there this afternoon, I thought you'd like to know. I'm hoping he might've seen something."

"And I'm praying he's not bleeding his life out in the dirty street!"

Mrs. Downie's mouth dropped open, her hands frozen still in the dough. The housekeeper had never raised her voice before.

"Forgive me, Mrs. Downie," the housekeeper said contritely. The outburst had surprised even her. "I couldn't bear it if anything happened to the wee lad."

"I'm sure the lad is fine," Mrs. Downie said. "He'll be tucking into me neeps and tatties come supper time." Wiping the flour from her hands on her apron, Mrs. Downie retrieved a copper pan filled with a mix of chopped rutabaga and potatoes.

"See, it'll all be ready and waiting for him. In the meantime, I'll make us a cup of tea. Then everything will be as right as rain."

Mrs. Robertson collapsed into the nearest chair. She wasn't herself. Concern for the lad, the stress of the wedding, and three additional houseguests with no additional staff added to her biggest headache. Come three days and their future—hers, Mrs. Downie's, and Mr. Tims's—was uncertain. Only Ethel was assured a place.

"I do hope you're right, Mrs. Downie. I do so hope you're right."

"You came!" Stella said, flinging herself into her aunt's open arms.

Her aunt wrapped her in a warm embrace. Aunt Ivy's cheek, pressed against Stella's, was soft and smelled of the same bergamot-scented face powder.

Who cared if they were in the middle of the sidewalk, blocking the entrance to the inn? Who cared if news of her public demonstrations of affections reached Lady Atherly's ears? Aunt Ivy was family and Stella hadn't seen her in years.

"Of course, I did. I wouldn't have missed my sister's baby's wedding for the world."

Aunt Ivy had been a fixture in Stella's life while her mother was alive, a frequent visitor to Bronson Ridge Farm. She'd been widowed young, left childless, and never remarried. When Stella's mother died, Ivy attempted to stand in for her sister as much as Stella's father would allow. But after a particularly loud argument (over what neither would ever say), he forbade Aunt Ivy to step foot on the farm again. Soon after, he dispensed with Stella's nannies and governesses too. Stella, loosened on the stable hands, was on her own. But Aunt Ivy had never stopped writing, never stopped sending birthday and Christmas presents, never stopped trying to find a way back into Stella's life.

"Now, let me get a good look at you." Aunt Ivy gripped

Stella's shoulders and held her out to full arm's length. The two women studied each other.

Seventeen years Stella's senior, Aunt Ivy had filled out a little in the middle, her face had become plump and round, wrinkles lined her high forehead and creased the edges of her mouth, crinkled strands of gray marred her smooth chestnut brown hair. Aunt Ivy had aged. Yet she was still Aunt Ivy, with a welcoming smile and the same kind brown eyes. Until this moment, Stella hadn't realized how much she'd missed her.

"You've grown into a fine lady." Stella beamed at Aunt Ivy's compliment. "How do you reckon your daddy managed not to ruin you?"

The carriage rolled to a halt beside them. The hired draught horses nickered softly, as if in on the joke.

"Hello to you too, Ivy," Stella's father sneered from the window. The sun had slipped behind the increasing cloud cover, casting him in deep shadow. But Stella could imagine his scowl. "What are you doing here? I don't remember inviting you to the wedding."

"You didn't." Aunt Ivy, not bothering to face him, continued to size up Stella. "Your lovely girl did."

Stella had sent her the invitation, unbeknownst to her father, out of kindness and fondness for her aunt. She never imagined Aunt Ivy would come.

"Well, I hope you're not planning to stay with us," Daddy said.

"No, I rented a room here at the inn," Aunt Ivy said.

"Good, because we've got guests. You remember the Swensons, don't you?"

"Of course." Aunt Ivy took in the carriage for the first time. Though a young gentleman in a boater hat and walking cane had admired it openly as he crossed the street, what Aunt Ivy thought of the famous coach, she didn't say. "I'm so glad y'all were able to make it for the wedding as well."

"Wouldn't have missed it!" Mr. Swenson said, lifting his hat from the crown in greeting.

"You're looking well, Mrs. Mitchell," Mrs. Swenson said, leaning forward to catch the sunlight, a tight-lipped smile on her face.

"As are you, Mrs. Swenson," Aunt Ivy said politely, without regarding the woman. Instead, she craned her neck, trying to spy who else was inside. "Is that the little miss I see in there? How are you, Miss Penny?"

Penny, who, when they were little, would beg to stay at Stella's house when Aunt Ivy was visiting, stuck her head out. "I'm just grand, Miss Ivy."

For a fleeting moment, Penny beamed with joy. Penny had been starved for affection as a child, and Stella believed Aunt Ivy was one of the few people Penny was fond of. The smile suited her. Too bad it wouldn't last.

Aunt Ivy approached the carriage, giving the closest horse a pat on the thigh, reached in, and pulled Penny into an awkward embrace. Penny's face reddened with embarrassment as she timidly patted the older woman's back. But longing lingered on Penny's face when Aunt Ivy released her hug, disentangled their hats, and stepped back.

"You almost beat us to Pilley Manor. We're heading that way now," Stella said. "I'm sure we can fit you in."

"The carriage is too crowded," Daddy said.

Mrs. Swenson nodded vigorously in agreement. "Then, we'll walk."

Stella wrapped her arm around her aunt's and studied the dear face again. She so much resembled Stella's mother. "We'll catch up on the way. Wait until you meet Lyndy!"

Aunt Ivy's arm tensed beneath Stella's hold. "I would love to, but . . ."

"I'm sure your aunt needs to settle in," Mrs. Swenson said. "I know Penny and I are exhausted."

"Yes, Mrs. Swenson's right. I do have a few things I'm fixing to do," Aunt Ivy said, patting Stella's hand before gently freeing her arm.

Stella didn't understand. Hadn't her aunt traveled the ocean to visit her? Hadn't they already spent years apart? What was more pressing than spending time together?

"But I'll visit later. I promise. We have so much to talk about. I have so much to tell you." Aunt Ivy shot a sideways glance at Stella's father. She cupped Stella's cheek with her hand, leaned forward, and whispered, "When we can be alone."

Aunt Ivy's touch was soft, her breath was warm and smelled like cinnamon, but the cryptic tone in her voice sent a chill down Stella's spine.

CHAPTER 7

Stella resisted the urge to run. She wasn't dressed for it. She'd been changing for dinner when Lyndy's message arrived. The moment Ethel placed the combs in her hair, she'd slipped on her gloves, grabbed the first thing in the cloakroom—her duster coat—and threw it over her dinner gown.

She still couldn't believe it. Uncle Jed, here? According to Lyndy's note, Uncle Jed had arrived unannounced on the Earl of Atherly's doorstep. First Aunt Ivy, now Uncle Jed. Stella was going to have more kin at the wedding, after all. And Uncle Jed hadn't even been invited.

She followed the well-worn track across the Forest from Rosehurst to Morrington Hall. Reaching down and running her hand through a cluster of heather, Stella released its sweet smell. The sun, bursting momentarily from behind darkening clouds, shot rays across her path. She raised her face, closed her eyes, and the images of this morning's shocking accident melted away when replaced by what Stella pictured the expression on Lady Atherly's face when she'd met Uncle Jed. Or Stella's father's reaction when he learned the news.

From the beginning, her father had made it clear, as he had after her mother died, that he had no intention of associating with their extended family. Wedding or no wedding. He hadn't invited a single member of the family, besides Aunt Rachel, of course. He figured inviting his friends, the Swensons, was good enough. Mrs. Swenson would stand in for Stella's aunts to help Stella navigate the pitfalls of last-minute wedding details. Penny Swenson could be a bridesmaid. But Aunt Ivy now was here, and Uncle Jed had come unexpectedly anyway.

Stella, bursting with excitement, grabbed a fistful of her duster coat and dress and picked up the pace, scampering along the spongy, moss-covered path. Stella couldn't wait to see her uncle.

The brothers had never been close, in age—Stella's father being much older than Uncle Jed—or in temperament; Uncle Jed was kindly and fun. But neither difference explained the bickering, the constant arguing between them whenever the two were in the same room. From what Stella had gleaned from stable hands and housemaids over the years, something had happened that each brother thought was the other's fault. No one knew what it was. Or they wouldn't tell the impressionable child that Stella was. Perhaps now, she'd learn the truth.

She followed the path through a wood populated by towering, ancient trees and out into the grazing lawns and horse paddocks bordering the estate's grounds. Morrington Hall loomed large in the distance. She threw the stone stables a wistful glance, the urge to visit Tully, her beloved horse, almost eclipsing her desire to see Uncle Jed. Stella hadn't ridden Tully in two days. But soon, very soon, when she took up permanent residence here, she'd be able to visit and ride Tully any time she wanted.

Permanent residence. Stella blew out a long exhale. *This is really happening.*

She giggled nervously when she crossed through the formal

garden, the roses neatly trimmed, the fountain of a cherub holding a bushel of round fruit, cheerfully spraying its sparkling water into the pool below. It was so much improved from the neglected garden Stella had first encountered. With the upcoming wedding and its promise of a substantial increase in funds, Lady Atherly had arranged its revival. A sign of what was to come. Stella plucked the head off a yellow rosebush and headed for the front door.

"Good evening, Miss Kendrick," Fulton, the butler, said, after answering her knock and gesturing for her to enter the hall. "I trust you are well?"

"Thank you, Fulton. I am. But what about you? I heard you've had unexpected visitors, relations of mine, in fact."

His face revealed nothing of what he thought of those relations when he took Stella's duster coat and hat. "Lord Lyndhurst is entertaining them in the drawing room if you'd care to join them."

"Thank you, Fulton." Stella smiled at the butler before hurrying down the hall to the drawing room.

Stella paused in the doorway. There, in the light shining through the French windows across the Persian carpet, the portraits of Lyndy's ancestors glaring down at him, was Uncle Jed, on all fours on the floor, a small girl, who must be Gertie, riding on his back. Sir Alfred, a pleasant pal of Lyndy's, stood near the mantel with a handsome gentleman Stella didn't know, both men trying desperately not to show their amusement at the antics of the man on the floor.

But where was Lyndy? Where were the rest of his family?

Gertie, with her arms around Uncle Jed's neck, her legs wrapped tightly around his middle, squealed when her father reared up to his knees, lifting her vertically into the air. They were playing horse. Stella had loved it when he'd played horse with her when she was little. Before he and her father had fallen out.

"Uncle Jed!" she cried, rushing into the room.

Uncle Jed paused in midrear when her cousin Sammy leaped from his spot on the couch and rushed to embrace Stella. She held the boy, kissing the top of his head, which reached the nap of her neck. When had he gotten so tall? Suddenly self-conscious, Sammy took a giant step back. He brushed the hair that had fallen across his forehead. Uncle Jed, reaching around, set Gertie on the floor but remained on his knees.

"My, you're a sight, aren't ya?" Uncle Jed declared. "You're as pretty as a spotted horse in a daisy pasture."

Stella beamed, until the corners of her mouth hurt. "Uncle Jed, Sammy, Gertie, I'm so happy to see you. How are you? How was the trip over? What a wonderful surprise. My wedding wouldn't have been the same without you. Do you know my Aunt Ivy is here too?" Sensing the other two men watching her, Stella addressed them. "Hello again, Sir Alfred. I assume you've already met my uncle?"

"Yes, indeed," Sir Alfred said. "Like you, we came early for dinner."

"So, you are Miss Kendrick, are you?" the stranger said, stroking his beard, trying to appear as if he weren't sizing her up. But the twinkle in his eye, so much like Lyndy's, gave him away. "I've heard much about you and your . . . horse riding skills."

"You must be Sir Owen, Lyndy's cousin," she said. Sir Owen nodded in acknowledgment. "I've heard much about your . . . sportsmanship." Sir Owen laughed at Stella's description of what Lyndy had called his cousin's "dedication to the sport of wooing." An approving smile spread across his lips.

"Who's that lady, Daddy?" Gertie whispered loud enough to be heard by all. The question stung. Gertie wasn't old enough to remember the last time Stella had seen her.

"That," Uncle Jed said conspiratorially, "is your cousin, Stella. She's a grand lady now." Gertie's eyes widened with curiosity and new respect.

"Oh, Uncle. I'm not a grand lady."

"Not yet, maybe, but soon." He turned back to whisper in Gertie's ear. "She's to be a countess one day."

Stella corrected him. "Morrington Hall already has a countess, Lady Atherly. Have you met her yet?"

"The lady of the house met us but made her excuses, what with the dinner tonight and all."

Stella was grateful Lady Atherly was taking her time dressing for dinner. How many of Stella's social encounters happened under her future mother-in-law's disapproving gaze? Much like Mrs. Swenson's when they'd met Aunt Ivy earlier on the street. But not this happy reunion. And what did Stella care if Sir Alfred and Sir Owen were witnesses?

"I suppose we'll meet the lord of the manor at the wedding."

"You'll meet him tonight, Uncle Jed. And Lyndy's sister, Lady Alice. I can't imagine Lady Atherly will object to you attending dinner." Stella could imagine it but hoped for once she was wrong.

"And Aunt Rachel? How is the old girl?"

"Feisty as ever." Stella chuckled. "She's not up for long dinner parties, though, so you'll see her tomorrow."

"If she's my cousin," Gertie continued in her loud whisper as if the adults' talk was trivial compared to her ruminations, "does that make me a princess?"

The adults all laughed at the little girl's aspirations, but her brother wasn't so amused.

"No, silly," Sammy scolded. "Stella isn't a queen but a countess. That makes you a contessa." Stella smiled at the boy's earnest but erroneous correction, but she wasn't about to explain the rules of hierarchy to a ten- and six-year-old.

"No, Gertie," Stella said, squatting down to be at the girl's level. "But since you're here, you can be the flower girl at the wedding. Would you like that?"

The girl hesitated, waiting for her father's permission. When he gave the nod, she lowered her head solemnly and curtsied. "Yes, thank ya, Countessa Stella."

"Just Stella will do. You are my flower girl now, after all." Stella had said it lightly, but the little girl's shoulders straightened. Gertie sought her brother's attention, scrunching her face at him as if to say, *I'm the flower girl, and you're not.*

"Now, we must formalize our relationship with a hug." Gertie rushed into Stella's outstretched arms, the little girl's soft warmth melting against her. Gertie smelled of toffee and dust. Scents reminiscent of Stella's childhood too.

When she reluctantly released the little girl, Stella said, "Where is Lyndy? Why did you come to Morrington Hall instead of Pilley Manor? How did you know about the wedding?"

"Same old Stella," Uncle Jed said, revealing a broken tooth with his smile. "Asking a lot of questions. I see becoming a fine lady hasn't stilled that tongue of yours."

Sir Owen chuckled.

"It is part of her charm, I'd like to think," Lyndy said, strolling into the room with James, the footman, trailing behind. The footman carried a silver tray with a tea service and a tray laden with a variety of sandwiches: watercress, smoked salmon, cheese and pickle, mint cucumber, and a few cheese scones. The corners of his lips rose when his and Stella's eyes met. His lingered, longingly taking her in. Her breath quickened. Then the moment was gone. Lyndy strode over to sweep Gertie into his arms. She squealed with delight. "And yes, we have already made our acquaintance."

Stella had never seen Lyndy with children before. She had a sudden urge to kiss him.

"Help the man, Sammy," Uncle Jed ordered, indicating the footman who was laying out the tea things. James's head shot up in alarm.

"That's kind of you, Jed, Sammy," Lyndy said, "but you've had a long journey and had to miss both your luncheon and tea. I think James would prefer if you left the serving to him."

Uncle Jed, with a playful wink, shrugged at Sammy, looking to his father for direction.

"Then serve away, James," Uncle Jed said, waving Sammy back to his seat. "By all means, serve away."

Stella poured the tea while Lyndy poured something stronger for Sir Alfred and Sir Owen. Leaning against the mantel, with heads bent, the two gentlemen occasionally shot glances toward Stella between sips of sherry. What they might be discussing, Stella didn't want to guess. As Uncle Jed, Gertie, and Sammy devoured the sandwiches, Stella settled into the settee next to Lyndy, inching as close as she dared. Taking advantage of the lack of female chaperones, Lyndy kissed her lightly, his lips warm on her cheek. Stella blushed at the crooked, knowing smile on Sir Owen's face.

Flustered, she unnecessarily smoothed the panel of rose-colored silk against her lap, carefully avoiding the floral sequins swirling down her skirt. "You never did say why you came to Morrington Hall first, Uncle Jed."

"I thought this is where you lived," Uncle Jed said, before shoving another tea sandwich into his mouth. He was her father's brother, but it was the first gesture he'd made reminiscent of her father. Neither of them had the best table manners.

"No, Daddy, Aunt Rachel, and I live at Pilley Manor in town."

"So Lyndy said," Uncle Jed said, wiping his beard with a napkin. "But that is what the wedding announcement in the *Courier-Journal* implied."

"Help yourself to the scones," Lyndy said. "The children might like them with butter."

Uncle Jed appreciatively slathered one with the herbed butter and handed it to an eager Gertie. The little girl licked a drip of butter from her finger before taking a bite. Stella, careful not to stain her dress, daubed tomato chutney on a scone; they were still warm from the oven.

"Try this, Uncle Jed." Before coming to England, she'd never had savory scones or chutney. But having been introduced to both, she hadn't had one of either she didn't like.

When Uncle Jed took Stella's offering, Lyndy shifted to face her. "How was your trip to Southampton?"

She snatched up a scone for herself and took a nibble. She couldn't resist. "Eventful." She mentioned meeting the Swensons' ship. She described the carriage crash. "Daddy wouldn't let me learn the extent of it, but there were at least two men on the ground." She leaned in closer to whisper, not wanting the children to hear. "One of them was trampled to death." She sat back and took another bite of her scone. "And that's not all. You'll never guess who else has come for the wedding. My—"

"Where is he?"

A man's angry voice, rumbling from the great hall, cut Stella off. Stella knew that temper all too well. She dropped the half-eaten scone on her plate, her appetite ruined.

With nails pressed into her palms, Stella rose from the settee to calmly face her father when he marched into the room, Fulton scooting in a few paces behind. Lyndy joined her side.

"I'm sorry, milord, but—" the butler said, minutely shaking his head. Lyndy dismissed the butler's apology, and irritation, with a flick of his hand. He knew her father too well to fault the butler for the intrusion.

Her father's face was red and splotchy, perspiration beading on his forehead. How had he gotten here? If Stella didn't know better, she would've guessed he ran. She glanced out the French window. The Daimler was in the driveway. Had he driven himself? Stella couldn't believe it. She'd been chauffeuring him around for years. And then Theo Swenson's head, goggles dangling from around his neck, popped up from the driver's seat. He held the tin of chocolates Stella had stashed in the glove compartment.

"What are you doing here so soon, Daddy? Dinner's not for another hour."

"So, it's true," Daddy said, ignoring Stella as he passed by her to stare down Uncle Jed. "Someone said you were here, but I didn't believe it."

"Hello, Elijah," Uncle Jed said through a crooked smile.

"You have some nerve coming here, Jed."

"I say!" Sir Owen chuckled behind them, baffled by her father's rude entrance. "What's he got the hump over? Someone pour this man a glass of sherry." Lyndy shot his cousin a warning glance. He was trying to lighten the mood, but Sir Owen didn't know Stella's father.

"I don't want sherry!" Daddy said, pinning Sir Owen with an ugly glare while pointing an accusing finger at Uncle Jed. "I want this lying backstabber, this leech, to crawl back into whatever hole he weaseled his way out of."

Sir Owen pinched his lips shut in shock. Stella guessed the aristocrat had never been spoken to that way before. Stella was unfazed. Her father had been bad-mouthing his brother for years.

He swung his finger around to point at Stella. "And you! I could cut you out of my will for inviting him."

Like the name-calling, Stella had heard this threat before too. "I didn't invite him, Daddy," Stella said. "I invited Aunt Ivy but—"

"Invited yourself, did you, Jed?" Daddy scoffed. "I should've known."

"But I'm so glad he did," Stella said. "Won't it be nice to have more family at the wedding?"

"This man stopped being family years ago. Besides, my brother doesn't care about the wedding. He didn't come here out of his love for you. His wallet is all he cares about. That's why you're here, isn't it, Jed? Stop deluding the girl and tell us what handout you're expecting this time."

Uncle Jed, his head cocked to one side, smirked. "You've done me wrong, Elijah. I'm here to celebrate with our Stella." He eased out of his chair to match his brother's height and shrugged. "What uncle wouldn't want to kiss the bride on her wedding day?" He winked at Stella.

It was what Stella wanted to hear, but for the first time, Uncle Jed's words didn't ring true. Had he crossed an ocean to ask for money? Stella noted the frayed cuffs on Uncle Jed's coat, Sammy's worn shoes. But then how did he pay for the voyage over? She never put much faith into her father's rantings, but suddenly she wasn't sure whom to believe.

Daddy snorted in disgust. "You never did anything that didn't end in you taking my money."

"But he brought Sammy and Gertie with him," Stella said. He wouldn't have dragged the children across the ocean to press her father for money. Would he?

"I don't care if he brought John D. Rockefeller," he said. "You'll never convince me he came for any other reason than to leech off me."

"Either way, they're here. So, of course, they'll attend the wedding," Lyndy said, taking up her cause. Stella rewarded him with a smile.

"Who's paying for this shindig?" her father reminded Lyndy. Sir Owen sniggered behind his hand at her father's mention of money. In polite society here, it wasn't done. But her father didn't care about that. He cared that everyone knew how rich he was. "I am. And I say he and his aren't welcome."

"Never could handle being outshined, could ya, Elijah?" Uncle Jed goaded. Stella's chest tightened. She wished he wouldn't do that. "Just like ya never could accept that Kate liked me best."

Kate? She'd never heard Mama called that. And what did Stella's mother have to do with it? What was Uncle Jed insinuating?

"How dare you!" her father bellowed, launching himself at Uncle Jed.

He barreled into his brother's stomach headfirst, knocking him off his feet. Uncle Jed's pointed-toe boots, one with the sole flapping loose at the tip, upended the side table. The silver tea service, the tray, the uneaten sandwiches and scones, and a half-finished cup of tea flew into the air and clattered with a crash to the floor. Stella swooped in to grab Gertie from the couch while Lyndy grasped Sammy's hand, yanking the poor boy to his feet and out of harm's way. Her father and uncle collided as one with the plush chair Uncle Jed had occupied, tipping it over. The men spilled onto the carpet in a huddle of thrashing arms and legs as they tried to punch and shove and kick each other.

"Stop it!" Stella shouted, cradling Gertie, the girl's tears dampening her face. "Stop it!"

The men ignored her, instead, they rolled around, through the mess of broken porcelain, squashed sponge cake, and spilled tea, first one getting the advantage and then the other. Only the sudden blare of a piercing whistle got them to stop.

Stella swirled around at the sound. Lady Atherly, the bright glint of her diamond tiara in stark contrast to her gray and black evening gown, gaped in horrified astonishment. At Stella, not the men. As if their juvenile behavior was Stella's fault. Beside Lady Atherly was Inspector Brown, the nickel-plated whistle still held to his lips. Lord Atherly, his pair of gold-plated lorgnettes held up to his face, peered over his wife's shoulder.

"Enough!" Lady Atherly declared.

Uncle Jed shoved Stella's father off him. With a welt already forming on his cheek and chunks of broken cheese scone lodged in his beard, he pushed himself up off the floor. Stella's father, holding the back of his hand to a cut on his chin, held out the other, to no one in particular, expecting to be helped to his feet. When Lyndy wouldn't budge, to his credit, Sir Owen obliged.

"I do apologize for disturbing you, Lord Lyndhurst," Inspector Brown said, masking all but a hint of sarcasm. "I see that I've come at a bad time. But, as I explained to Lord and Lady Atherly, I'm afraid I have news that can't wait."

CHAPTER 8

❧

"Bloody hell, Brown," Lyndy exclaimed. "What is it this time?"

Stella couldn't have said it better. She liked Inspector Brown. She'd even invited him, over Lady Atherly's objections, to the wedding. But the way her day was going . . .

"I realize you're entertaining guests," the inspector said, noting her father slouched in the armchair rubbing his head and Uncle Jed dabbing a cut with a handkerchief, "but I must speak with you, and Miss Kendrick." Inspector Brown indicated the children, clutching each other's hands and cowering on the couch, with a nod.

Stella cast a questioning glance at Uncle Jed. Too wrapped up in his misery, he hadn't consoled his children. Perhaps the brothers were more alike than she'd hoped.

"Preferably, in private."

Stella knew it. His news was going to be bad.

"Of course," Lyndy said.

"I say, Lyndy," Sir Owen inquired flippantly. "Do you get called on regularly by the local constabulary?"

Sir Alfred stomped on Owen's foot to silence him when the policeman preceded them out the door. Lady Atherly pinched her lips in disapproval and settled on the edge of the chair farthest from Uncle Jed. Lord Atherly hid a snicker by turning his back and pouring himself a glass of sherry.

"One moment, Inspector," Lyndy called before crouching down before the children.

"Why don't you two play checkers," he said. "Or Sammy can continue reading *The Tale of Two Bad Mice*." The little illustrated book lay on the inlay side table. Someone must've brought it in from the library. "Would you like that?" He brushed a tear from Gertie's cheek, and the girl nodded.

Stella's heart fluttered at his tenderness. How could she ever have thought him callous and cold?

Sammy, who hid his distress better than his simpering sister, said, "I'll read to Gertie, Cousin Lyndy."

"Okay, then. Stella and I shall be right back." Lyndy handed Sammy Miss Potter's latest book before gesturing to Stella to proceed him out into the hall. In the doorway, out of sight of those in the drawing room, she stopped. When Lyndy bumped into her, she grabbed him by the lapels and pressed her lips hard against his. The inspector's bad news could wait.

"Oh, I've missed you," he whispered when she ended the kiss.

"It's only been two days," she said, her smiling lips an inch from his. "There's been lots to do." She pulled away, teasing him. But secretly she couldn't bear the distance. She'd come to crave his closeness—more than she wanted to admit. The past two days had been lonely without him. "Soon, we'll be together every day, and then you'll get sick of me." She joked but held her breath, awaiting his answer.

Lyndy's breath was hot when they again leaned into each other, their foreheads touching. "I shall never tire of you. Ever."

"Uh-um," the inspector, a few yards away down the hall, politely cleared his throat.

Had he heard every word? So what if he had?

Stella gave Lyndy a quick peck on the cheek for good measure before joining the inspector beneath the Gainsborough painting that so captured the inclement English landscape. With its billowing clouds and shadowed trees, she swore she could feel the raindrops whenever she passed.

Stella glanced down the hall to the etched glass windows on either side of the door. The evening light was unusually dim, and shimmering splashes of rain dotted the panes. *How appropriate.* The inspector chose his position well; the Gainsborough reflected the storm that was brewing inside and out.

"Now, what's this all about?" Stella asked. Brown held up a finger to silence her.

Footsteps echoed in the hall as someone crossed the wooden parquet floor in the grand saloon beyond. A servant, most likely, going about their business. The policeman waited until the hall was silent to begin.

"There's been a carriage accident—"

"On the Southampton wharf," Stella finished for him. "Inspector, I was there. Daddy and I were meeting family friends from Kentucky who've come over for the wedding. I saw the whole awful thing."

Stella never imagined this was the inspector's news. But why? As her father had reminded her, it had nothing to do with them.

"Then perhaps you know why I'm here?"

"I have no idea," Stella said, searching the policeman's round, weathered face. "I assume the two men died of their injuries?"

"The cab driver may yet survive, but the other fellow was dead when I arrived. It is because of the dead man that I'm here."

"But isn't this a matter for the Southampton police?" Lyndy said.

"You're correct, my lord, but they've requested my assistance. Both Sergeant Clark of the Southampton police and I thought it better you were interviewed by someone you were already acquainted with."

"That's kind of you, Inspector, but certainly you needn't come all this way to ask Miss Kendrick what dozens of others must've witnessed."

"Lyndy's right, Inspector," Stella said. "Of course, I want to help, but I don't know what more I can tell you."

"I'm hoping you can explain this." Inspector Brown pulled a tattered newspaper clipping from his jacket pocket and handed it to Lyndy. Stella leaned over to see what it was. It was the announcement of their wedding that had run in the *Courier-Journal* in Louisville. The same one Uncle Jed had mentioned. "We found it on the trampled man."

"So, the man has a copy of our wedding announcement," Lyndy said, handing it back to the inspector.

"The odd thing is, this newspaper clipping and a packet of matches were the sole items we found on the dead man's body. He had no wallet, no money, no passenger tickets, no grocery receipts."

"And you think we might know who he is?" Stella said.

The inspector pulled a small black and gray photograph from his pocket. "I apologize for the grim scene, but it's all we have. A police photographer took this earlier. Do you recognize this man?"

Stella's stomach flipped in revulsion at the muddy horseshoe print outlined on the man's broken, bloody face. What a horrible way to die. But a spark of recognition steeled her to study the photo more closely. The curls on his head sprang about as if they had a life of their own. His sharply pointed nose was grotesquely crushed to one side. A bandanna lay discarded on the ground by his head. She did know this man. And not just from the accident.

"I don't know his name, and I have no idea what interest he had in our wedding, but I saw him on the wharf. Earlier, before the accident. He was at the center of the commotion near the fruit market. Lots of other people witnessed it too. I think even the police got involved."

The inspector nodded. "Yes, we've confirmed he was in an earlier altercation. Lord Lyndhurst?" Stella handed the photograph to Lyndy. Lyndy's head drew back stiffly in surprise.

"My lord?" the inspector said expectantly, almost eagerly.

"Lyndy?" Stella asked. "Do you know him?"

"I do. I'm surprised you don't recognize him as well." Lyndy showed Stella the photograph again.

"Should I?" Stella was confused. The first time she'd seen him was on the wharf. Or so she thought.

"He's an American jockey," Lyndy explained. Stella still didn't remember him.

"And his name, my lord?" Inspector Brown insisted. "Do you know the man's name?"

"Prescott, if I remember correctly," Lyndy said, handing the inspector back the photograph. The name was familiar, but Stella had no memory of meeting him. Her father rarely invited jockeys to Bronson Ridge Farm.

"I can't thank you enough, my lord," Inspector Brown said, slipping the photograph away.

"Quite." Lyndy put his hand on the small of Stella's back and turned to leave. "See yourself out, Inspector?"

"Of course, but if you could answer one more question."

"I'm happy to have helped," Lyndy sighed, impatient to dismiss the inspector. He held up his hand when the inspector opened his mouth to continue. "But before you ask Inspector, I know him only from the racing papers. He was well known on the turf. But that's the extent of it, I'm afraid."

"If that is true, Lord Lyndhurst, answer me this." Inspector Brown pressed his lips together in a grimace. "If you didn't know this jockey, then why was he, if not for his death, on his way to kill you?"

"Me?" Granted, Lyndy could imagine a few who might enjoy taking him down a peg or two, but murder? The idea was preposterous. Yet the firmness of the policeman's jaw, his steady stare, made the hair on the back of Lyndy's neck rise. The man was deadly serious. "Why would this jockey want to kill me?"

"So, you have never had any occasion to meet or interact with the deceased then, my lord?" Inspector Brown asked.

Lyndy shook his head, emphatically. "No. Never."

"But you do know who he is." Lyndy had skimmed an article about the Woodhaven Downs scandal the jockey had been embroiled in a few months back. That was the extent of his knowledge.

"Yes, but I assure you," Lyndy said, addressing the fearful questions clouding Stella's countenance more than those of the policeman, "I can think of absolutely no reason he'd want to cause me harm."

Stella smiled, halfheartedly, to reassure him, but Lyndy recognized the effort it took. Her apprehension was palpable.

"To be fair, my lord, the victim wasn't overheard saying your name specifically, but a man at Morrington Hall. I assumed when you said you knew who he was, that the man he mentioned was you. Could anyone else at Morrington Hall be acquainted with him then?"

Who else was there? Papa? Papa barely knew the difference between a quarter crack and a quarter pole, let alone have any occasion to wrong an American jockey to the point of violence. Fulton? Gates? Could one of the servants be dabbling in something they shouldn't? Lyndy wouldn't believe it. Could the jockey have meant a wedding guest? He had been carrying a copy of the wedding announcement. But how would Prescott know who was staying at the house?

"But Prescott's dead now," Lyndy said, hoping to avoid Brown's questioning the staff or worse, their wedding guests. "Surely, so too is the threat."

"We do hope so, my lord," Brown said. "But since we don't know what he was planning and why, we can't rule out that he hadn't set in motion something that could be harmful to you or someone here. That's why it's imperative we discover everything we can about him."

Stella, who'd been crinkling her porcelain-like brow in concentration, laid her hand lightly on Lyndy's arm, her face lit up with recognition. "Prescott. Pistol Prescott! I remember him now."

"Pistol?" Inspector Brown said. "Is that a moniker for his racing acumen?"

"If memory serves," Lyndy added, "Prescott didn't have a winning record until recently, which was part of why he got caught up in the scandal. Sudden success is suspect."

"You're right," Stella said, laughing mirthlessly. "His full name is . . ." She hesitated, correcting herself. "Was Jesse James Prescott. He got the nickname Pistol, not for his speed as a jockey but because he was never without a pocket revolver, one he claimed once belonged to Jesse James, the outlaw, and his namesake. But being named after the outlaw and wanting to kill someone isn't the same thing. What reason could he possibly have to want to hurt anyone?"

"We didn't find a gun, of any kind, on the victim," Brown said, without answering her question.

"He must've lost it when the horses trampled him," Stella said.

"No, we searched the whole area. We never recovered an unclaimed gun." The inspector's countenance clouded, and Lyndy took a hard swallow. "Tell me more about this scandal, if you would, my lord."

CHAPTER 9

❧

Mrs. Robertson, her keys jingling at her side, paced back and forth the full length of her small study, wringing her hands. The distant roll of thunder echoed in her ears.

Where was the wee lad? His supper had long since grown cold.

With the Kendricks returning from Southampton with their guests, and still no sign of Robbie, the housekeeper had told herself to buck up and see them settled in. With Miss Kendrick dashing away after receiving a note from Lord Lyndhurst, the old auntie taking to her bed, and Mr. Kendrick and Mr. Swenson off in the motorcar soon after, only the Swenson women were left to attend to before they too departed for dinner. Mrs. Swenson wanted a fresh set of linens, Miss Swenson insisted a bath be drawn, and the Swensons' maid had to be shown about. When Ethel had it all in hand, Mrs. Robertson retreated to her study, pouring over her accounts. With the upcoming wedding and the arrival of wedding guests, there had been a flush of new expenses to tally. But the carriage accident had been on everyone's tongue. Two men had died, they said, many more had been injured. Only her long years in service had kept her fears from showing on her face. And still, there'd been no Robbie. Abandoning her receipts, she paced, imaging any manner of ill that could've befallen her dear nephew.

The clatter of carriage wheels on the drive drew Mrs. Robertson to the window. It was Lord Atherly's. Two wee children scrambled out, a lass and a laddie. Stumbling with fatigue, the wee lass hooked her finger over the bridge of her nose and sucked on her thumb. They waited in the drive, shivering in the cooling night air. Ethel went out to meet them and wrapped an arm around each bairn's shoulder, cooing words of assurance. Mr. Tims, not unkindly, shooed them toward the front door while the coachman unstrapped more luggage.

More guests? Where were their parents? Where was Mrs. Robertson going to put them? Who was going to look after them? Ethel already had too much to do. Mrs. Robertson would need to hire a nanny. As the housekeeper mentally considered and rejected several available village lasses, the top of a man's head bobbed by along the path to the tradesmen's entrance. *Thank God!* She'd know that jaunty step anywhere. She clasped her hands to her chest in gratitude and strode quickly from her room.

"Robbie, it that you?" she said, throwing open the door. She had a mind to scold him for making his poor auntie fret, but for the bandage covering the side of his head, his flaxen hair matted with something resembling blood, she held her tongue. Instead, she cooed and fussed, snatching his arm and pulling him into the safety of the servants' hall. "You're injured, lad. What happened?"

Before Robbie could speak a word, the housekeeper forced him gently down into a chair. Mrs. Downie left checking what was cooking in the bain-marie by the window and set a cup of tea on the table. The housekeeper, eyeing the bandage, longed to brush the hair from his forehead as she was wont to do when he was a wee one. But her nephew, gratefully reaching for his tea, was a grown man now, broad at the shoulders and a full head taller than she. Even so, allowing him the time to relish the hot, sweetened tea without pressing for answers tested the limits of Mrs. Robertson's immense patience. Despite the bristly whiskers on his upper lip, he was still his sister's bairn; she could barely contain her concern.

When Robbie set down his cup, Mr. Tims strolled into the room, his perpetual frown flicking at the edges at the sight of her nephew at the table.

"We have unexpected houseguests, Mrs. Robertson."

"Yes, I know."

"Mr. Kendrick's brother and his family. Ethel has begun settling the children in. They will need supper, Mrs. Downie." The cook nodded but made no motion toward the kitchen. She too wanted to hear what Robbie had to say. "Mr. Kendrick, the junior, is dining with the Kendricks at Morrington Hall. He will need a room made up."

"Of course, but would you be so kind as to give me a few wee moments? As you can see, my nephew has arrived and he's injured."

"I do hope you are well, young man?" Mr. Tims inquired, eyeing the bandage on Robbie's head. The lad nodded over his cup of tea.

"Thank you. It looks worse than it is."

"If that's all, Mr. Tims?" Mrs. Robertson said, wanting to hurry the butler along. "I will be there presently."

Mrs. Robertson turned to Robbie the moment the butler's back had disappeared through the door. "You feeling a bit better, lad? Can you tell us what happened?"

Without asking, Mrs. Downie had ensconced herself at the table at Robbie's right, her arms folded to support the weight of her ample bosom, so Mrs. Robertson lowered herself into the chair on his left. Thank goodness Ethel had taken charge of the children. The maid would be able to attend to much that needed doing, leaving Mrs. Robertson time before she was called away.

"Aye, Auntie. I am sorry to have kept you waiting. I know you'd had a meal prepared and everything."

"Don't you worry about that, love," Mrs. Downie replied. "I'll warm it up for you in no time." And good to her word, she pushed back from the table and disappeared into the kitchen.

"By now, you must've heard the news about the accident at the docks at Southampton?" Robbie said, lightly touching his bandaged head. Mrs. Robertson nodded. "As you see, I got a wee bit caught up in it. Had to spent much of the afternoon speaking to the police. That's why I'm late."

"But how did you get injured, lad?"

"When those horses rounded the corner at a gallop, I knew to keep well away. But then this man stumbled by me. He had to have noticed them coming. I don't know why he kept going, but he did, straight into their path."

Mrs. Downie, shuffling along quickly, reappeared with a plate covered with a plain white tea towel, and another with a large slice of Dundee cake. She set the plates before Robbie and lifted the cloth, revealing a heaping portion of steaming neeps and tatties, a roll, and a slice of pheasant pie she must've set aside from the Kendricks' luncheon. If Mrs. Downie didn't tell, neither would Mrs. Robertson. The cook placed a knife, fork, and napkin beside the plate.

"You were saying, love?" Mrs. Downie said, settling back into her seat. After her kindness, Mrs. Robertson didn't have the heart to remind the cook she had business elsewhere.

Sighing appreciatively, Robbie shoveled several ravenous bites into his mouth before continuing.

"I grabbed at the poor lad's coat, hoping to stop him, but he was small and wiry and moving forward fast. And his coat was thin. When it slid off his arm, I should've let go. But I dinna. Instead, the coat freed itself and slipped off him. Without the sudden loss of the lad's weight pulling me forward, I lost my balance. I was still clutching the coat when I slammed against a brick wall."

"You poor lad," Mrs. Robertson said.

"At least you didn't find yourself beneath the horses' hooves," Mrs. Downie said when Robbie took a few more bites of his dinner. "We wouldn't be talking right now if you did."

"Aye, it could've been worse," he said, after wiping his lips with his napkin. "They gave me a tincture for the pain, but the wretch I tried to stop is dead."

Mrs. Robertson glanced at the tiny watch on her chatelaine. Ethel would be needing her soon. She rose from the table, confident Mrs. Downie, who had poured Robbie another cup of tea, would hover protectively over the lad as he finished his dinner.

"I'm sorry, but I've got to attend to these new guests. Then we'll see to settling you in. I want to hear all about your trip to America."

"Of course, Auntie." He smiled at her, then winced at the pain. Inwardly, Mrs. Robertson flinched in sympathy. Brave lad, trying to save that man.

When Mrs. Robertson dragged herself away, Mrs. Downie asked, "Do you think that man did it on purpose? Jumping in front of those horses like that?"

What on earth? Mrs. Robertson's heel hit the wooden floor plank hard as she came to a halt by the door. Mrs. Robertson pivoted around, preparing to scold the cook for voicing such scandalous conjecture when Robbie's thoughtful expression stilled her tongue. Could there be some truth to it?

"I've been asking myself the same question," he said. "I dinna think so at the time, but after all the police's questions called to mind the momentum he had, racing toward his doom if you like. It did make me wonder."

"Perhaps he was simply rushing about, preoccupied with a

task we'll never know, and didn't spot the carriage coming?" Mrs. Robertson said, hoping to put an end to the conjecture.

Robbie hesitated, as if to say more, then changed his mind about it. "More likely than not, Auntie," Robbie said, before taking an enthusiastic bite of his cake.

"Or someone in the alley pushed him," Mrs. Downie said.

"Mrs. Downie!" The housekeeper couldn't let the cook by with that comment. Of all the wicked, ridiculous things to say. Why on earth would anyone do such a thing? Mrs. Downie had always been a bit of a gossip, but this was going too far. "That is the most absurd thing I have ever heard you say."

The cook shrugged. "You would never have thought we'd have three murders in the Forest in so many months, either." Robbie paused his fork halfway to his mouth in surprise. "You have to admit, Mrs. Robertson," Mrs. Downie said, hauling herself up from the table and clearing away Robbie's dinner plate, "it's not as preposterous as it sounds."

What could Mrs. Robertson say? Mrs. Downie was right.

"I remember a mention of doping, which isn't uncommon, and race fixing, which is, but it was the audacity of the ring-in schemes that made the headlines," Lyndy said of the scandal.

"Ring-in schemes?" Inspector Brown asked.

"That's when someone switches look-alike horses either before or after a race," Stella explained.

"And how was Mr. Prescott involved in all this?" Brown asked.

Lyndy shrugged. "I'm afraid the details beyond what I've already mentioned have long left my memory."

"My father will know more about it," Stella said.

"I'm not certain he would. It all happened about the time you would've left New York," Lyndy said.

A creak of a floorboard behind him caused Lyndy to turn around. A man with a well-trimmed beard and damp tan duster coat hovered in the door to the grand saloon. Goggles dangled from around his neck. Glancing at the stranger's stylish leather shoes, Lyndy suspected he wasn't someone's chauffeur. But then who was he? How did he get past whoever was manning the front door? And most importantly, how long had he been standing there? When he spotted Lyndy staring at him, he strolled toward them like he lived there.

"Well, hello, Stella, darling. Which one of these fine gentlemen is to be your lord and master?"

Lyndy liked the ring of the title *lord and master*, but from the icy expression on her face, Stella wasn't as equally pleased.

"Hello, Mr. Swenson," she said, her tone flat and unimpressed. "May I introduce Lord Lyndhurst and Inspector Brown of the Hampshire Constabulary."

Lyndy turned a keen eye on the newcomer. So, this was Swenson. Mr. Theodore Swenson's reputation on the turf for breeding champions was second only to his friend and fellow Kentuckian, Elijah Kendrick. Several chaps Lyndy knew had had good runs with Swenson thoroughbreds. Lyndy aimed to get the man's opinion on Orson and Tupper tonight at dinner. Assuming he was more reasonable than Mr. Kendrick.

"I am pleased to know you, Lord Lyndhurst," Mr. Swenson said, offering his hand.

"Inspector." Brown acknowledged the newcomer with a tilt of his head. "And congratulations on your upcoming wedding, my lord. You and Miss Stella will make a fine match."

"Thank you, Mr. Swenson. How kind of you to make the journey."

Inspector Brown turned to Lyndy. "With your permission, my lord, I'd like to show the photograph to other men on the estate, starting with the stable staff."

"Of course, Inspector," Stella said, answering for Lyndy. "Whatever you need to do."

Lyndy had hoped to keep the staff out of this but was loath

to contradict Stella. "I trust you'll keep the disruption to a minimum. This close to the wedding, I wouldn't want to put undue stress on the staff."

"You can rest assured, my lord, we will conduct our investigation as swiftly and discretely as possible. We will get to the bottom of this."

Stella rested her hand on Lyndy's shoulder reassuringly, lightening his mood.

"Let us hope so, Inspector. All Miss Kendrick's and my plans shall be for naught if someone comes to the door and shoots me with Jesse James's gun."

Lyndy regretted his flippant remark the moment he said it. Stella's hand clutched Lyndy's shoulder in distress. Only Theo Swenson laughed.

"I dare say, I will do everything to prevent that from happening," Inspector Brown said, taking Lyndy's flippancy for fear. "I would like for one of my men to stay close if that would be amenable?"

Lyndy was about to object—who needed a policeman underfoot? But the truth of what he said blossomed as a wave of heat in his chest. Lyndy, though he wouldn't admit it even to himself, suffered a twinge of trepidation.

Sensing Lyndy's apprehension, the inspector added, "You won't even know he's here."

"If you think it best," Lyndy conceded. Relief washed over Stella's smiling face.

"Good. Then I will take my leave," Brown said. He dipped his head almost imperceptibly and left.

"Shall we join the others, Mr. Swenson?" Lyndy said, gesturing for Stella and the horse breeder to precede him toward the drawing room.

"Ah, none of this 'Mr. Swenson' stuff, son. Call me—"

"Theo!" Mr. Kendrick said when they entered, brightening as if he hadn't been brawling on the floor with his brother a few minutes ago. "Where have you been? You didn't happen to see the baron arrive with Challacombe, did you? He said he'd come before dinner. I wonder what's keeping him."

"Didn't see your baron, Elijah. I was too busy admiring your automobile," Mr. Swenson said. "I'll have to get something like it before I head home."

Mr. Kendrick's lips spread into a wide grin, his cheeks still flush from his fight. Mr. Swenson tugged the goggles over his head. Handing them and his duster to Fulton, who had tracked him down, he added, "And who are all these fine people?"

Lyndy proceeded to introduced Theo Swenson to his parents and friends. Mother graciously welcomed him, inquiring after his wife and daughter, who'd be arriving shortly. Owen quickly offered him a drink. Theo Swenson and Jed Kendrick shook hands as if they were old friends.

"Has the policeman gone?" Mother asked, as Lyndy took up his half-finished glass of sherry and settled in with his friends near the fire. An inexplicable chill had grabbed hold of him.

"He has."

Mother's shoulders relaxed and returned to the conversation she'd been having with Sir Alfred about his mother's new garden. Should Lyndy divulge that the policeman was questioning the staff and that he'd be placing a police guard on the house? Typically, Lyndy relished the pinched expression such a revelation would cause. But not tonight.

"Where are the children?" he asked.

"I've sent them to Pilley Manor with the luggage," Lady Atherly said.

"Daddy," Stella said, "Inspector Brown was telling us about the man who was killed in Southampton."

"And?"

"It was Pistol Prescott."

Owen gulped down the last few drams in his glass. "The disgraced jockey from America?" Of course, Owen would know of him too. "What was he doing in Southampton?"

"That's what the police are attempting to discover," Lyndy said.

"Did you hear about the scandal Pistol Prescott was involved in?" Stella asked, pressing her father for an answer.

"Of course I did. It was disgusting. Half a dozen jockeys and trainers tainted the sport with their doping, race fixing, and filthy ring-in schemes. All of them lost their jobs, their licenses, and thankfully won't ever work on the track again. Most were lucky not to end up in jail."

No wonder the man wanted to murder someone. Lyndy suppressed a strong desire to pace. *But why me or someone at Morrington Hall? None of us were involved.*

"Prescott was lucky he didn't get tarred and feathered. Good riddance, I say."

"Come now, Elijah," Theo Swenson said. "No man deserves getting trampled, no matter what he's done." Mr. Kendrick shrugged.

"But what do you think he was doing in Southampton?" Stella asked, tenacious in her questioning as always when she was unsatisfied with the answers. It was a quirk about her Lyndy had come to admire. Except when he was on the receiving end, of course. "And why would he have a clipping of our wedding announcement in his pocket?"

"Maybe your daddy invited him," Jed taunted, knowing full well his brother, with all his faults, would never associate with anyone who cheated on the racetrack. It was one of Elijah Kendrick's few redeeming qualities.

"As usual, you are making too much of this," Mr. Kendrick said, ignoring his brother. "The man was in the wrong place at the wrong time. End of story."

"But that may not be the end of the story," Stella said. "What you don't know is that Prescott threatened to kill someone before he died."

Lyndy sighed in silent relief. They hadn't spoken of it, but how grateful he was that Stella hadn't mentioned the minor details about whom. Again, he was struck by how she could read his mind.

"But we don't know why," she added. "And now Pistol Prescott's gun is missing."

"That is a bad business," Papa said, no doubt recalling how much he'd been rattled when someone had stolen his valuable fossils.

"Is that what you meant by someone shooting you with Jesse James's gun?" Theo Swenson said. For a second time, Lyndy regretted his remark.

"What's this, Lyndy?" Mother said, her voice pitched higher than usual. "What does Mr. Swenson mean?"

"Sorry to worry you, ma'am," Theo Swenson said. "Having fallen on hard times, Prescott probably pawned the gun. Anyone with half an eye for such a thing would know its worth and offer him more than he could refuse."

"But—" Stella began.

The neighing of horses and the crunching of wagon wheels in the gravel drive announced the arrival of two carriages before they passed by the French windows. The rain pattered lightly against the glass, but Lyndy could tell there was no horse wagon attached to either of them. Not the baron then.

"But nothing," Stella's father said. "Like I said, you make too much of everything. If that man were still alive, blocking the aisle of the church, waving his gun at your viscount on your wedding day, I still wouldn't be bothered. You didn't know Prescott like we did." He looked to Mr. Swenson for affirmation, who nodded knowingly. "The man was a coward. He couldn't have squashed a flea."

"You agree with him, Mr. Swenson?" Stella asked.

"I do, darling. You shouldn't trouble yourself a minute longer over the likes of Jesse Prescott."

"For once, I agree with your daddy," Jed said. "A lady like

you've become shouldn't get wrapped up thinking about such filthy things as guns and killings."

Stella caught Lyndy's eye, sharing his amusement at the irony. Stella's uncle had no idea what "filthy things" she'd been involved in.

"Well put, Mr. Kendrick," Mother said, smugly glaring at Lyndy. "I've often advised your niece to stay clear of anything that might taint the Earl of Atherly's good name."

"More than her son has already done, that is," Owen said good-naturedly.

Everyone shared in the laugh, everyone except Mother, of course, and Mr. Kendrick, who'd lumbered from his chair to stare out the rain-streaked windows. "Where is the damn baron with that champion horse?"

CHAPTER 10

Constable Waterman wanted to go home. He'd never been fond of Southampton. The crowds of passengers had thinned, but the wagons laden with crates of cotton and silk, sacks of sugar and grains, barrels of butter, and tins of tea would clatter down the town quay for hours yet. A product of the Forest, Waterman wasn't used to the cramped buildings, the chaos, the noise, the stench of the city docks. Give him a boisterous drift, when Commoners annually round up their Forest ponies, or the gentile bustle of Lyndhurst High Street any day. But his wife, Meredith, and his warm cottage would have to wait.

Waterman lifted his boot over a fresh horse pile and knocked. He pulled the collar of his policeman's jacket up against the chill. A fire truck wailed past. He covered his ears, but they were still ringing when the shopkeeper, a man with a pencil-thin mustache and hair thickly slathered with pomade, cracked open the door.

"Good evening, sir. I'm Constable Waterman, making inquiries after this man." He presented the photograph. "Could he have been in your shop today?"

The merchant grumbled at having been called away from his tea. When pressed, he gave the photograph a passing glance, denied ever seeing anyone like that, and promptly shut his door. And so it went. After knocking on dozens of doors, Waterman had nothing but mud on his boots and reddened knuckles to show for it. He plodded on to the next building on the quay, the cold rain *tap-tapping* on the crown of his helmet.

With Inspector Brown off to face them at Morrington Hall, Waterman had stayed to assist the Southampton men. Sergeant Clark had first assigned Waterman to interview onlookers, an endless string of passengers, drivers, tradesmen, and dock-workers who'd helplessly witnessed a man get trampled. If it had been a routine carriage accident, Sergeant Clark would've interviewed the drivers of the two vehicles involved, informed the dead man's family of the tragedy, typed up his report, and called it a day. But with the cab driver unconscious in hospital, the wagon driver out of view when the accident occurred, and an unidentified victim, last heard threatening to kill someone, Sergeant Clark needed all the help he could get.

After a couple of hours, and learning nothing new, Waterman had spoken to a Robbie McEwan, a Scot who had arrived on the ship from New York that morning. He'd witnessed the dead man stumble into the path of the horses, and in trying to save the chap got his head banged up. Mr. McEwan wasn't acquainted with the victim, but had witnessed him coming from the direction of the alley behind Snook's, the fruit market. It was the only lead they had. Then news came that Inspector Brown had identified the dead man as Jesse James Prescott, a jockey from America, and that locating the victim's gun took priority. That's when it got complicated. With Sergeant Clark interviewing the proprietors of Snook's, the rest of the South-ampton men searching for the pistol, Waterman had been left to conduct the house-to-house inquiry.

Only five more blocks to go. Waterman blew warm breath into his cupped, numb hands.

Waterman gratefully huddled beneath the shelter of a second-floor balcony, the sign above his head swaying with the breeze that had picked up off the water. THE RIVOLI INN. He tried the handle, and happily, the door opened into a lobby, equipped with a registration desk, two wicker rocking chairs by the expansive front window, two by the hearth, and a lush fern in a tall brass plant stand. The glow of the crackling fire colored the whitewashed walls with shadows of orange and gold, and colorful but faded area rugs dotted the plank floor—a workman's hotel, simple, clean, and welcoming. But no one was about.

The constable tapped the bell on the desk; its ring echoed in the empty room. A middle-aged woman, her black hair pulled back tightly into a bun, emerged from a side door, brushing something from the starched white apron she wore over a plain black dress.

"How can I help you, Officer?" Her accent was thick with a singsong lilt that said she wasn't born in this country. Not unheard of in this bustling port city that beckoned a good life for those willing to work for it. France or Italy, perhaps? Waterman was terrible with accents.

"I'm Constable Waterman, and you are?"

"Marie Prudhon. This is my hotel."

"Very good, Mrs. Prudhon. I'm hoping to trace the movements of the man killed in the carriage accident this morning."

"Oh, bad business, no?" she said sympathetically. "You think he might've been staying here?"

"It's just routine. I'm asking everyone along the quay." Except for the sighting near the fruit merchant, they had no idea where Jesse Prescott had been or why he was on the docks. With such dismal luck tracking down any information in that regard, Waterman could only assume Prescott arrived on a ship this morning.

"What was the man's name?" she asked, opening the large leather guest register book.

"Jesse Prescott." She retrieved a pair of spectacles from her apron pocket and settled them on the tip of her patrician nose before using her finger to trace the lines of names written across several pages.

"I am sorry, Monsieur Waterman. I have no one registered in that name."

"Perhaps he visited someone here?" Waterman retrieved the photo from inside his breast pocket but didn't turn it around immediately. "I must warn you; this isn't a pretty picture."

"Let me see," she said, reaching for the photograph. "Yes, I know this man." Waterman swelled with self-satisfaction and was mentally congratulating himself for his persistence when the hotel matron added, "I should've known."

"Should've known what?" Had he congratulated himself too soon?

"Follow me." She tossed the spectacles back on the register, skirted the desk, and headed for an unmarked door Waterman hadn't noticed on the other side of the room. The matron produced a jumbled set of keys from her apron pocket. She swiftly found the right one and unlocked the door. After pulling it open, she stepped aside, revealing a small, tidy linen closet. A worn leather steamer trunk sat in the middle of the floor. Faded stenciled letters read *JJP*.

"I wondered why he never came back," Madame Prudhon added. "Said he would be a couple of hours. He had a boat to catch, you see."

A boat to catch? Where was Prescott going? Had he premeditated his need to escape? Or perhaps the jockey hadn't arrived this morning as Waterman assumed, after all. If so, where had he been staying? When had he arrived? What had Prescott been up to?

"Did he say where he was going?"

"Back to America."

"If he didn't stay with you, why do you have his trunk?"

"He stopped in hoping to store his trunk. I said he could, for a small fee, of course."

"Of course."

Waterman knelt in front of the trunk. "Don't happen to have the key, do you?" he asked, flipping the brass lock on the hinge with his finger.

The matron shook her head. Then she raised a finger. "Ah, but I have the next best thing." She crossed back over to the desk and returned with a flat-head screwdriver. She inserted the screwdriver into the keyhole. After a moment of jiggling and twisting, the lock flopped open. When Waterman raised his eyebrows in surprise, she shrugged. "Monsieur was not the first to leave behind locked luggage."

With the lock swiftly dispatched, Waterman lifted the lid. He did so slowly, conscientious of the dangers of the unknown. But the trunk held no surprises. Only the usual: undergarments; a couple of pairs of cotton shirts; a cheap, dark gray, worsted suit; a pair of boots; a shaving kit; and a packet of miscellaneous racing papers. The one unusual item was a pair of dark blue denim pants with metal rivets; Waterman had never seen anything like them.

Waterman pulled out the items one by one. When he stared at the bottom of the empty trunk, he pulled up the cotton fabric lining it. No hidden compartment, no billfold, and most importantly, no gun. Frustrated, he gathered up the pile of Jesse Prescott's belongings and tossed them carelessly back into the trunk. Two small pieces of paper fluttered to the ground. Cursing himself for not thoroughly checking the pockets, Waterman picked them up. One was a torn receipt for a wager at last week's St. Leger Stakes. Prescott had bet on Challacombe to win. The other was a round-trip ferry ticket to the Island, dated two days later.

Finally! Something to take back to Inspector Brown. Waterman could already taste the steak and kidney pie warming in the oven for him when he dodged back into the rain.

*　　*　　*

"My, my, who do we have here?" Sir Owen whispered when the two Swenson women swept into the room. Penny, yawning, snapped her mouth shut when she caught sight of Sir Owen staring at her. She sheepishly batted her eyelids at him, a coquettish smile on her brightly rouged lips.

"Mrs. Sarah Swenson and Miss Penelope Swenson," Fulton announced.

Sir Owen, captivated by Penny's beauty, and the tight bodice of her sky-blue silk and lace evening gown, winked at Sir Alfred, who bolted up to his full height.

Stella rolled her eyes. *Men!*

After the introductions were made, the two Swenson women immediately separated, Penny gravitating toward the younger men clustered around the mantel, Mrs. Swenson joining the ladies.

"How kind of y'all to invite us to your beautiful home," Mrs. Swenson said, admiring the vaulted ceiling, the portraits on the walls, the crystal vases overflowing with fragrant blossoms. "Elijah's descriptions don't do it justice."

I bet they don't. Daddy never boasted about anything he didn't own.

"We were afraid you wouldn't make it," Lady Alice said, having returned from calling on a neighbor. "What with the rain, and the wind, and the roads being quite muddy."

Stella hadn't noticed the wind whistling outside. She peered through the windowpanes, blurred by the rain. Flashes of distant lightning danced across the sky.

"And you've had a long day," Lady Atherly added politely.

"What's that when you've invited us to dinner at Morrington Hall?" Mrs. Swenson said. "Of course, we wanted to meet y'all. With Stella and Penelope growing up together, that makes us practically family."

Stella distinctly remembered Mrs. Swenson complaining about the invitation, that is, before she discovered potential husbands for Penny would be there.

"Are all these spectacular bouquets from your garden? I caught a glimpse of it as we came in. It looked wonderful, even in the dim light. I hope you'll invite me back when we get better weather."

Lady Atherly's face softened. Whether she knew it or not, Mrs. Swenson had found the one possible way into Lady Atherly's good graces—praise her garden.

"Please, won't you sit?" Lady Atherly said, indicating the seat beside her. She'd never offered for Stella to sit that close.

Within minutes, Mrs. Swenson and Lady Atherly were companionably discussing the wedding plans, which Stella had wholeheartedly given into Lady Atherly's capable hands. What did she care what flavor the cake would be or what flowers she would carry? She was thrilled Uncle Jed and Aunt Ivy had come, but all she wanted was to start her life with Lyndy, free of her father's control. When the discussion included seating arrangements at the reception, Stella interrupted.

"I'd like to thank you, Lady Atherly."

"For what, Miss Kendrick?" Despite the wedding being a few days off, Lady Atherly still refused to call Stella by her Christian name. Would she ever?

"For inviting my uncle to dinner. I know he arrived unexpectedly."

A laugh rose from the group across the room. Penny, who had weaseled her way between the two young bachelors, held a drink in one hand and the other against her heaving chest. As if the men needed help noticing Penny's ample bosom. Lyndy, taking a sip of his sherry, rocked on his heels. Stella had seen him do it countless times. It was an endearing sign of his boredom, his restlessness, his desire to be anywhere but cooped up in the drawing room listening to other people talk. It was a sentiment they shared. With the exception of enjoying Uncle Jed's company, Stella too wished she were somewhere else. Riding Tully in the rain would be an improvement over listening to Penny's hollow laughter.

Lady Atherly dismissed Stella's gratitude with a flick of her wrist. "No need to mention it again." The tone in her voice was light, but Stella caught her meaning. The dismissal was for Stella as well.

"If you'll excuse me," Stella said as Lady Atherly turned back to her guest.

"From what you've told me, you have the wedding plans all sewn up, Lady Atherly," Mrs. Swenson was saying when Stella leaped from the settee. "And you're so kind to have taken the poor motherless child under your wing."

If I hear her say that one more time . . . Unfortunately, the conversation with Penny and the younger men was no better.

"So, what is it about the bride-to-be you like best, Lyndy?" Sir Owen was asking when Stella silently took a place among them. Lyndy greeted her with a soft peck on the cheek.

Penny regarded them with a familiar expression of part disgust, part jealousy. "I imagine it's her money." Penny laughed lightheartedly, but she intended the comment to hurt. And it did.

"Oh, my!" Sir Alfred sputtered. Lyndy yanked on the sleeve of his dinner jacket.

"What? Did I say something wrong?" Penny asked with false innocence.

"I'm afraid that's a touchy subject, Miss Swenson," Sir Owen playfully admonished.

"I'd marry Miss Kendrick if she hadn't a penny to her name," Lyndy blurted.

"Now you're talking nonsense," Penny said dismissively.

It was nonsense, and Stella and Lyndy both knew it. He would never have been allowed to marry her if she wasn't bringing a fortune to the marriage. His duty required it. Lady Atherly demanded it. With the Earl of Atherly siphoning off more funds than the estate earned to fulfill his dream of finding ancient horse fossils in Wyoming, Morrington Hall was in desperate need of an infusion of cash.

But Stella loved to think it was true, that Lyndy meant what he said.

"As we have just met, Miss Swenson," Lyndy said through clenched teeth, "I would think you are in no position to comment on—"

An intense flash of brilliant light radiated through the windows. For a second, the drawing room was transported from evening back to midday. A boom of thunder exploded a moment later, shaking the ground and rattling the paintings on the walls. Penny screamed, her eyes squeezed tight and her hands covering her ears. With the second clap, a crackling that set the hairs on Stella's neck on end, Penny dropped into a squat and curled up into herself as tightly as possible. Sir Owen knelt at her side and wrapped a comforting arm around Penny's back as Penny rocked back and forth in terror until the crashes of thunder rolled off into the distance.

"It's past now, Penelope, darling," Mr. Swenson said over the clinking of the crystal chandelier as it swayed from the storm's impact.

That's when Stella smelled smoke.

"My God! The stables are on fire!" Sir Alfred shouted, pointing out the window.

Tully!

With a single thought in her mind, Stella jumped up and raced Lyndy toward the French doors. They bumped shoulders when each sought to get outside first. Lyndy pushed the doors open. Caught by the wind, the doors clattered against the wall. The crash of a crystal vase, the shouting, and the heavy footfalls of the others dashing around behind her weren't enough to slow her down.

Once she was outside, the wind tugged at Stella's hair and gown, whipping the dress's train like a whirligig behind her. The rain, driving sideways, stung like tiny cold pellets against her exposed skin; her silk gown protected her only slightly better from the elements. Her beaded pumps, once ivory, were now a muddy mess. But the smell of burning wood, the blaze of the fire, raging even in this storm, propelled her forward. Horses whinnied in fear, but thank heaven, the stone stables stood apart and unharmed from the fire. Lightning had struck the ancient oak fifty yards behind the stables, the one they called the Earl Oak, five hundred years old if it was a day. Towering sixty to seventy feet above them, its branches, burning as bright as a giant beacon, soared toward the sky like a man imploring aid from heaven.

Lyndy caught up to her and snatched her hand as he passed. Together, they dashed for the shelter of the stable yard. Gates, the stablemaster, the grooms, and the stable boys, rivulets of rain dripping from the brim of their hats, raced around putting out any stray embers landing on the roof or in the straw bale stores. With no hat or coat, Stella was drenched to the bone, her hair sticking to her cheeks, her dress scandalously clinging to every curve of her body. *At least the horses are safe.* She shivered.

Lyndy, his hair and clothes just as wet, snatched up two gray woolen horse blankets from a pile on a bench and wrapped one around her. The rough blanket scratched against Stella's exposed neckline and arms, but she hugged it tighter around herself to ward off the chill. To her surprise, Lyndy stripped off his jacket. The pale skin of his chest and stomach shined through the wet, white dress shirt. He toweled off his hair, which for a moment resembled an angry porcupine before he straightened it with his fingers. No longer dripping, he wrapped his blanket and his arms around Stella's shoulders. After the dash to the stables, her breath was rough and labored. Lyndy's nearness, his warmth, didn't help things.

"I've known you to go to great lengths to skip Mother's social events," Lyndy said, tucking a soaked strand of hair behind her ear. His fingers trembled, and she could feel the pulse of his racing heart against her. "But this? However did you arrange for a lightning strike?"

Stella smiled at him, relishing this moment alone.

"I noticed you willingly followed me, my lord," she teased when he bent his head to kiss her. His lips were warm, and surprisingly dry. He slipped his hand into her hair as if hoping to pull her even closer. And then distant thunder crackled, and the horses whinnied again.

"We need to go calm the horses," she said against Lyndy's lips.

Lyndy blinked slowly and sighed. His cheeks were flush; he too was breathing hard. "That's not all I need to calm." He spoke so softly, Stella wasn't sure he'd said it.

He laced his fingers with hers once more, and they walked toward the stalls that housed the horses. They passed a window, and the fire outside cast a glow across Lyndy's features. He'd never looked so handsome. Another horse whinnied.

"They're still afraid," she added.

And so was she. She knew so little about Pistol Prescott's intentions. Had the threat of violence died with him? Or was Lyndy, or someone he loved, still in danger?

Stella quickened her step, longing to comfort and be comforted by Tully, her beloved horse.

CHAPTER 11

❧

"Gentlemen," Baron Branson-Hill said when Lyndy and the men clustered together under umbrellas held up by the footmen. A little rain wasn't going to stop this private showing.

After returning from the stables, Mother, to both their surprise, excused Stella from attending dinner. Whether Mother worried about Stella's health this close to the wedding, didn't want to interrupt the flow of the evening by waiting for Stella to change, or was content enough in Mrs. Swenson's company, Lyndy couldn't say. But he was glad of it. Stella needed the evening to get warm; he needed the evening to cool down. In the stables, his desire almost got the best of him.

Only three, no, two more days, Lyndy thought, when Finn, his valet, helped him into dry clothes. And then the baron had arrived, having laid up in Rosehurst during the worst of the storm—a welcome, well-timed distraction indeed.

"May I present the winner of the 1905 St. Leger Stakes . . ." The baron, as thin as a hat stand but filling the space with his presence, paused for dramatic effect. "And my latest acquisition, Challacombe."

Challacombe sauntered down the ramp of his horse wagon, following Leonard, the head groom's lead, as if expecting to be applauded. Considering the horse's lustrous bay coat, exquisite muscle tone, and white star on its forehead, Lyndy nearly obliged. The animal was a stunner.

"Well, I'll be," Jed Kendrick said. "That horse is a beauty."

"Here, here, Baron," Owen said. "He's lovely."

"Yes, absolutely magnificent," Sir Alfred agreed.

Challacombe, head held high despite the rain, swished his tail and basked in the attention. Lyndy whispered to Leonard, who slipped him the nub of a peppermint stick, a treat for the horses, thanks to Stella. All their horses loved it. Would this champion racehorse enjoy it too? Lyndy stepped out from under the umbrella and approached the horse. Challacombe eyed him cautiously, snorting a warning until Lyndy slipped his open palm under the horse's giant, soft lips. After one sniff, the horse lapped up the peppermint and nudged Lyndy's hand for more.

"Yes, a fine specimen," Theo Swenson said, stroking his beard. "I know now, Elijah, why you wanted me to see him. Now I am sorry to have missed the St. Leger Stakes."

Baron Branson-Hill beamed with pride at this barrage of compliments. "He is the highlight of my collection."

"I always thought you were a nincompoop," Stella's father said, wiping the proud look from the baron's face.

"I beg your pardon?"

"I said, you are a nincompoop."

"I think the baron heard very well what you said, Mr. Kendrick," Lyndy said.

"Yes, indeed, milord, I did. But why, may I ask, Mr. Kendrick, do you insult me in this way?"

"Because you don't know a horse's ass from its elbow."

"Kendrick!" Lyndy chided. "Take care, man."

"Is that kind of talk necessary, Elijah?" Theo Swenson said.

"You're right, Theo," Mr. Kendrick conceded. "You've got yourself a fine Thoroughbred here, Branson-Hill."

The baron's shoulders relaxed, and he combed his fingers through his thinning brown hair. "Well, I should say so. The stallion is a champion, after all. And I'll admit I paid a tidy sum for him."

"That's what I'm talking about," Mr. Kendrick said. "You've been had, Baron. That horse is a ringer."

"What?" A chorus of protests mingled with the pattering of the rain under the hollow of the umbrellas.

"Are you suggesting someone has switched this horse for Challacombe?" Lyndy asked. Much the same as what Jesse Prescott did in Kentucky? Could it be a coincidence?

"I say!" The baron crossed his arms across his chest, his fists clenched. "How dare you say such a thing. I know of no man who would stoop to such ungentlemanly behavior."

"Good for you, Baron, that you keep such admirable company," Mr. Kendrick said. "But whatever you say, I say you've been cheated."

"It takes one to know one," Jed Kendrick muttered.

"What's that, Jed? Did you say something?" his brother said.

"I said you should know. Since ya cheated me out my rightful inheritance."

"Not that again," Mr. Kendrick sighed as if this were a long-standing feud.

"What think you, Lord Lyndhurst?" Baron Branson-Hill asked.

"I don't know of such treachery occurring on this side of the pond," Lyndy said. Should he mention the dead jockey? No, better not add to the baron's humiliation.

"Perhaps this sort of thing happens in America," Owen said, throwing in his assurances, "but no Englishman would stoop so low."

"Absolutely not," Sir Alfred said, agreeing.

Mr. Kendrick shrugged. "Wouldn't they? If they could get away with it? Don't you think, Theo?"

"I'm afraid it's true," Theo Swenson said. "But it's not your fault, Baron, most people are fooled."

Lyndy inspected the horse more closely, running his hands down the animal's legs, across his back and barrel. The horse's coat was slick with rain. Lyndy had seen Challacombe race but had never gotten this close to the stallion. He couldn't tell the difference.

"But not you, Theo," Mr. Kendrick said. "You saw it right away too, didn't you? I mean, this horse could be that two-year-old you raced at Saratoga last year."

"You mean Charmer? By God, you're right." The two men shared a laugh.

"I have to admit I saw another look-alike at Salisbury last year," Owen said, reaching out to pat the stallion on its back. "Damn fine horse, just the same. Won its race, if I recall." Owen was kindly trying to ease the baron's embarrassment. It didn't work.

"With all due respect, Mr. Kendrick, Mr. Swenson, I don't accept your conclusion." The baron, a rail of a man, trembled. From the cold or his anger, Lyndy couldn't guess which.

Lyndy raised his hand but stopped short of patting the baron's shoulder. Lyndy had never had cause to regret the dictate that kept people from wantonly touching each other in public. *Until I met Stella, that is.* The baron, his shoulders sagging, rain dripping from the end of his nose, looked pathetic. A reassuring touch on the arm would've gone a long way.

"I reckon we should go back in," Theo Swenson said. "The wind's picked up, and I, for one, am not used to this chill." To emphasize his point, he blew into his hands before rubbing them together.

"This ringer sort of thing doesn't happen in England. My horse is the real Challacombe." Despite the baron's insistence, he waved at the groom to stable the horse, without a glance at his "champion," and trudged back toward the house.

"I'd say, 'he got what he paid for' "—Mr. Kendrick chuckled when the rest of the men sought the warmth of the front hall— "but in this case, he didn't, did he?" Had the baron heard the brute's comment? Lyndy hoped not.

"That's right, Elijah," Jed Kendrick said. "Ya know just what to say when a man's down, don't ya?"

"Are you still here, Jed?" his brother asked, as he handed his rain-drenched coat to Fulton. "I thought leeches preferred being wet."

Jed snatched his brother's coat back from the startled butler, flung open the door, and threw the coat out into the rain.

"Jed, what were you thinking?" Theo Swenson, pointing at the black coat lying in the gravel, voiced Lyndy's silent question. Jed Kendrick was, by all accounts, an amiable fellow. Unlike his brother.

"You'll need a conjurer, not a valet to clean that," Owen quipped, as always trying to lighten the mood.

"You . . . how dare you . . ." Mr. Kendrick stammered with rage, his pointed finger shaking violently toward his brother. "Your children will starve before I give you another penny. Do you hear me? They'll starve in the poor house. And I want you gone from Pilley Manor before I get home!"

Jed Kendrick grabbed his brother's finger and shoved him backward. "Go to hell!"

Off balance, the older, rotund brother stumbled against a side table, knocking the silver calling card tray clattering to the floor. Jed, a smug grin widening on his face, ducked back into the rain, stomping his muddy boots over his brother's coat as he went.

Stella brushed a curl from the little girl's forehead. Gertie looked too peaceful, curled up in the blankets, to carry her to the bedroom Ethel had prepared for the children. Stella slipped down to the carpet beside the little girl. She crossed her legs, hidden beneath the yards of billowy sea-green silk of her favorite tea gown, as she'd seen photographs of the native people of the Great Plains do. After shedding her soaked, clingy evening gown, Stella had put aside convention, and her corset, and donned the most comfortable dress she owned.

As Stella settled in near the warmth of the crackling fire, Ethel scurried around the library, picking up the mess until her arms were full of the makeshift toys the lady's maid had managed to scrounge up. According to Ethel, Pilley Manor had never housed small children before, being the dowager house. If a dowager countess wished to enjoy the company of her grandchildren, she would visit them at Morrington Hall. As Ethel explained, "no self-respecting dowager would be seen entertaining children" at Pilley Manor. So it was up to Stella and Ethel to find suitable "toys." Instead of blocks, Ethel rounded up cookie tins and butter molds. With no spinning tops or cup and ball games on hand, Stella produced string to play cat's cradle. And to replace toy soldiers or dolls, Ethel borrowed several porcelain figurines from the back of a curio cabinet. Gertie clutched her favorite as she slept, a shepherdess with an attached tiny lamb.

"What are you reading, Sammy?"

After a simple supper of cold pheasant pie, string-bean salad, pickles, bread, and butter with Aunt Rachel and the children, Stella and Ethel had played with the children in the library. Long before Gertie succumbed to exhaustion, Sammy abandoned the games and crammed himself into a corner of the sofa to read a book he'd pulled from the shelf.

"Hmm?" Sammy's head drooped, his hair flopping across one eye. The boy was exhausted.

"What's your book about?" Stella asked again.

In response, Sammy lifted the book from his lap so Stella

could read the title: *Castles of England and Wales*. He continued to study one of the black and white sketches of the castles. The clock on the mantel chimed the nine o'clock hour.

"I believe it is bedtime, don't you?" Stella said. "Time to put your book away?"

Sammy ignored her.

"You heard your cousin. It's time for bed, Master Kendrick," Ethel said, with authority. When he didn't respond, she reached down and tugged the book from the boy's grasp.

"Hey, I was reading that."

"What will your daddy say if you are still awake when he gets home?" Stella added. How many times had nannies threatened her with such a statement? Would it motivate Sammy any more than it had her? Probably not but was worth a try.

"I don't want to go to bed. I'm scared."

Of Uncle Jed? Stella didn't believe it. More likely an excuse to avoid a proper bedtime. "I know you're not afraid of your daddy."

Sammy hugged his knees, resting his chin on the threadbare patch of his pants. Tomorrow Stella would send someone to get new clothes for both children.

"Not my daddy. I'm scared of the cowboy. He said he was gonna kill someone."

Cowboy? What was he talking about? Could he have seen Pistol Prescott? Overheard his threats? It was possible. Sammy and his family had arrived on the same ship as the Swensons.

"What man?" Ethel said. "No one's going to kill anyone."

"Are you talking about a man on the wharf?" Stella asked, pushing up from the floor and perching on the edge of the sofa beside him. "Why do you call him a cowboy? What else did he say?"

"Never mind." Sammy tried to shrug off her questions.

"Sammy, if you know something, you have to tell me."

The boy shook his head. Stella skimmed the room for something, anything to draw the boy back out. The book about castles lay on the oak side table. Stella snatched it up and flipped it open. She paged through it until she found the picture she needed.

"Did you know there's a castle less than eight miles from here?"

"So?" Sammy grumbled.

"It's this one." Stella tapped on a sketch. Beneath the pencil sketch of a sprawling stone fortress beside the sea were the words: *Keyhaven Castle*. "What if I took you there tomorrow?"

The idea was inspired. Stella had hoped to comb the halls of the castle, built hundreds of years ago by King Henry the VIII; there was nothing remotely like it in the States. But with all the obligatory house calls, teas, balls, and dinner parties these last few months, she hadn't found the chance to explore it yet. This way, she could invite Lyndy, and Aunt Ivy and Uncle Jed, if he wanted, to join her and the children, have Mrs. Downie pack them a picnic and make a day of it. Otherwise, Stella would be stuck helping Lady Atherly and Reverend Paine finalize the wedding plans.

"You mean it?" Sammy said, sitting up, dropping his knees with a thud on the floor. Gertie shifted in her blankets but didn't wake up.

"I don't know, miss," Ethel said, catching on to what Stella was trying to do. "It's old and abandoned and well known to be haunted." Sammy fidgeted in his seat but kept his attention firmly on the picture. "You don't want to go there, do you, Master Kendrick?"

"Yes, Miss Ethel, I sure do."

"Are you brave enough that ghosts of prisoners and dead soldiers won't keep you away?" Stella said.

Sammy squared his shoulders and puffed out his chest. "Braver."

"Then tell me what about this cowboy frightens you so much."
Caught by the women's trick, Sammy's shoulders drooped, and he
sank back into the sofa.

"Do I have to?"

"You do if you want to go to Keyhaven Castle tomorrow."

Sammy exaggerated a sigh in defeat. "It was on the pier, like
you said, Cousin Stella. The man scared me, saying he had a
score to settle with someone named Morrington. I never saw
anyone so angry before, at least not until Uncle Elijah and Pa
started fighting."

That brawl was ridiculous—two grown men. And in front of
the children, no less. But it explained how angry Pistol Prescott
must've sounded.

"That's when I started to worry," Sammy added.

"But why are you worried?" Ethel asked. "Your name is
Kendrick, not Morrington."

"But don't you see, Miss Ethel?" he said, sheepishly regarding Stella from the corner of his eye. "That angry man was talking about the fella Cousin Stella is gonna marry. He had me
calling him Lyndy, but I know his surname because when we
got to his mansion, they all said, 'Welcome to Morrington's
Hall.'"

Stella wanted to hug the boy, laugh about his mistake, tell
him there was nothing to be afraid of, but she stopped short.
Boys his age didn't enjoy hugs, even from their mothers. Or
being laughed at. He wouldn't appreciate being lied to either;
the danger to someone at Morrington Hall could be real.

"I assume your father heard everything you did and told the
police?" Ethel asked.

Sammy shook his head. "Why would Pa do that? You can't
trust the police."

Stella, who never crossed paths with a policeman until the
day she found the dead vicar a few months back, couldn't fathom
such an attitude. Why on earth would a boy of ten think that?

"But your daddy would be helping the police with their investigation."

"He'd never do that. Pa doesn't like the police."

"Even just to tell them something he overheard?" Ethel said, crossing her arms across her chest in disapproval.

Sammy squinted and made a face at Ethel as if she was missing the point.

"Pa and me weren't eavesdropping, if that's what you think," the boy said, sounding offended. "That cowboy told these things to us."

"When was that?" Stella asked.

"When Pa asked him for a light and directions to Morrington's Hall."

Stella gaped at the boy, bowled over by his revelation. Uncle Jed had encountered the jockey before the accident. He'd spoken to him, even knew of his threats. So why hadn't he told her? She'd asked her father about Pistol Prescott, had voiced her concerns over Prescott's threatening remarks, but Uncle Jed hadn't said a word.

"All the more reason to tell the police," Ethel admonished.

"That's why I didn't want to talk about it," Sammy said, injured by the maid's disapproval. "I wasn't even supposed to tell anybody," he muttered under his breath when Gertie moaned in her sleep.

Why would that be?

Ethel crouched down, slid her arms beneath the blanket and the girl, and easily hoisted them both onto her shoulder. When the maid, with her precious burden, tiptoed from the room, Stella ignored her earlier caution and wrapped her arm around Sammy, pulling him into a cuddle. He resisted for a moment, his muscles taut, his head turned away, but he eased into her embrace when he realized she wasn't letting go.

"I'm glad you told me," Stella whispered. She laid the book

in his lap, opened to the page for Keyhaven Castle. "And I'll be happy to take you to Keyhaven Castle tomorrow." Sammy snuggled closer, his eyelids drooping as he read the history of the castle.

And I'll be even happier when I get some answers from Uncle Jed.

CHAPTER 12

⁓

It was no use. Stella couldn't sleep.

She threw off the heavy bedclothes, slipped out of bed, and padded over to the wardrobe. The bed had been warm, almost stifling, but the chill in the air raised goose bumps on her skin. She snatched a pink, flower-embroidered satin robe from the wardrobe and wrapped it around her. Her wedding dress, on the back of the door, floated like a ghost in the moonlight. She caressed the silky fabric, listening, as she had for hours, to every hum, every creak, every tick of a clock.

Thud! Click!

Finally! Uncle Jed was back.

When Stella's father and the Swensons had returned from Morrington Hall, Uncle Jed wasn't with them. According to Penny, smiling and aglow from the evening, Stella had missed an eventful night. Between "Sir Owen this" and "Sir Owen that," Stella gleaned her father and Uncle Jed had quarreled again. Only with Mrs. Swenson's gentle persuasion did her father concede to let Uncle Jed and the children stay. But Uncle Jed never returned.

Stella had so many questions for him. Why had he kept quiet about speaking to the jockey and about Prescott's threats that frightened Sammy so? What else was Uncle Jed hiding? Had Prescott revealed something to him: what score he needed to settle, whom he planned to kill, or why he had a clipping of her wedding in his pocket? Stella imagined Prescott traveling the ocean, scheming, and planning to carry out his evil task. Or had he made idle threats in a heated moment? Could Uncle Jed tell which when he talked to him?

Tightening the sash around her waist, she stepped into the hall, her feet bare against the hall carpet, and tiptoed toward the stairs. She had no intention of waking the children sleeping in the guest room beside hers. But someone else was already awake. A bedroom door creaked open, a line of candlelight streaking across the hall and onto the opposite wall. Stella waited, but no one emerged. She couldn't remember whose room it was—one of the Swensons. When the door slowly closed, the light retreated with it. Unlike her, whoever it was chose to return to bed rather than satisfy their curiosity. Stella padded on.

Reaching the bottom step, she stopped, startled to hear muffled voices drifting from under the library door. She approached slowly, avoiding the loose board that creaked, and put her ear against the door.

". . . get caught?" A man's voice whispered so low Stella only heard part of what was said. Who was it? Uncle Jed? Probably. Was he talking to himself? And what was he going to get caught doing?

Stella was reaching for the doorknob when a different voice said something. The words were unintelligible through the thickness of the door. Who else was up at this hour? Frustrated, Stella knelt and peered through the keyhole, but the room was bathed in only the dim light of the fire's embers. She couldn't see a thing. She held her ear against the keyhole, but the people stopped talking.

Should she open the door? Could she justify barging in on whoever was on the other side? If it was Uncle Jed, she could. But what if it was Mr. Swenson, or worse, her father? How would she explain her nosiness?

Her knees, pressed against the hardwood floor, began to ache as she tried to decide what to do.

Bam!

Stella jumped when the front door swung open. With muffled voices and hurried footsteps, the people in the library scurried around. Not wanting to be caught snooping, Stella leaped to her feet and dashed toward the stairs. Uncle Jed staggered through the front door.

"Uncle Jed?" Then who was in the library?

"Hello, my girl, fine evening we're having."

He tossed his hat toward the hall tree. It missed by several feet and floated to the floor. He stumbled forward, tripped on the edge of the hall carpet, and bumped against the wall. Stella hurried over to steady him. He waved her attempts off, his breath reeking of whiskey.

"Fine pub ya have in this town too." He swayed, zigzagging across the hall toward the library.

"Your room is upstairs, Uncle Jed."

"Elijah forbade me to sleep under his roof, but he didn't say I couldn't drink his liquor."

"Daddy changed his mind. You're welcome to stay."

"Then, I'll just get me a little nightcap first." He grabbed for the doorknob, and overcompensating, stumbled into the library when the door opened. Stella was a step behind him.

The room was empty, but one of the French windows was ajar. Whoever had been in here had left by the window. Leaving Uncle Jed to pour himself another drink, Stella crossed the room, passing the pile of makeshift toys. She glanced over her shoulder at a clink of glass and a thud. Uncle Jed had collapsed in the overstuffed chair, his legs stretched out before him, his head, with his mouth wide open, plopped against the headrest, his arms flopped over the armrests like a rag doll. A glass of whiskey lay beside him on the floor, tipped over and empty.

So much for getting her answers tonight.

She latched the window, her breath fogging the glass, and stared out at the moonlit night, calm and clear after the storm. The distant call of a nightjar pierced the silence. She traced a question mark in the condensation and glimpsed Sir Owen disappearing around a hedge.

Sir Owen? What was he doing here?

Side by side on the bench nestled against the wall in the Pilley Manor garden, Stella shuddered as Lyndy traced the outline of her lips. And not from the chill morning air. Dried leaves rustled in the oak overhead. Holding her chin gently with the tip of his finger, he dipped his head to kiss her.

"Now, now, you two," Aunt Rachel called from her spot under the tree, startling the pair apart.

Stella and Lyndy had met almost every day after breakfast alone in this secluded spot. To talk, to commiserate, to snuggle, to kiss. And no one had ever disturbed them. Why Stella's aunt had decided to join them this morning, Stella could only guess.

"It's fine you're so sweet on each other, but you're going to have to wait." Aunt Rachel's eyelids drooped, then closed when a ray of warm sun lit her wrinkled face. Her thin, parchment-like skin seemed to glow from within. "And don't get thinking I'm going to fall asleep. With the wedding so close, I promised your mama, Lyndy, that I'd keep an eye on you." Her left eye popped open. She squeezed it shut, opening her right one instead. "Just haven't figured which one yet."

Lyndy glanced askew at their chaperone, who cackled at their expense. "Two more days," he whispered.

"Should've eloped while you had the chance," Aunt Rachel said, resting her head against the back of her wicker chair.

Maybe we should have. Nothing about the days leading up to the wedding had been blissful.

When she was a little girl, picturing her wedding, Stella couldn't have imagined the exotic landscape, the ancient church, the aristocratic husband, the castle-like estate that was to be her home, the most beautiful dress in the world. It was like a fairy tale. And with Uncle Jed, Gertie, Sammy, Aunt Ivy, Aunt Rachel, the Swensons, and her father all here to sit on her side of the aisle, she should be basking in love. Instead, her friends and family had done nothing but bicker and lie and sneak around since they got here. And according to what Lyndy told her about the fight between Daddy and Uncle Jed last night, the belligerence and animosity were getting worse.

And that was nothing compared to the questions. Peace of mind was elusive enough, on the cusp of trading her old life for a new one, without adding to the uncertainty. Why did someone send the souvenir spoon anonymously? What could be more important to her beloved Aunt Ivy than spending time with her? Why would Uncle Jed, whom she remembered as carefree and loving, deceive her about Pistol Prescott, and not tell the police everything he knew? What was Sir Owen doing in the library late last night (presuming that's why he was sneaking past the bushes) and with whom? What were they afraid of getting caught doing? Why did Daddy and Uncle Jed hate each other so much? How could the tragedy Stella witnessed, the trampling of a stranger, be a possible blessing in disguise, his death saving someone she cared about?

Considering the wedding had been the impetus for it all, Stella wasn't so sure they had made the right decision not to elope. She laced her fingers with Lyndy's and smiled halfheartedly. At least she didn't doubt her decision to marry her viscount.

"Too late now," she chuckled mirthlessly. "Though if Mrs. Swenson repeats the 'poor motherless child' quip one more time . . ."

"At this point, the best we can do is avoid Mother and Mrs. Swenson until the wedding," Lyndy said.

"I'm ahead of you there," Stella said, brightening. With such an adventure in store, she sloughed off her melancholy like a dirty pair of gloves. "I'm planning an outing to Keyhaven Castle. Care to join me?"

"That's a brilliant idea. I haven't visited there in years."

"We're bringing a picnic and making a day of it."

"We?"

"Pretty much everyone."

Stella still wasn't sure how it had evolved into such a large party. She'd planned for her, Ethel, and the children. But Aunt Ivy was coming, happily accepting the invitation to spend time together, and so too was Uncle Jed, to "make sure promises were kept." *Whatever that meant.* Her father had no intention of joining them until, overhearing Stella and Sammy discuss it at breakfast, Mr. Swenson had shown an interest and persuaded her father to come too. Stella wished Mr. Swenson had the urge to take a trip to London or, even better, Timbuktu. Maybe her father would be miles away by now. But instead, he threatened to spoil the day.

"Everyone except Mrs. Swenson, that is," Stella asked. "Your mother invited her to luncheon with her and Reverend Paine."

"Better her than us," Lyndy said.

"And better you than me at that haunted castle," Aunt Rachel chimed in. "I wouldn't step foot in that place if you told me I'd come out a giggling schoolgirl again."

"It's not haunted, Aunt," Stella said. "That's just what Ethel told Sammy."

"Even so." Aunt Rachel shifted nervously in her wicker lounge chair. "You got enough chaperones. You don't need me tagging along."

"Well, if we need more strong protectors," Stella said, chuckling at her aunt, "Sir Owen and Sir Alfred are welcome to come too. Though that would mean putting up with Penny." Penny had declared she'd go if Sir Owen went, though Stella had never invited her.

"Alfred has a prior engagement," Lyndy said when a bee buzzed past his head on its way to the last of the small blush-colored roses climbing the trellis against the wall, "but I'm certain Owen will be game. We used to explore ruins as boys. And you can ask him to explain himself."

The first thing Lyndy had told Stella when they sat down was the suspicions surrounding Baron Branson-Hill's "Challacombe." She never condoned the baron's way of acquiring horses simply to parade them around, but she empathized with the sting of betrayal the baron must be experiencing. The first thing Stella had told Lyndy was about finding Sir Owen outside last night.

"I can't fathom what he was doing here."

Lyndy wasn't being completely honest. Was it his lack of eye contact or the way his jaw muscles simultaneously slackened as his forehead tightened? Either way, Stella had learned to detect when he couldn't bring himself, for his sake or someone else's, to voice an ugly thought that had crossed his mind. Stella also knew, if it were important, he would tell her eventually.

"Brown came by again," Lyndy said, obviously changing the subject. He'd lowered his voice when Aunt Rachel's soft snores echoed the garden's birdsong. He slid closer again until their thighs and shoulders touched.

"He did?" Why hadn't Lyndy told her this sooner? "What did he say?"

"Not much, I'm afraid. The police still haven't found the gun. A bystander must've pilfered it. But they did discover he'd been in the country for a week. Seems he went to the Island at least once and attended the St. Leger Stakes." Stella focused her memory. Had she seen him there? Could something have happened there that caused him to want to kill someone at Morrington Hall?

"Tupper," was all she said.

"What?"

"Tupper placed at the St. Leger Stakes. That's the connection between Morrington Hall and Pistol Prescott. We need to figure out who the jockey bet on and whether he won or lost. We have to know—"

"So, it is conceivable . . ." Lyndy interrupted, his voice trailing to a whisper, disbelief permeating his voice and facial expression. "I could've been the man's intended victim."

Stella squeezed his hand to reassure herself as much as him, but his hand was clammy and cold. She forced a smile at him, but staring off into the middle distance, he didn't notice.

"But like Daddy told me at breakfast when I voiced my concern, 'The man's dead. He couldn't squash a bug when he was alive, let alone shoot a gun. I'd bet the farm his ghost won't do any better.'"

"I never thought I'd say this . . ." Lyndy pointed to Aunt Rachel. As she slumbered, a brave squirrel gathered the acorns littering the ground under her chaise lounge. "But your father is right. If we consider it rationally, we have no more to fear from the dead jockey than Aunt Rachel does Keyhaven Castle."

Ivy Mitchell stepped through the iron gates of Pilley Manor. Servants passed her, lugging chairs, rugs, and the wherewithal of a picnic to a dogcart. Two children chased each other, whooping and hollering. A barking mongrel dog playfully dodged through everyone's legs. Only the saddled horses, kept at bay by the grooms, stood still.

Surely, they aren't all fixin' to go to the castle? Stella had mentioned the children and a maid.

Elijah Kendrick, his arms folded across his chest, sauntered to Ivy's side. He wore a tweed coat and riding boots. Without a sideways glance, Elijah kept his attention focused on the commotion. "I don't know why you came all the way here just to disappoint the girl," he said.

Ivy adjusted the fingers of her glove. "I'm here now, aren't I?"

If Ivy had known Stella's daddy would be along for the ride, she wouldn't have come now either.

"Didn't have any more 'things to tend to'?" he scoffed, throwing her words back at her. "Couldn't come up with another pathetic excuse not to visit the girl?"

Ivy bristled at the implication. Of course, Ivy wanted to come before now. She'd missed Stella like paper misses a pen (just look how lovely Stella had become), but she couldn't. She had something she had to do first.

"Mock if you like, it was the truth. I did have important things to attend to. Unlike you, I don't lie to your daughter."

He laughed, a deep bellow that jiggled his whole body. What had Katherine ever seen in this man? He was uncouth, with gray hairs sticking out of his ears, barely taller than her but carrying more weight and wearing a perpetual smirk that marred his face. Ivy had attended Katherine's wedding, and granted, on that day, Elijah Kendrick had cut a handsome figure. He was also successful and lorded over the most successful horse breeding operation in Kentucky. He'd entertained and charmed the likes of the then Prince of Wales, who'd bought one of Elijah's most promising stallions once during a visit to the States. But that charming man was long gone. Beside her stood a self-indulgent bully who cared little but for his vainglory. Without Katherine to keep him in check, he'd failed at self-restraint, in his choice of words, his appetite, or his acquisitions. Who else would pay millions to buy a British title for his family?

"But you haven't told her the whole truth either, have you, Ivy?" Elijah said, his tone light, as if reminding her which spoon to use for ice cream.

Elijah was right. But unlike him, Ivy was lying to Stella for the right reasons.

"When you tell her the truth, I will," Ivy said.

Elijah turned to her for the first time. "You'd have me ruin the memories the girl holds so dear? My, you are more ruthless than I gave you credit."

Ivy wanted to wipe the self-satisfied smile off his face.

"You don't care about Stella's memories. You know as well as I do that if she knew the truth, you wouldn't be able to control her. This wedding would never take place, and you would never see the inside of Caroline Astor's ballroom."

"I don't control anyone. I facilitated the match, and the girl recognized the necessities of it. She's nearly twenty-three with no other prospects, after all."

"Then maybe I should tell her everything if you aren't going to."

"Be my guest."

Ivy hadn't expected him to say that.

"As long as you don't leave out the part you played."

"I've done nothing wrong."

"Oh, no? Do you want to find out if the girl would see it the same way? She idolizes you. You would not only taint the memories of her mother, but she'd never trust you again. If you can live with that, I bow to your ruthlessness."

Ivy blanched. She'd never considered Stella wouldn't understand her motives. But would she? Or would Stella believe Ivy conspired with her father all these years?

Noticing her reaction, Kendrick smirked. "Maybe you're right. Maybe, when we toast the happy couple at the wedding, I tell the girl everything. That way, everyone will know. Clean slate and all that. Then we'll find out where the blame lies."

"Blame lies for what?" a voice asked from behind Ivy.

Ivy spun around abruptly at the sound of Stella's voice. How much had she heard? "Nothing," Ivy stammered.

"It didn't sound like nothing," Stella said when a groom approached with a stunning dapple-gray mare. Could that be Stella's pet horse? The mare had been a foal the last time Ivy saw it.

"Is that Tully?" Ivy said. "How lucky you are she's here with you."

Stella crinkled her beautiful face in dissatisfaction at Ivy's deflection.

"I am." Stella stepped into the groom's cupped hands and hoisted herself into the mare's saddle. "And I'm lucky you're here too." Stella's tone was sincere but suspicious. Before Ivy could reassure the girl, before she could express how delighted she was to be here, Stella steered her horse away, called away by the others.

Was Elijah right? When Stella learned the extent of what Ivy was hiding, would she ever trust Ivy again?

As if reading her mind, Elijah smirked. "Maybe you shouldn't have come after all, eh, Ivy?"

When he lumbered off toward his waiting mount, Ivy stared at the shiny bald spot at the back of his head, resisting the urge to fling her handbag at it.

CHAPTER 13

Stella smelled the salt in the air long before the sea came into view. They had taken a route that crossed the windswept shrubby heath from Rosehurst toward the small coastal village of Keyhaven, a cluster of whitewashed cottages and red-tiled brick buildings facing a picturesque harbor with more boats anchored in the bay than buildings on the shore. Past the village, the marshes spread out before them, vast mats of floating grass blurring the edge between land and the Solent, the deep, wave-crested, miles-wide channel between them and the Isle of Wight. But for a few wispy clouds, the sky and the water matched in color; crystal-clear blue. What an inspired plan. A prewedding picnic. All her concerns, her questions, her doubts about Uncle Jed, Aunt Ivy, the dead jockey, the anxiety of getting married in two days, drifted away like the yachts on the water, their sails flashing bright white in the sun.

"I don't see any castle," Daddy said from the landau he shared with Aunt Ivy, Penny, and Mr. Swenson.

The other Americans followed her father's lead, searching the approaching coastline for turrets and flags, but there was nothing.

"Me neither," said Sammy, disappointed.

Stella halted Tully beside Lord Atherly's carriage where Sammy, his sister, and Ethel squeezed in beside each other. Uncle Jed had offered to drive. He'd wanted to use the Daimler, but Lyndy had assured everyone the terrain was no place for an automobile.

Stella turned to Lyndy when he and Beau rode up beside her. "Lyndy? Where is it?"

"You don't see it because it isn't on the coast here," Lyndy said. "It's out on a spit, a curling, narrow peninsula of sorts, that juts out into the water a good mile or more."

"Better to defend the mainland from foreign invaders coming by boat," Sir Owen added, astride Lister, Lord Atherly's Cleveland Bay. "King Henry had a string of them built along the coast."

"What are we waiting for then?" Sammy said impatiently. "Let's go."

Sir Owen, as eager as the boy, took the lead. Stella and Lyndy, on horseback, followed him single file down a well-worn track of gravel and sand onto a narrow strip of land. The two carriages and the dogcart with the picnic supplies bumped along behind them. As they rode, Stella couldn't keep her head still; there was so much to see. On one side of the spit was the calm, bay-like River Keyhaven, sheltered from the breeze off the water by the thick mats of grass that lined both sides of the river. Dozens of boats—white yachts with spindly, tall masts; small fishing vessels; and dinghies anchored to the bottom—bobbed gently in the river. Waterbirds—redshank, little egrets, curlews, and various terns and gulls—swooped over the water, fished the shallows, or paddled about enjoying the sunshine. And was that a seal popping its head out of the water?

The other side of the spit, no less impressive, was dominated by the Solent and the hazy outline of the humpback hills of the Isle of Wight beyond. In the distance, an ocean liner, its smoke-stacks like black lines smudging the sky, having left Southampton behind, headed out to the open sea. Stella's thoughts immediately leaped to the dead jockey, his threats, his missing gun. Why was she still worried about him? As her father had assured her, and she Lyndy, Pistol Prescott was dead, and his threat gone with him. Wasn't it?

She patted Tully on the neck and turned away from the ship, from the distant, vague shimmer of Southampton in the east, to observe the meandering western coastline, captivated by the sun's glare on distant chalky white cliffs.

"There it is!" Sammy shouted, standing up in the carriage and pointing.

Ethel held Gertie tightly on her lap to keep the little girl from following her brother's example as Stella surveyed the landscape in the direction Sammy pointed. At the end of the spit stood a massive three-story crenelated stone tower keep ringed by two-story stone circular bastions. A moat, long since dried up, encircled the entire complex. Despite being abandoned, the British Union Jack flapped from a single flagpole jutting up from the central tower's roof.

"Wow!" Penny exclaimed when they drew nearer, the thick, gray stone walls looming large and high above their heads.

"You said it, Penelope, darling," Mr. Swenson said. "I don't think I've seen anything like it."

"And in this country," Daddy boasted, "places like this are a dime a dozen."

"Really?"

Stella had never heard such admiration in Penny's tone. Could Penny be genuinely impressed?

"I wouldn't say that, Mr. Kendrick," Sir Owen corrected. "But granted, we probably have a few more medieval castles in England than you do."

"I'll say," Aunt Ivy said, gaping up when they entered the shadows beneath its walls.

"And surely, this one is special. Some would say even sacred," Lyndy said. "When King Henry disbanded the Catholic Church, he literately dismantled the abbeys as well. The stones you see here once formed Beaulieu Abbey, right here in the Forest."

Stella steered Tully closer, reaching out to touch the massive stone blocks that made up the walls. The castle had risen from the abbey's destruction, like a phoenix. And here it stood almost five centuries later. Could this wedding be like the building of this castle, making something stable and beautiful after her father's betrayal and lack of affection?

"Pa, where are you going?" Sammy said.

Stella swiveled in her saddle as Uncle Jed handed the reins of the carriage to his son and leaped down from the driver's seat. The pebbles covering the spit crunched beneath his boots when he landed. He pulled a cigar from his waistcoat pocket and stuck it between his teeth.

"I need to stretch my legs." Without further explanation, Uncle Jed skidded down the moat's embankment, rounded the corner, and disappeared.

"Why did he come in the first place?" Daddy grumbled.

With no one left to drive, Ethel urged the children to climb out and walk. But Mr. Swenson kindly offered to take the reins for the last few dozen yards.

Owen, Stella, and Lyndy led the way across the drawbridge that spanned the grass-filled dry moat, the horses' hooves *clip-clopping* on the thick wooden boards. The chains of wrought iron rings attached on either side of the bridge harkened back to a more turbulent time when raising the bridge was often a necessity. Now the narrow two-story stone gate gapped open. The carriages rattled in behind Stella and Tully, the rumble of the wheels echoing against the high walls of the weed-choked cobblestone courtyard. When the party clustered together, no one spoke. For several moments, only the soft sound of the horses' breath, the cooing of roosting doves, and the distant lapping of waves broke the silence. Like everyone else, Stella was in awe. . . . Of the light streaming through the slit-like windows, designed for shooting through. Of the dozens of darkened doorways, hinting at the high number of people who once lived and worked here. Of the surrounding stone walls that blocked out the rest of the world.

Lyndy was right. Abandoned a long time ago, it did have an air of sacredness. And they had it to themselves.

"We'll have our picnic there," Sir Owen suggested, pointing to a patch of ungrazed, grassy lawn. "It's the only sunny spot."

Stella agreed. The day was too lovely to waste sitting in the shadows.

"I say we all wander about a bit before regrouping for the picnic," Lyndy said, slipping down from Beau.

"Come on, Gertie," Sammy said, grabbing his sister's hand and pulling her down from the carriage. "Let's explore."

"Don't go too far," Stella called when the children disappeared into one of the many unlocked doorways.

Stella and Lyndy helped unhitch the carriage horses while Ethel and James, the first footman, unpacked the dogcart. After Stella made sure all the horses were free to graze, she noticed everyone but Lyndy and the servants had made themselves scarce. Even Penny, whose wide-brimmed straw hat Stella glimpsed disappearing into the central tower, was surprisingly eager to explore.

"Shall we?" Lyndy offered Stella his arm and led her away from the central keep.

He ducked into the first door they encountered. It was a dark, cavernous room covered in the rubble of an old coal pile. What Stella mistook for gravel on the floor soiled her boots and the hem of her dress with soot. That room lead into a narrow hall with a wet, slick ceiling so low Stella could reach up and touch it. Everything was made of stone.

As the hall twisted and turned, they passed room after room, dark, damp, and empty. Lyndy lead them down a wide staircase that ended in a flooded basement. From there, they climbed single file up a winding staircase, where countless feet had worn deep hollows into the edge of the stone steps. When light spilled into the stairwell, they followed it through an open doorway. The room was large with several fireplaces and brightly lit and dry, the sun streaming through several well-placed windows. Inexplicable nooks, carved deep into the stone, haphazardly punctuated the walls. Stella tried to picture the room when fires raged, tapestries hung on the walls, and the floors were covered with carpets. Was this the living quarters of the medieval soldiers? Their dining room? Or was this where they planned their defenses? Now it was eerily quiet and cold.

"We're finally alone," Lyndy whispered, his breath warm against her ear. He pulled the pin from her hat and tossed it to the floor. Wrapping an arm around her waist, Lyndy pressed his lips against her cool skin, kissing slowly, from her ear to the nape of her neck. His other hand reached into her hair, supporting her head as he guided her gently backward. After the warmth of his embrace, the heat of his lips, the icy cold of the stone through her linen dress as he pressed her against the wall rocketed down her spine. But instead of pushing away from the wall, she pulled him closer. She placed her hands on his cheeks, the hint of stubble tickling her palms, and lifted his face from her neck to her lips. He hungrily pressed his mouth against hers, the hard, cold stone forgotten. A pulse of heat shot through her belly as she sought to bury herself into him.

"*Whaaaaaa!*" At the sound of the distant, guttural yell, Stella and Lyndy jerked apart.

"What the devil?" Lyndy cursed, his face flush, his eyes bright and glistening.

Stella, bile rising in her throat where moments ago Lyndy had planted kisses, stared at him in horror. "Oh, my God! What was that?"

"It sounded like a man crying out in pain."

"We have to go."

Stella bolted for the door. But instead of the winding staircase she expected, she was in another narrow, darkened hall. She swiveled around to turn back and collided against Lyndy a few steps behind her, lace from the collar of her dress snagging on his waistcoat button.

Lyndy pointed over her head toward a door down the hall she hadn't noticed before. "It came from the direction of the central tower. We'll get there faster that way."

"Then let's go," Stella said, yanking her collar free.

Lyndy squeezed by her and grabbed her hand. With their fingers tightly lacing together, he guided her toward the direction of the cry.

Stella squinted when she and Lyndy emerged from the dark into the castle courtyard. "Ethel?"

"Right here, miss." Ethel knelt on the checkered picnic rug laid out on the grass and clutched the children, one in each arm. Gertie sniffled in fear. Plates filled with fresh fruit, finger sandwiches, and chunks of cheese lay on the rug before them.

Stella was relieved the children were safe. She counted the horses, and except for a few nervous whinnies, they too seemed fine. So, what happened? Stella asked her maid.

"I'd begun to feed the children when someone cried out," Ethel said. "I didn't know who or why so I thought it best to stay put and keep the children with me."

"Was it a ghost?" Sammy asked, his voice shaking.

"No, Sammy," Stella said gently. "Someone is hurt somewhere." She surveyed the courtyard. "Where is everyone else?"

"I haven't seen anyone but James and the children since you all left," Ethel said, pulling out a handkerchief and wiping away Gertie's tears.

Mr. Swenson, his face flush from running, burst through a nearby doorway. "What happened? I heard someone call out."

"I don't know, but it came from up there." Ethel pointed to the top of the central tower.

Without hesitation, Stella aimed for the wooden stairs that spiraled around the outside of the stone tower. Lyndy and Mr. Swenson were right behind her.

"Who yelled?" Aunt Ivy, leaning over the edge of the bastion wall, called down to those below. "Is everything okay?"

"We don't know," Stella answered, trying to keep her focus on not losing her step.

If there had been a railing for the stairs, it had disappeared long ago. As they climbed, Stella trailed her hand along the rough stone wall, purposefully positioning her foot on the next step. When the stairs ended halfway up the tower, Stella stepped tentatively through the open doorway, not relishing exchanging the bright day for darkness. Who knew what she would encounter inside? But with the gun slits positioned at equal intervals around the circular, vaulted room, it was lighter inside than Stella expected. Still, she had to let her sight adjust.

The first thing she noticed was Penny, backed up against the wall, her arms hugging her knees, the brim of her hat bent against the stone, her face flush, tears streaming down her cheeks. Stella rushed to her side and knelt before her on the hard stone floor.

"Penny! Are you all right? What happened?"

Penny sniffled and gulped for air. She wordlessly pointed past Stella's shoulder, her finger shaking toward an inner spiral staircase across the room. Hidden by the stairwell wall, it hadn't been visible when she'd entered. In the shadows at the foot of the stairs lay a man's body. His feet, legs, and knees, bent in unnatural angles, draped upward across the bottom few steps. With his arms sprawled out before him, his head and torso lay flat on the floor below. A smoldering cigar, its glowing red tip unmistakable in the dark, lay inches from the man's outstretched fingers. He wasn't moving or making a sound.

Uncle Jed!

This couldn't be. Stella had only reunited with him yesterday. Whatever suspicions she had about him, he was still her uncle. And the children. How was she going to tell Sammy and Gertie their father was dead?

Stella leaped to her feet. Mr. Swenson grasped her arm when she moved toward the stairs, hoping perhaps to shield her from the worst, but she wouldn't be deterred. She pulled away and crossed the room, Lyndy following closely. With tears welling up, blurring the body before her, Stella knelt, slipped her hand under the man's cheeks, still warm to the touch, and gently raised his head off the floor. She rotated his face toward her.

It wasn't Uncle Jed.

"No!" she cried, letting go and slumping onto her hip. Stella gasped for breath. Her fingers and hands and face tingled and grew numb.

"Bloody hell!" Lyndy muttered from behind her.

The man stared upward, unblinking, his mouth a frozen grimace of shock and pain. With a burning pain in her chest, she reached for his hand. Callouses, earned as a hardworking youth and never lost, hardened the inside of his palm. She squeezed it, trying to remember the last time she'd held his hand. In life, he'd shunned her touch and her affection. In death, he no longer had a say.

No! Daddy! No!

Stella curled over the body of her dead father and released all the tension between them, sobbing until her body was wracked with convulsions and she couldn't breathe. So lost in her grief, she never questioned how it happened or why. She'd lost both of her parents now, orphaned two days before her wedding, and she'd never felt so alone in her life.

And then the weight of Lyndy's hand on her shoulder brought her back. Back to the tower room, back to cold seeping up through the floor numbing her hip and legs, back to the world where a man she'd met a few months ago loved her more than her father did.

Lyndy pressed a handkerchief into her hand.

Seeking the comfort of the light and hungering for the fresh air that wafted down the wide stairs spiraling above her, she wiped her cheeks and lifted her face. There, at the top of the stairs, framed against the blue sky, was Sir Owen. He stared down at her from the roof, his hand held against his cheek, blood running down his fingers.

CHAPTER 14

Inspector Brown peered down at the mangled body. The loss of life was a terrible thing, even to a terrible man. No one, not even Mr. Elijah Kendrick, deserved to end up this way.

When he received the call to the castle, Brown's first thought was a reckless lad had tried to scale the walls and had lost his footing or had been caught down in the dark recesses of the castle basement with high tide coming in. And with his resources bent on tracking down the puzzling circumstances behind the life and death of Mr. Jesse James Prescott, Brown inwardly cursed the lad who was wasting his precious time.

Brown never understood the lure of Keyhaven Castle with its dank, empty rooms and gray stone walls. Give him low timbered ceilings, a fire, and a lively pub any day. But it wasn't unknown that Keyhaven Castle, since the days of his youth, had been a magnet to the idle youth, the site of much misadventure too often ending in injury. Twice during his seventeen years as a policeman, he'd been called to the castle to find a dead body. Never had it been for a murder.

"But, I thought he simply fell?" Mr. Theo Swenson, the

middle-aged gentleman questioning Brown's conclusion, squatted against the wall comforting a young woman Brown was unfamiliar with. But despite Mr. Swenson's full beard, the family resemblance between the two was pronounced.

Brown would've considered the young woman with dark auburn curls softening her brow reasonably pretty. But the lip rouge smeared on her lips and the hair sticking to her tear-streaked cheeks ruined the effect. A few feet to the side of the Swensons was Sir Owen, a bloody handkerchief held to his cheek. Brown would find out what that was all about soon enough.

"I'd have thought so too, at first," he admitted.

One glance at the awkward angle of the body at the bottom of the slippery, worn stairs and anyone would conclude the man had broken his neck in a fall—an accident. But on close inspection, the case wasn't everything it seemed.

Just like that of the jockey in Southampton.

The circular, cavernous room, devoid of any decoration, carpeting, or wall coverings, reminding Brown of a spacious jail cell, was lit by a paltry light that eked through the air slits cut symmetrically every few feet around the entirety of the room. But someone had left the door open at the top of the stairwell. And the sun streaming down from the roof had lent Brown the necessary illumination he needed to inspect the body, the stairs, and the people clustered throughout the musty room more closely. And what he saw pointed to murder.

Brown, still crouched beside the body, his knees against the stone growing stiff and painful, pointed to the strange semi-circular impressions around the murdered man's neck. "See these markings?"

But wait, what was that? With his knees protesting, Brown leaned in closer. In a wrinkled fold of the man's neck, and near the bruised markings, was the darkest of specks. Considering coal still blackened the floors of several of the castle's storage rooms, it could be a flake of coal dust the man picked up in his wanderings. But it was nowhere else, not his boots, his trousers or jacket, his face, or elsewhere on his otherwise scrubbed clean neck. So how did it get there? Brown lifted the man's right hand. The dirt and tiny pebbles one would expect to find lodged in the dead man's palm if he'd tried to break his fall were absent. But there was a faint smudge of black on his palm and under one of his fingernails. More coal? Brown wished he had his hand lens. He'd be sure to have Dr. Lipscombe make a note of it.

"Of course, I'll have to confirm my suspicions with the medical examiner," Brown continued, "but I believe this man was strangled before he fell."

"But we heard him," Miss Kendrick said.

Brown glanced up. "What?"

Poor lady. These were the first words she'd uttered since he arrived. Brown had never seen her so despondent, and that was saying something. Puffy, red eyelids marred her comely face. Clutching a handkerchief, she leaned into Lord Lyndhurst, his arm tightly around her shoulders. Brown suspected it was the viscount's firm hold alone that kept the lady from her dead father's side. And rightfully so. Miss Kendrick had encountered more than her share of murdered bodies, this being the most personal yet. But what did she mean "we heard him"?

"Heard whom, Miss Kendrick?" Brown asked gently.

"Daddy." Her voice was unnervingly flat like she was speaking from another room. "Lyndy and I both heard him cry out when he fell."

How could that be? A strangled man doesn't cry out.

"Are you certain?"

All heads nodded in agreement.

"We all heard it," the petite woman hovering by Miss Kendrick's elbow said. She barely reached Brown's chin, and he was not known for his height. "He called out when he fell."

Brown pinched the bridge of his nose. Could it be that when

someone was attempting to strangle him, Mr. Kendrick won the struggle to free himself, only to lose his balance and break his neck falling down the stairwell? Even so, and Brown wasn't admitting that was the case, it didn't make the man's death any less villainous.

"And you are . . . ?" Brown asked.

"Mrs. Mitchell. Ivy Mitchell. Mr. Kendrick was my brother-in-law."

Constable Waterman, who had inconspicuously guarded the door to prevent anyone from leaving, licked the tip of his pencil before writing her name in his notebook.

"Hello? Where are y'all?" A man's cheerful voice echoed as his silhouette formed in the outside doorway. Waterman jumped, swiveling around at the sound.

Who the devil was that? Brown thought he'd accounted for everyone. Most likely a chance sightseer who'd picked a most unfortunate time to visit the castle.

"Stay where you are, sir," Brown called, shooing his constable to intercept the new arrival. But before Waterman could respond, Mr. Jedidiah Kendrick, the dead man's younger brother, stepped over the threshold.

"Sammy and Gertie said they heard a ghost," he laughed. "What an imagination that boy has."

His chuckle died in his throat when he noted Waterman's unmistakable domed helmet. He attempted to retreat, but Waterman grabbed his arm.

"Whatever my brother says, I know nothing about it."

It was an odd response. But one Brown had encountered time and again. If Brown were a waging man, he'd bet Mr. Jedidiah Kendrick was no stranger to the police.

Then the younger Kendrick spotted Brown kneeling beside his dead brother's body. He shook off Waterman's firm grip, and in three long strides was upon Brown before Waterman could waylay him again.

"Keep your distance, sir," Waterman warned.

"Lord in heaven! What happened?"

"I'm so sorry, Jed," Mrs. Mitchell said, putting her hand on his arm. "Elijah fell down the stairs."

Brown pushed up off his knees and brushed his trouser legs. The first time Brown had met Mr. Jedidiah Kendrick, the brothers were having a punch-up on the floor. He hadn't expected him to be a member of the excursion party. Brown scrutinized the younger Kendrick's face. Was that an upturn in the corner of the man's mouth?

He is one to watch, that one.

"Right! My sincere condolences, Mr. Kendrick." Out of the corner of his eye, Brown noticed Miss Kendrick wince at Brown's use of the address so frequently used for her father. "But I'm afraid I'm investigating your brother's death as suspicious."

The brother didn't blink. Did that mean he knew something? Or that he didn't care? Or both?

"I'd prefer to conduct more thorough interviews elsewhere," Brown continued, as he ushered everyone, with Constable Waterman's help, to the other side of the room, where the curly-headed young woman had already positioned herself. Out of sight of the dead man. "So, for the present, I'll only ask where everyone was when Mr. Kendrick cried out."

"I didn't hear any cry," Mr. Jedidiah Kendrick said.

That surprised Brown. Everyone else had been adamant they heard the older Kendrick cry out. "May I ask then where you've been since you arrived at the castle?"

"I was out on the trail we came down." The younger Mr. Kendrick pulled a cigar out of his pocket. He bit the end and spit it out the nearest gun slit.

Brown had found a cigar near the dead man's body. He hadn't thought twice about it; the castle grounds were littered with crushed cigar stubs. Even discovering it warm didn't alarm him, knowing Mr. Elijah Kendrick frequently smoked them.

But now, with the brother clenching one in his teeth, Brown may need to reconsider its significance.

"Why?" the brother asked.

Brown ignored the question and faced the young couple. Lord Lyndhurst still protectively wrapped his arm around Miss Kendrick's shoulder. Miss Kendrick's unblinking gaze wandered to the stairwell wall, which her father lay hidden behind. Wasn't their wedding two days away? Brown could guess the turmoil the father's death would create. But there'd be worse consequences if he didn't catch the man's killer.

"Where were you when you heard the shout, my lord?"

"Miss Kendrick and I were, uhmm . . ."

Brown squinted at the viscount. Why the hesitation? It wasn't like the self-assured noble Brown had come to know.

"Exploring the castle." Miss Kendrick finished the young man's sentence, her tone reflecting her blank, faraway look.

Never once entertaining the thought she was culpable, Brown nevertheless regarded her with interest. She was bareheaded, and strands of hair fell down the back of her neck. The hem of her skirt was blackened as if dragged in coal soot. Could she have introduced the coal fleck to her father when she found him? Perhaps.

When Brown prepared to ask, Lord Lyndhurst glared at him, daring Brown to inquire further.

"I was in the coal storeroom opposite when Elijah called out," Mr. Swenson volunteered. "Miss Kendrick, Lord Lyndhurst, the servants, and the children were in the courtyard when I arrived."

"That's right," Mrs. Mitchell added. "I could see them all from my vantage point."

"And where were you, Mrs. Mitchell?" Brown inquired.

She pointed up toward the roof, her gaze following her finger as if she could see through the timbered ceiling. "Up there. I'd been admiring the amazing view."

Brown studied Mrs. Mitchell's face—round, pleasantly plump with a few telltale wrinkles and a gentle upturn of the eyebrows. A kind face. Yet not that of a woman steps away from the dead body of a man she admired. Mrs. Mitchell would shed no tears for her brother-in-law. But was she capable of killing him?

Brown dismissed the thought as soon as it arose. She was far too small to get her hands around the dead man's neck long enough to leave marks; Mr. Kendrick would've tossed her aside like a child's doll.

"Could you see the victim from your vantage point?" Brown asked.

She cocked her head to one side, thinking. "No. But I'd heard him talking earlier, or grumbling more like it, when I was on the roof above him." Again, she pointed up. "I was surprised how easy it was to hear him. I would've thought the stone walls would dampen the sound."

Her aunt's answer aroused Miss Kendrick. She shifted her focus, albeit slowly, from the stairwell wall to her aunt, a glint of her old spark in her eyes. Brown was glad of it.

"Who was he talking to?" Miss Kendrick asked. "What was he saying?"

"I got the impression he was talking to himself. I didn't catch any distinct words. As Elijah is—was prone to grumbling over just about anything, I thought nothing of it and continued up to the roof and across the bastion wall."

"That leaves this young lady," Brown said, motioning toward the woman seated on the floor huddled against the stone wall beside Mr. Swenson.

"My daughter, Penelope, Inspector," Mr. Swenson supplied.

"That leaves Miss Swenson, and you, Sir Owen." Brown regarded the young gentleman standing off to the side as if hoping Brown might forget he was there. Or was he perhaps planning to escape the tower when everyone's head was turned?

Although Brown suspected the young man didn't remember him, he and Sir Owen had crossed paths before. Brown had just made inspector when a "misunderstanding" involving the daughter of a local commoner and Sir Owen occurred. The pair had borrowed two of the young lady's father's New Forest ponies and run off together. Fearing for his daughter's reputation, not to mention the safety of his ponies, the father called in the police. Sir Owen and his lady friend were halfway across Hampshire before a constable caught up with them. It was Brown who'd had to escort the lad back to Morrington Hall and his fuming parents who were guests of the earl's. Being his first encounter with the estate, he never met the earl and his family when he'd given Sir Owen back into the care of his then governess.

"Where were you, sir, and what caused you to injure your face?"

Sir Owen squirmed under the scrutiny, pulling at his collar with one hand while diligently holding the handkerchief in the other, as a roomful of people waited in anticipation for his answer. Dried blood stained the back of his hand and fingers.

"I was, we were . . . Miss Swenson and I, that is"—he nervously laughed when he motioned toward the woman against the wall—"were exploring the rooftops."

"You saw Mrs. Mitchell then?" Brown asked.

"I did, yes."

"I saw them as well, Inspector," Mrs. Mitchell said. "But right before Elijah cried out, you, Sir Owen, were at the top of the stairwell, alone."

"I'm afraid you're mistaken, Mrs. Mitchell," Sir Owen said with a hint of the indignation Brown expected from a man of Sir Owen's stature. "Miss Swenson and I were together the entire time."

"Unchaperoned then, sir?" Brown pushed.

Sir Owen's cheeks reddened, fittingly abased.

"Is this true, Miss Swenson?" Brown said, turning toward

the young woman on the floor against the wall. "Were you and Sir Owen together at the time of Mr. Kendrick's scream?"

The young wretch shook her head in denial but said nothing.

"What?" Sir Owen started, pivoting to stare at the young woman in alarm. "Miss Swenson, what are you doing? We were together. Of course we were."

Miss Swenson shook her head vehemently this time.

"But—"

"Are you calling my daughter a liar, sir?" Mr. Swenson demanded.

"No. I don't know. Yes?" The gentleman laughed nervously.

"Were you or weren't you up on the roof?" Brown asked.

Sir Owen straightened to his full weight. "I was. I don't deny it. And neither do I deny I was at the top of the stairs, as Mrs. Mitchell said. I left Miss Swenson's side for a moment. Like the others, when I heard a man shout, I wondered what the bloody hell happened."

So he had lied. Miss Swenson wasn't with him at the top of the stairs. Tall and athletic, Sir Owen could've overpowered the dead man. But what motive did he have? And could he have done it without Miss Swenson witnessing the struggle?

"How did you get that cut, sir?" Brown asked, motioning to the bloodstained handkerchief Sir Owen pressed to his cheek.

The gentleman hesitated, glancing at Miss Swenson again before answering. "I walked into one of those wrought iron hooks."

Brown knew the hooks he meant. Keyhaven Castle was dotted with them. Paired at eye level on the walls, they once held rifles and the various long tools needed to load the cannons, up off the damp floors. The hooks were wrought iron and sharply pointed. They could indeed inflict such a deep scratch if an unsuspecting man of Sir Owen's height encountered one in the dark.

"May I see it?"

"I say," Sir Owen said, taking a step back when Brown approached. "Haven't the ladies endured enough ugliness for one day?"

"I agree, Inspector," Lord Lyndhurst said. "Sir Owen explained his injury. He explained what he was doing at the top of the stairs. That should suffice."

"I'm afraid I disagree with you, my lord," Brown said. "Your future bride's father has been murdered. You of all people should understand what it requires to bring his murderer to justice."

"Yes, I do. . . ." Lord Lyndhurst shifted his weight, like a man restraining himself. "And I've held the highest respect for you, but . . . tread carefully, man. This is my cousin you are accusing."

"Accusing? Are you accusing me of murdering Miss Kendrick's father?" Sir Owen choked out the words. Hints of fear and trepidation mingled with the disbelief in his voice.

But instead of answering, Brown turned his back on the others and rounded the corner. He slid down to one knee beside the dead man again and examined his hands once more. This time Brown studied the rings on the dead man's fingers. He wore four. On his left hand was a simple band of gold engraved with vines, presumably his wedding band, and a silver signet ring with the letter *K* carved into it. On his right, he wore a rectangular yellow and white gold ring set with aquamarine stones and diamonds and a pinky ring with a massive square-cut emerald, either of which could inflict a gash to a man's face during a struggle. But was there blood on any of them? Brown couldn't tell. Not in this light. Another task he'd have to leave to Dr. Lipscombe.

Brown pushed up from the floor and rejoined the others. Not wanting to take any chances, he waved Constable Waterman to his side.

"Sir Owen Rountree, I am arresting you in connection with the suspicious death of Mr. Elijah Kendrick."

"What?" Lord Lyndhurst, dropping his arm from Miss Kendrick's shoulders, stepped to his cousin's side. "This is preposterous."

Sir Owen, stunned into silence, stared over his shoulder in an attempt to witness the constable secure him in handcuffs.

"Sir Owen?" Miss Kendrick asked. But whether she questioned why the gentleman did it or why Brown thought he had, Brown couldn't tell. Either way, she didn't sound convinced.

"I didn't do this, Miss Kendrick, Inspector. I swear to you I would never do anything like this. Besides, I told you. I was with Miss Swenson the entire time. Tell them, Penny."

Penny? The use of Miss Swenson's Christian name implied a familiarity between the two that made her silence damning.

"Take him away, Constable," Brown said.

CHAPTER 15

❧

Her father was dead.

Stella had wanted him to go away. Had been counting the days when he'd go back to Kentucky. She never imagined this.

Stella had cried more in the past hour than she had her entire lifetime. Her head pounded, her whole body ached, but the tears had dried up, her nose had stopped running, and she welcomed the reassuring rocking of Tully beneath her as they rode. Out in the fresh air with the sun on her back, away from the dank, dark, closeted castle tower room, she was able to face the truth, the complete and brutally honest truth. That, alongside the shock, the guilt, and the grief, was a lightness, an unexpected sense of relief.

She shivered. Had the breeze cut through her dress, or was the chill from something else? Seeking reassurance, Stella leaned forward to stroke Tully's shoulder. She was startled to find her horse's sleek coat foamed with sweat.

How long had they been riding? Where were they? The landscape caught her off-guard. They'd crossed the spit, passed the marshes, climbed the banks of the shoreline, navigated the path through the shrubby coastal heath, and had entered Whitley Wood not far from Rosehurst. The journey had been a blank. She couldn't remember any of it.

What Stella painfully remembered was the police wagon rumbling away, carting both Sir Owen and her father's body back to Lyndhurst: one to the police station, the other to Dr. Lipscombe's examining table. With an autopsy, Brown promised they'd determine precisely how her father had died.

Does it matter?

She turned in the saddle, expecting a slow cavalcade of carriages, like a funeral procession, following behind. Only the dogcart with Lister, Sir Owen's mount, tied to the back, followed. But where were Ethel and the children? Uncle Jed? Aunt Ivy? The Swensons?

"Most of the others went back to Pilley Manor." Lyndy, answering her unvoiced question, swayed comfortably in the saddle as he rode alongside her. "I'm taking you to Morrington. I don't think you should be alone right now."

Stella agreed. She wasn't sure she could ever go back to Pilley Manor. There were too many memories of her father there.

When they approached Morrington Hall, sunlight reflecting off the chimneys jutting above the trees, Stella was struck by the resemblance of the first time she'd traveled up this drive. She, pushing the gas of the Daimler, eager for a glimpse of the manor house, her father grumbling at her to slow down. Stella had had no idea then the secret her father held, how he'd sold her off like one of his horses, for his own benefit. She'd resented him for it, almost hated him. Now she just felt drained.

A pig, pink and barrel-shaped with large black spots, emerged suddenly from the wood, its snout to the ground, industriously wiggling and sniffing out its quarry—fallen acorns. It crossed the driveway, oblivious of the horses, and disappeared into the trees on the other side. Lyndy clicked his tongue, urging the horses, distracted by the pig, to move on.

Stella adored the New Forest. How lucky she was to call it her adopted home. *And how happy I am with Lyndy.*

Thankfully, the engagement hadn't been the nightmare Stella feared it would be. She'd grown to respect, admire, dare she even say love, her betrothed. But her father couldn't have known that, nor did he care. And it didn't excuse how all of this came about. He'd done it for selfish reasons, wanting a British title he could brag about, that would guarantee an invitation into the highest society. How trivial the resentment, the anger, the disappointment she'd felt at his betrayal seemed now. None of it mattered. In two days, Stella would become Viscountess Lyndhurst, and her father wouldn't be there to witness it or brag about it to his friends. Nor would he ever see the inside of Mrs. Astor's ballroom.

When they arrived, Stella allowed Lyndy to lift her down from the saddle, as Mack, the scruffy stray, barked at the horses, leaping and dodging, encouraging them to play. In his excitement, Mack leaped up on Lyndy, stamping his jacket with two muddy paw prints. Lyndy ruffled the dog's head before shooing Mack away. Tully whinnied softly and nudged Stella with her muzzle, seeking the peppermint treats she so loved. Stella didn't have any and instead threw her arms around Tully's slick, muscular neck, tears spilling down her cheeks and onto the mare's glossy coat. Stella clung to her horse until she felt calm again. Then she stepped back and handed Leonard the reins. The groom clicked his tongue, encouraging the horses to walk toward the stables. The dog scampered after.

Heartened by the warmth and enthusiasm of the animals, Stella brushed the tears away with the back of her hand and offered Lyndy a reassuring smile. He offered his arm, and the two strolled toward the house.

A small crowd of people: Lord and Lady Atherly, Lady Alice, Mrs. Swenson, Reverend Paine, a half dozen servants, had clustered in the hall and accosted them the moment Fulton opened the door. They'd been waiting for them. Reverend Paine was the first to approach as Lyndy handed the butler his hat. Stella had no idea where she'd left hers.

"My dear, dear Miss Kendrick." Holding his folded hands over his heart, the vicar wore his sense of importance as blatantly as the spectacles on his face. "May the Lord bless you and watch over you."

Barely in his middle thirties, the Reverend had gained his current living due to tragedy. But the circumstances hadn't humbled him. Instead, the vicar had perceived his predecessor's sudden demise, and his subsequent promotion, as an act of God, or so it seemed to Stella, and fully embraced his role as spiritual counselor to Lord Atherly and his family.

"I am so very, very sorry to hear about your father. Poor soul. I pray he's now at peace. If you would like, I can pray with you at any time."

Stella, not surprised the news had reached Morrington Hall before she did, mumbled something noncommittal. Daddy, at peace? Stella couldn't imagine it. Especially the way he went out of this world. Besides, Reverend Paine was the last person she wanted to engage in conversation with right now. But the vicar wasn't done.

"How very sad, how tragic. Cut down in the prime of his life. To think I was here finalizing the wedding service. And now it must be postponed."

Postponed? No. This wedding was what her father wanted.

"Daddy wouldn't want it postponed."

Mrs. Swenson, her silk skirts rustling, swooped in to gather Stella in a comforting embrace. She smelled of lilacs and lemon. "Oh, you poor, poor orphaned child."

Stella, typically one to initiate personal contact, stiffened at the woman's touch.

"We're so sorry for you," Mrs. Swenson went on, motherly fingering a loose strand of Stella's hair. "Aren't we, Penny?"

Without waiting for her daughter's reply, she added, "You must feel awful."

"As bad as she looks, I reckon," Penny muttered.

Stella hadn't given a single thought to her appearance, but leave it to Penny to notice how disheveled she was. It was the least of Stella's concerns.

"I did so like Elijah," she added. "And to be murdered . . ." She dropped her voice to a whisper on the last word as if the very mention of it was scandalous. "But," she continued at a more natural volume, "we can all rest easier knowing he's in a better place."

Stella knew no such thing and wished the woman would go away.

"I agree with Reverend Paine," Lady Atherly said when Mrs. Swenson released her grip and stepped aside. "The wedding must be postponed. The mourning period prohibits going ahead as planned."

In her dark blue day dress, Lady Atherly appeared already dressed for mourning. Yet she'd said nothing about Stella's father. No condolences. No outpouring of false sympathy, no pretense of regret her father was dead. Instead, Lady Atherly had found another excuse to put off the wedding. She was nothing if not consistent. In an odd way, it was refreshing, and Stella respected her for it.

"Of course you do, Mother," Lyndy scoffed. "You've been trying to break off our engagement since the moment you met Mr. Kendrick."

"God rest his soul," Reverend Paine chimed, raising his gaze toward the ceiling.

"Now, now, Lord Lyndhurst," Mrs. Swenson chided gently. "Your mother is trying to do what's best. Elijah is dead, and a member of your family is accused of killing him. Consider how scandalous it would be if y'all defied convention. Stella needs to mourn him properly."

"Owen didn't kill anyone," Lyndy insisted.

But Mrs. Swenson continued as if she hadn't heard. "But your gracious mother didn't say to cancel the wedding, now did she? She said to postpone. And for what it's worth, I agree."

"No one asked for your opinion," Lyndy sneered.

Stella squeezed his arm. Arguing wasn't helping lessen her unhappiness. She knew of only two ways to do that.

"We will be getting married," Stella whispered, adamantly voicing one way. "For Daddy's sake. It's what he wanted."

Lyndy nodded curtly in agreement, pulling her tighter to him until the length of their sides touched as if daring anyone to separate them.

"We can discuss this later." Lady Alice was suddenly at Stella's side, carefully prying Stella from her brother's grip. "Stella's had a shock. We all have. I think she needs to be lying down."

"You are absolutely right, Alice," Lady Atherly said. "Fulton, see that Miss Kendrick's old room is prepared." Stella had stayed here when she'd first arrived in England, seemingly a lifetime ago. "And see that Ethel comes from Pilley Manor straightaway."

Stella rewarded Lady Alice's surprising kindness and fortitude with a smile of gratitude. She'd rescued her from the well-meaning but suffocating attention.

Mrs. Swenson twittered about, counting off reasons why Stella should come back with her to Pilley Manor, to be with kin, to let her and Penny console her, to change into something more suitable, but everyone ignored her. After Lyndy gave her a reassuring peck on the cheek, she drifted after the butler up the grand staircase, trusting her feet to know the way, for her mind was preoccupied, making plans, deciding the best way to proceed.

To track down the truth about her father's murder.

* * *

The moment the door closed, Stella flipped off the stifling sheets and blankets and put her feet on the floor. They all had good intentions. But laying idly in bed wasn't part of her plan. She pulled the satin and lace nightgown Ethel insisted on borrowing from Lady Alice over her head. With her clothes banished to the laundry, Stella dressed in the white shirtwaist and embroidered light and dark blue skirt (also borrowed from Lady Alice) her maid had laid out before she left.

Stella put her ear to the door. Ethel's footsteps no longer echoed on the other side. Counting silently to ten, she opened the door and slipped into the hall. Memories, of sneaking out of her room in Kentucky as a girl, rushed into her mind. She hadn't done it often, but each time warranted the necessary risk, or so she'd thought at the time. When Tully was a foal, for a reason she could no longer remember, her father had forbidden her to go to the stables for three days. But Tully had been colicky, so Stella had risked the willow switch to check on her.

The memory stung. Her father's cruelties had stamped her heart, like a brand on a cattle's hide. But with him dead, so too were her hopes he'd ever make right what he'd done. But then how was she going to mourn him properly, as Mrs. Swenson suggested? How was she going to make peace with him as a daughter should, and move on with her life?

By catching his killer, for a start.

Stella tiptoed down the hall to the servants' door at the far end. When the thick green baize door closed behind her, she sighed in relief. No one upstairs could hear her. No one downstairs would stop her. She scurried down the narrow, dimly lit stairs toward the servants' hall, the braid down her back bouncing like a horse's tail ready for the show ring. The comforting fragrance of freshly baked bread met her at the bottom. Her stomach rumbled. Having to forgo the picnic, Stella hadn't eaten since breakfast. She spied Mrs. Cole's kitchen maid laying out a plate of yeast rolls for the servants' tea. Stella hastened in and snatched a roll from the plate, still warm to the touch. The maid squeaked in surprise. With a finger across her lips, Stella helped herself to an apple from a plate of fruit. Ignoring the maid's gawping stare, Stella left the servants' hall and hurried toward the tradesmen's entrance. She yanked it open. A warm, fresh breeze ruffled her shirtwaist and the tendrils of hair on her forehead. She stepped into the sunshine and paused to inhale the sweet musky autumn air, noting the lingering scent of burnt oak still tainted it. She crossed the gravel yard, skirted the stone walls separating the back entrance from the gardens, and headed down the garden path.

"Miss!" Charlie, the stable hand, exclaimed when she strode into the stable. He stammered a moment, uncertain what else to say, and dashed toward the harness room, where Mr. Gates was often found.

"Miss Kendrick," Mr. Gates said, popping his head out, a frown on his taut, sun-weathered face. "What tragic news about your father."

Of course, he would know, she reminded herself. Everyone from Lymington to Fordingbridge must know what had happened by now.

"You have our sincere condolences. If there's anything . . . ?"

"Thank you, Mr. Gates." After talking so much in her head, the sound of her voice sounded hollow and far away. "If it's all the same to you, I would like to go for a ride."

"Of course," he said as if they were all carrying on as usual. "Charlie! Saddle up Tully. That's a good lad." Charlie tipped his cap at her. "And be quick about it."

Charlie dashed off to his task. Stella and Mr. Gates waited in the dim light of the aisle in awkward silence. The scent of the hay, the leather polish, the horse dung mingled in her nose as she waited. A wave of security, like a mother's embrace, washed over Stella at the sight of Tully swishing her tail and bobbing her head in greeting. Shunning offers of help, she hoisted herself into the saddle, feeling more grounded on Tully's back than she did with her feet on the floor.

She nodded Mr. Gates her thanks, clicked her tongue, and she and Tully were off. The moment they cleared the stable door, Tully, as if sensing Stella's need, picked up her pace. By the time they'd passed the paddocks and reached the open heath, Tully was cantering. Soon they reached a line of towering oaks, planted in a row hundreds of years ago. Stella guided Tully down the dirt track that paralleled the tree line, not knowing where it led, and let Tully break into a run. Dust kicked up and wind rushed at her face. Stella's braid kept time, rhythmically thumping against her back, the peach ribbon tied at the end fluttering like a flag, as Tully raced across the landscape.

And for a long time (how long she had no idea), she thought of nothing but keeping her seat. But when she leaned into a jump over a small seasonal pond, the horror of Pistol Prescott's last moments burst into her mind. Was it only yesterday he'd died? That she'd learned of his threats toward someone at Morrington Hall?

Now Daddy is dead too.

Exhausted, tears whipped from her cheeks by the wind before she could wipe them away, her thoughts spiraled out of control.

Both were horsemen from Kentucky. Could it be a coincidence? Mr. Swenson and Uncle Jed were also both horsemen from Kentucky. For that matter, so was she. Were their lives in danger too?

Shoving such ridiculous ideas aside, Stella concentrated on the long black strands of her dapple-gray's mane, whipping around her neck. But the questions continued to hound her.

Who did kill her father? Sir Owen? Almost anyone she could think of, Uncle Jed included, had more of a reason than

Sir Owen did. And what about the jockey? Was the jockey's death an accident, as her father's first appeared to be? Maybe someone pushed him into the oncoming runaway carriage? But why? And who had Pistol Prescott wanted to kill? Was it a co-incidence her father was now dead too? Until now, she and everyone else had assumed it was Lyndy or Lord Atherly or even perhaps one of the male servants at Morrington Hall. Could her father have been the jockey's intended victim? Maybe Pistol Prescott had made the same mistake Uncle Jed did by thinking Stella and her father were living at Morrington Hall? But that assumed someone else was involved, someone who followed them to the castle and finished what Pistol Prescott started. But if so, why not use Pistol Prescott's gun? Why do it at the castle? Why do it all? Nothing made any sense.

As her questions twisted in and around themselves, Stella urged Tully to run faster, as if she could outrun them, or find answers waiting over the next rise. They entered a stand of spindly old gorse bushes, bare but for their prickles, like cactus in the desert. She leaned low to avoid the shrubs, her face inches from Tully's neck. When they left the gorse, a gust of wind whipped strands of Tully's mane across her face. Stella didn't notice the outstretching branch of a young oak tree before it was too late.

CHAPTER 16

Inspector Brown wrinkled his nose. The overuse of furniture wax did nothing to hide the pervasive odor of stale cigar. With their glassy stares warily guarding the door, the deer heads mounted on the dark paneled walls did nothing to put him at ease. Did they know something he didn't? In a rare moment of optimism last spring, after using it during another murder investigation, Brown believed he'd seen the last of Lord Atherly's smoking room. But he was fortunate Lord Atherly had kindly offered the use of it again. What was regrettable was Brown's requiring it at all.

Staring at the large antlers perched above the door, Brown mentally checked off his witness list.

The first to be interviewed was Ethel Eakins. Having been put through the paces during the last investigation, Miss Kendrick's lady's maid had eagerly cooperated. She'd supplied herself, the footman, and the children alibis (a necessity Brown had never seriously entertained). Otherwise, she could do nothing more than confirm encountering Lord Lyndhurst, Miss Kendrick, and Mr. Swenson in the courtyard soon thereafter.

She had no knowledge of Sir Owen's or Mr. Kendrick's movements. James, the footman, the second to arrive, corroborated everything the maid had said.

Mr. Swenson, too, was forthcoming, confessing to getting separated from Mr. Kendrick after touring the castle together when the victim wanted to linger over the view from the battlements. The punishing winds, Mr. Swenson explained, had made his ears ache. Like the maid and the footman, Mr. Swenson had only recently met Sir Owen and had no idea why he'd have cause to kill Mr. Kendrick. After an admonishment to contact him if they thought of anything else, Brown had let each go after a few minutes.

Jedidiah Kendrick had proved more difficult. Brown tried every tactic he knew to pry information from the tight-lipped and oddly belligerent bugger, appealing to his love for Miss Kendrick, reminding him of his civic duty, threatening him with time spent in a jail cell. But Brown guessed the reticent American had been interrogated before. He resented being imposed upon by the police, even if it meant convicting his brother's killer. Why that surprised Brown, he couldn't say. But after an insufferable hour of hearing the man claim, repeatedly, nothing more than having roamed the spit, never observing nor hearing anything pertinent to the murder, Brown knew better than to press on. The man was hiding something. Of that, Brown had no doubt. But learning the nature of it was beyond Brown's patience and ability. For now.

Lord Lyndhurst, when he arrived, refused to sit down. He refrained from pacing but exuded a barely suppressed desire to. With his arms folded against this chest, the viscount denounced Brown for arresting Sir Owen when Miss Kendrick's Uncle Jed was by far the more obvious suspect. Hadn't anyone told Brown of the second altercation between the two brothers last night? Lord Lyndhurst had asked. When Brown admitted ignorance, the young lord described a heated row where the victim threatened to throw his brother's children out on the street, and "Uncle Jed" pronounced his desire for the victim to "go to hell."

Why then had Jedidiah Kendrick accompanied his brother on today's excursion? Brown wanted to know. Had the two reconciled? Or had other factors come into play? Lord Lyndhurst couldn't tell him.

Brown cursed himself, then, for not pressing the younger Mr. Kendrick further.

Not wanting to make the same mistake twice, Brown questioned Lord Lyndhurst further, pressing for details: where had he been, whom was he with, what else had he seen? Even he refused to give Brown details, volunteering nothing more than he'd kept company with Miss Kendrick the entire time and knew nothing of what had transpired in the tower. It was as plain as beans on toast that Lord Lyndhurst had a secret he was anxious to keep. But Brown, having gotten to know the gentleman, chalked it up to one of a more personal nature than a criminal one. They parted congenially, both men agreeing that questioning Miss Kendrick could wait.

When Brown had spoken to Mrs. Ivy Mitchell, the victim's sister-in-law and the second to last to arrive, he'd detected an undercurrent of triumph, as if she were glad the victim was dead. But to Brown's chagrin, she'd supplied him with little more insight into Sir Owen's movements, his motive, or that of the others, than she had at the castle.

He'd spent hours questioning the excursion party. And he was getting nowhere.

Brown, rubbing the crick out of his neck, returned his attention to the woman sitting in the dark leather-covered captain's chair across from him, powdering her nose from a silver compact with blue enamel flowers. She was the last on his list.

"Try harder if you please, Miss Swenson." Brown was losing his patience.

She'd changed from her traveling suit into a pale purple tea gown and tapped her foot impatiently as if he'd called her away from an engagement with far more important men than he. Gone was the petrified creature who huddled in her father's arms. The young woman had regained her composure and an all-together unhelpful attitude.

"I've already told you." Miss Swenson snapped the compact closed. No amount of powder could hide her red, puffy eyes. "I don't remember where I was when I heard the shout."

Brown wasn't unsympathetic. The young woman had discovered the murdered man's body. It was her defiance that made him press her. What wasn't she telling him?

"Sir Owen was most adamant you were with him at the time." Brown could picture the deflated young gentleman when Constable Waterman installed him in the cell. "Are you telling me that isn't true?"

"As I said before, and I will say again, he's lying." She shifted in her seat.

"Were you with someone else then?"

Anger flashed across her face. "What are you implying, Inspector?"

"I'm not implying anything, Miss Swenson. I'm trying to establish the whereabouts of all the members of Mr. Kendrick's party. If you were not with Sir Owen as he claims, then I must conclude you were alone. Am I correct?"

"Yes, I was alone." The young woman flipped open the compact again. She studied her reflection in the compact mirror, the silver case glinting in a stray ray of sunshine.

"Then, you too have no alibi." His statement lingered in the silence between them until she snapped the compact shut. Brown leaned forward in his chair, hoping to stress the precariousness of her position. "Sir Owen claims you as his alibi. Which, if true, would make him yours as well. But if you were both alone at the time, as you insist, then you are both suspects."

Miss Swenson squared her shoulders, but a trace of arrogant desperation colored her voice. She shoved her compact back in her bag.

"Owen was the one gaping down at Mr. Kendrick from the top of the stairs. He was the one with the scratches on his face. Not me." She crossed and recrossed her ankles. "Why are you even questioning me? You have your killer. Why can't you leave me alone?"

Brown pinched the bridge of his nose. If only murder inquiries were as simple as that. *Or any investigation for that matter.* Yes, Sir Owen sat accused of killing Elijah Kendrick, but where was the evidence that would convict him? What was his motive? And with Jedidiah Kendrick having more obvious animosity toward the victim, and Miss Swenson having discovered the body, who's to say Sir Owen wasn't at the wrong place at the wrong time?

But Brown wasn't about to satisfy Miss Swenson with an answer. She was the one who had a bit of explaining to do.

"Did you have any reason to want Mr. Kendrick dead?" he said.

She shot up out of her chair. "What? You think I . . . ?" She sputtered in surprise a moment, glaring down at him. "I promise you, Inspector. If I wanted anyone dead, it wouldn't have been her father."

Miss Swenson snatched up her handbag and, without requesting permission, flounced out of the room.

Brown nestled back into his chair and stared up at the deer heads again. *Her father.* Had Miss Swenson realized what she'd said? From Brown's reckoning, she probably had no idea she'd revealed her animosity toward Miss Kendrick. He slapped his cap on his head and stood.

"Right! Now we're getting somewhere."

Brown had finished at Morrington Hall and was eagerly anticipating tea with his wife when he spied Mrs. Mitchell along Lyndhurst High Street. She ducked into a gabled brick building, nondescript, but for the distinctive red metal box mounted into the wall by the front door. The petite American had been his most valuable witness, placing Sir Owen at the top of the stairs at the time of Mr. Kendrick's fall.

He might've kept going, the taste of his steak and kidney pie already on his tongue, but for a nagging curiosity, which, when aroused, served him well. Brown guided Matilda toward the curb and parked the police wagon. He leaped down, wrapped the horse's reins around a lamppost, and headed back toward the post office. Mrs. Mitchell emerged when he approached the post office door.

"Good afternoon, Mrs. Mitchell."

"Inspector!"

The parcel she was carrying slipped from her grip at the sight of him. He bent to retrieve it, but she hurriedly snatched it up.

"Everything all right?"

"Yes, yes, thank you." The American lady's face flushed a bright red, and she glanced about her as if afraid to be seen speaking with him. If she'd been a horse, Brown would've described her as skittish. But why? "If you'll excuse me," she said, brushing past him and scurrying down the sidewalk, quickly disappearing into an alley between a tea shop and a dressmaker's.

Now, what was that all about?

Glancing over his shoulder, he checked Matilda was well secured to the post before pushing open the post office door. *Post office* was an oversimplification. Besides collecting and delivering the Royal Mail, sending and receiving money orders and telegrams, the office served as a savings bank as well as a government insurance and annuity office. Inside, banks of wooden, glass-fronted, numbered letter boxes created a wall on both sides of the open counter.

The jingling ring of the bell above the door brought the clerk to the counter straightaway. The middle-aged man exuded a sense of precision and orderliness, from his clean-shaven face, his blindingly white starched shirt, and sleeve garters down to his oiled hair that appeared to have been parted using a straight edge. Brown pulled out his warrant card.

"Inspector Brown, Hampshire Constabulary. There was a small woman, in her midforties, American, who—"

"You just missed her," the clerk interrupted.

"No, I spoke to her outside. She was carrying a parcel. I'd like to know what was in it."

"Why ask me? She came in with the parcel."

"She didn't collect it here?"

The clerk shook his head. "She didn't receive anything here."

"Then what business did she have?"

The clerk pointed with his thumb over his shoulder. Behind him in the corner was a highly polished desk with a potted geranium with delicate blue flowers. A lined ledger with a pencil in the binding crease lay open beside an electric telegraph.

"She sent a telegram."

"I need to know what it said and to whom she sent it." When the clerk hesitated, Brown pinned him with his most disapproving glare. "As I am conducting a murder inquiry, I advise you to assist me, Mr. . . . ?"

The clerk swallowed hard, his large Adam's apple bobbing up and down. "Stote. Bertram Stote. But I don't think it proper that I—"

"Mr. Stote, the contents of that telegram may prove vital. If you refuse to assist me, I may have to arrest you for impeding my inquiry."

Mr. Stote paled, spun around, sliding on the waxed plank floor, and snatched up the ledger from the desk.

"She sent it to, to . . ." He stammered nervously. The answer came in a rush. "To a one Mrs. Eugene Smith, care of the Star Hotel, High Street, Southampton."

Southampton? Could Mrs. Mitchell know someone staying there? Plenty of people overnighted in the city after they arrived in this country or before they shipped out. But with the unanswered questions surrounding Jesse Prescott's death, Brown couldn't brush the possible connection aside.

"How did the telegram read?"

"I'm not quite sure how to say. Even before you arrived, I wondered about it myself, but I'm not paid to question the customers, am I?"

The simple mahogany wall clock above the clerk's desk chimed half past five. Brown was late for tea.

"What did it say, Mr. Stote?" Brown repeated less patiently.

The clerk, a moment ago pale, sprouted two red blotches on his cheeks.

"It was simple, really. All it said was, *It's over. He's dead.*"

CHAPTER 17

~

"She's had a bad night of it, I suspect, milord," Gates whispered, "but she's a tough one. She'll mend."

Lyndy and the stablemaster peered over at Stella curled up in the corner of Tully's box stall, like a child, in the hay. Bits of golden-brown bracken clung to her skirt, brown and green splotches stained her white blouse, and a scratch, etched in dried blood, marred her perfectly porcelain forehead. She was fast asleep. Tully, although calmly chewing her oats and hay, kept a wary eye on the men. As if Stella were her foal, Tully had positioned herself protectively between her and the men.

"Have someone tell Miss Kendrick's maid we've found her mistress," Lyndy quietly instructed a passing groom. The maid was sick with worry.

Lyndy had kept one eye on the dining room door during breakfast. When Stella hadn't come down, he'd ordered a tray sent up. He'd been more concerned than he'd admit. Stella never missed breakfast. He shouldn't have been surprised then when Stella's lady's maid, breaking all rules of decorum, had burst into Papa's study, uninvited. Lyndy and Papa had been discussing hiring Sir Charles Nighy, Papa's solicitor, to free Sir Owen from his predicament. Papa, who strictly prohibited the female servants from entering his study, surprised Lyndy by allowing the maid to explain herself instead of sacking her on the spot. The poor distraught thing rambled on about last night's tray being left untouched and a nightgown left in a pile on the floor, all to say Stella had gone missing.

"Will do, milord," the groom whispered back.

Lyndy detected the surprise in the groom's tone, the approval in his eyes. His instinctual reaction was one of annoyance. Who was the groom to approve of him? But more to the point, why had the man been surprised? Was Lyndy's concern for Stella's maid so unexpected? That's what troubled him. It was uncharacteristic of him to notice or care. Was he becoming a better master? A better man? If so, he had the woman asleep in the straw to thank.

Thank heavens, she is safe and unharmed.

"What happened?" Lyndy strained to keep the concern from his voice.

Luckily, after a frantic few minutes in Papa's study, wondering what he would do if harm had come to her, Lyndy had gotten word from Mr. Gates that she'd been found.

"Charlie discovered her like this when he came to feed and water Tully."

Lyndy stifled his desire to scoop her up and carry her back to the house. If he had his way, he'd tuck Stella into his bed and never let her out of his sight again.

The stablemaster shook his head in regret. "I wished I'd kept a better eye out for her when she came in yesterday."

"You saw her here yesterday?" Lyndy had thought her resting in her room.

Gates nodded.

"She came around to take Tully out for a ride. Considering what had happened to her father, I wasn't surprised."

No, Lyndy wasn't surprised either, come to think of it. How

else would Stella outchase her worries than on the back of her horse? It's what he would do.

"It's not unusual she wouldn't require a groom on her return, preferring to brush and wash down the horse herself. But none of us heard her come back. And what kind of watchdog is Mack? The mongrel didn't even bark."

"One that knows his mistress," Lyndy argued, his fondness for the dog evident.

Mack, as if he'd heard his name, came loping down the aisle, his tongue hanging out of his mouth. Gates dashed to intercept the dog before he bounded into the open box stall. As Gates motioned for one of his men to take charge of the restrained dog, Lyndy rewarded Mack's loyalty with a few hearty pats on the head.

"You get Tully," Lyndy said softly once the dog was secured outside.

The horse swished her tail slowly, swatting flies, but her vigilance was undeniable; her gaze followed every movement the men made. Lyndy knew Stella's horse to be the gentlest of creatures, but a mare protecting her foal was unpredictable. Lyndy wasn't taking any chances.

Gates retrieved Tully's bridle and offered the mare a piece of peppermint as he slipped it over her head. With that in place, the stablemaster gently led Tully out of the stall. The moment he was clear of the horse, Lyndy was inside, on his knees in the straw beside his bride-to-be. Resisting the urge to pull her into his lap, he brushed strands of matted hair from her forehead, his fingers grazing her smooth, soft skin. He slowly traced the scratch with his fingertip.

"Wake up, my love."

He bent forward and lightly kissed her cheek and, with a rush of relief, felt her stir. Cold and stiff, she uncurled slowly, before pushing up onto her elbows. She vigorously rubbed her hands over her arms.

"Lyndy, I think Pistol Prescott wanted Daddy dead."

Her words hit him like a bucket of ice water.

"But he threatened to kill someone at Morrington Hall," Lyndy reminded her.

"I think the jockey made the same mistake Uncle Jed did, believing Daddy and I were staying at Morrington Hall. It was never about you or Lord Atherly. It was about Daddy all along. But why, I don't know."

"Does that matter now? Prescott's dead, Stella. Even if he had wanted to bring harm to your father, he didn't kill him."

Stella sighed in exasperation. "But someone did. And I'm not convinced it's Sir Owen."

"No, you're right. Owen didn't do it."

"But it's too much of a coincidence. The two deaths have to be related."

"Come on, let's get you back to the house."

Lyndy pushed up from his knees and held out his hand. Stella, smelling of hay and damp earth, clamped it and let him haul her to her feet. She brushed bits of straw and bracken from her blouse and skirts. Lyndy plucked bits and pieces from her braided hair.

"How did you injure yourself?"

Stella raised a hand to her scratched brow. "I was careless. A branch hit me when I was riding."

"But why stay here all night? You nearly frightened your maid to death." Not to mention how he'd suffered.

"Oh, poor Ethel. I should've left her a note. But I was so upset yesterday," she said, stepping out of the stall and glancing down the aisle. One of the other horses neighed in greeting. "Where is Tully?"

"Gates took her outside. You were saying?"

Standing in a pool of sunlight in the middle of the aisle, like an angel sent from heaven, she turned to face him. "Lyndy, I was devastated. I was confused. I was mortified. I was relieved. I had so many unanswered questions."

She dropped her head in her hands, distraught, ruining the angelic tableau. He stepped out of the box stall and joined her in the aisle. As he strode toward her, planning to wrap her in a comforting embrace, she slid her hands down her face and rested her fingertips on her delicate jawbone.

"You know how I felt when Daddy betrayed me and forced me into this engagement?"

Lyndy, who was most comfortable in motion, froze.

Why had she mentioned that? Wasn't that all behind them? Had her father's death made her change her mind? He'd barely considered it, but now, with the wedding postponed and Kendrick dead, of course, she could.

"Yes." The word came out strained and angry.

She didn't notice the sudden tension between them but continued as if confident of his sympathy. "That is how I now feel about his death. But not in the way I should. I don't mourn the loss of him. I mourn the loss of ever having a loving father. I grieve for how his death is now preventing us from being together."

Lyndy let out a long, steady stream of breath. He was so relieved, almost giddy. He tugged on his sleeve and joined her in the aisle.

"For a moment there, I thought you'd changed your mind."

Stella touched his arm, holding him in thrall with the warmth of that brilliant, all-in smile he adored so much.

"No, Lyndy. Daddy did a good thing bringing us together, even if he did it for the wrong reasons. But I wish we could start the life he wanted for us without his murder hounding us. It reminds me of what happened with Reverend Bullmore, except this time, it's so personal. Not just who died but who the killer is."

"I thought you didn't suspect Owen."

She hesitated. "I don't."

Lyndy could guess whom she suspected but didn't want to

volunteer the name. "We did it before; we'll do it again. We'll find out who killed your father. I promise."

"I knew you'd understand."

When her soft lips brushed against his, her warm breath mingling with his own, Lyndy would've promised her anything.

Stella lifted the brass knocker, taking gratification in the clanking *Rap, tap, tap*.

She was refreshed but wary. With trunks of her things brought up to Morrington Hall, she'd had a bath and with Ethel's help changed for riding. With a late breakfast to fortify her, she'd made up her mind. While Lyndy ferreted out answers in London (meeting with a friend who owned one of the racing papers, in hopes of learning more about Jesse Prescott), she would seek them closer to home—Pilley Manor to be exact. But when she'd arrived, the black ribbon hanging against the familiar red door, conjuring up all her conflicting emotions, she wondered if she was doing the right thing.

Would she be able to riffle through her father's things? Would she find anything about who did this to him, and why?

She glanced back at Tully, her reins wrapped around the hitching post. The horse was nibbling on what she could from the green, newly mowed lawn. Stella could easily hop back into the saddle and be gone, with no one the wiser.

And squander a chance to find answers?

The black ribbon hanging on the door fluttered when Tims, the butler at Pilley Manor, flung it open. Stella was poised to knock yet again.

"Miss Kendrick! I hope I didn't keep you waiting. I was made to believe you'd be staying indefinitely up at Morrington Hall."

The stoic butler was flustered. He'd always kept an eye out for her return, and, like magic, the door would open before she had a chance to knock.

"I am staying at Morrington," she said, reassuring him with all the smile she could muster when she stepped inside, "but I came back for a few things."

"Of course." The butler closed the door behind them. "Shall I inform your guests you are home?"

Home. Stella glanced at the silver tray piled high with black-lined calling cards on the side table in the hall. *This will never be my home again.*

Tims had never adapted to her unconventional ways, as the female staff had done, so she appreciated the butler's meaning, nonetheless.

"No, thank you. I'll find everyone myself."

When she handed him her riding hat and gloves, the butler coughed nervously. "And may I say on behalf of all the staff, how sorry we are about Mr. Kendrick."

"Thank you, Tims."

"Stella!"

The Swensons, as one, streamed down the stairs into the hall. Mrs. Swenson and Penny, already wearing their hats, were dressed for an outing, in white gloves and similar lace-layered day dresses but of different accenting hues—Penny's hem piped in yellow, Mrs. Swenson's sash in dark blue. Despite the black crape on the door, nothing about them indicated a death—no, a murder had descended on this house. Granted, they were visiting, and her father wasn't their kin, but still, the vividness of their clothes, the vitality in their faces irked Stella. Even Penny came across as fully recovered from the ordeal.

"You poor thing," Mrs. Swenson lamented.

Stella took a step back to avoid the woman's attempt at an embrace.

"Penny told me everything that happened, including Sir Owen's involvement, and to think we were considering Sir Owen as a match for our darling girl." She raised a hand to her chest as if to slow her fretting heart. "I shudder to think of it now."

When had that happened?

Stella had noticed the two flirting, but they'd only met yesterday. When had they had time to talk of marriage? Then again, Stella and Lyndy were engaged before they'd even met.

". . . and about that dreadful policeman interrogating her and Theo," Mrs. Swenson was saying.

"Inspector Brown is just doing his job," Stella said, wondering why he hadn't spoken to her yet.

"He could've been nicer about it," Penny fussed, adjusting the tilt of her straw hat. "I don't think he even believed me."

"Of course he did, Penelope, darling. Why wouldn't he?"

Penny shot her father a sideways glance but refrained from explaining further. Instead, she brushed past Stella toward Tims, holding the door open. Her parents followed when a carriage came into sight and rumbled up the drive. Two gray Irish Draught horses pulled it.

"Where are you going?" Stella asked. She wanted to add, "In Daddy's precious landau," but she held her tongue.

"Lady Atherly has been kind enough to invite us to Morrington Hall," Mrs. Swenson said.

"I reckon she wants to commiserate about the postponement of the wedding," Mr. Swenson said. "Aren't you joining us?"

Instead of answering, Stella asked, "Where's Aunt Rachel? Uncle Jed and the children?"

"How should I know?" Mrs. Swenson said, eying Stella critically. "By the way, if you want my advice, I wouldn't go around like that, Stella, dear. You are supposed to be in mourning. You aren't wearing all black."

Stella glanced down at her riding costume. Although her jacket and skirt were black, her blouse was white. *How appropriate.* She had mixed emotions about her father's death. *And it shows.*

"Shall we, Theo?" Mrs. Swenson said, reaching for her husband's arm. "And don't dawdle, Penny."

They crossed the drive toward the carriage, the pebbles crunching beneath their shoes. Stella turned her back on them, and Mr. Tims shut the door.

"Mr. Jedidiah Kendrick left moments before you arrived, Miss Kendrick," the butler said, answering Stella's earlier question. "He did not inform me of his plans."

Where Uncle Jed stole off to, Stella could hazard a guess, but she had no intention of tracking him down at the pub.

"The children are in the kitchen with Mrs. Downie, and Miss Luckett and Mrs. Mitchell are in the library."

"Thank you, Tims."

Stella found Aunt Ivy on the couch, her legs tucked beneath her, reading a letter while Aunt Rachel snored quietly in the overstuffed chair. On the low table between them was a small wooden-handled silver coffeepot and two cups, empty but the dregs. The crackling fire in the grate added to the peaceful domestic scene.

"It's so good to see you, Aunt Ivy," Stella said quietly, hoping not to waken her elderly aunt.

"Stella!" Aunt Ivy, startled by her sudden arrival, dropped her stocking feet to the floor and slipped the letter she'd been reading behind a tasseled throw pillow.

Great Aunt Rachel snorted, shifted her in the chair, and fell silent again.

"I didn't expect you so soon."

Obviously. But why? What was it about the letter she didn't want Stella to see?

"Thank you for coming here," Stella said as if the awkward moment hadn't occurred. "It's so nice to have you closer." Stella had proposed Aunt Ivy leave the White Hart Inn in Lyndhurst and stay at Pilley Manor. But after she'd declined Stella's first invitation to join her there, Stella wasn't so sure Aunt Ivy would agree.

"Anything for you, dear girl," Aunt Ivy said.

"What were you reading?" Stella wanted to point to the pillow hiding the letter but instead indicated the book lying open across her aunt's lap.

Ivy lifted the blue and yellow cover to show it to Stella, Mrs. Oliphant's *A House in Bloomsbury*. Stella had been reading it when Miss Naplock, the seamstress, had arrived for Stella's final dress fitting.

Was that only two days ago? It was hard to believe.

"I found it on top of this stack. You might remember, I'm a sucker for romances."

Stella did remember because she was too. Back in Kentucky, her father hadn't approved of ladies reading novels. But Aunt Ivy used to sneak them to her. Before Aunt Ivy stopped visiting them at Bronson Ridge Farm, that is.

"I hadn't read this one before," her aunt carried on. "I haven't been able to put it down."

"You've been here all morning then? Reading?"

Aunt Ivy nodded. "Considering what happened yesterday, I couldn't imagine what else to do. And I needed the escape."

But that couldn't be. When Ethel helped Stella dress, her maid mentioned she'd noticed Aunt Ivy coming out of the post office when Ethel was returning from Pilley Manor with Stella's trunks. Why was Aunt Ivy lying about that too?

"I did telephone Morrington Hall, but they reckoned you'd gone out."

"I was on my way over here. It's another beautiful day. The ride over was wonderful. I recommend it."

"I'm surprised you're up to it."

"I'm always up for a ride with Tully. Besides, I've come to go through Daddy's things."

Great Aunt Rachel suddenly groaned softly, as if in pain, before settling down peacefully again.

Aunt Ivy scooched over and patted the space beside her,

careful to put her back against the pillow hiding the letter. Stella took the invitation, dropping heavily onto the couch.

"And why's that?" her aunt asked. "What do you think you're gonna find?"

"Clues as to why someone killed him."

"I don't mean to be crass." Aunt Ivy placed her hand over Stella's. "Or speak ill of the dead, but do you need to go through his things to learn that? Your daddy wasn't a well-liked man."

"Don't you think I know that? Every person at the castle yesterday had a reason to dislike him," Stella said, sharper-tongued than she would've liked. She was suddenly angry, and Aunt Ivy was partially to blame. She yanked her hand out from her aunt's. "So much so that one of them killed him."

"I'm sorry, Stella. I didn't mean to upset you further. You've been through so much. I can't imagine how you must feel. What can I do to help?"

The offer was appealing. Stella was reluctant to do the task alone. She wanted to get it over with. But Aunt Ivy couldn't be entirely trusted. "I don't know."

"Well, I'm here." She smiled empathetically. "You holler if you need me."

I need you now, Stella wanted to say.

With the hidden letter burning a hole through the pillow, and her aunt's denial about being in town still ringing in her ears, Stella couldn't trust herself not to blurt out the questions sitting on the tip of her tongue. *What are you hiding? What were you and Daddy arguing about? Why have you been acting so strange?* It was no use asking. Aunt Ivy wouldn't tell her the truth anyway.

Stella rose, muttered an excuse, and left, closing the library door behind her. But not quite. Holding her breath, she peeked through the crack she'd left. Assuming the door closed, Aunt

Ivy snatched the letter from its hiding place and began reading again. A triumphant grin slowly stretched across her face. Stella's heart sank.

The Cheshire cat smile reminded her too much of her father's. And like when her father had smiled, nothing good would come of it.

Stella took a deep breath and opened the door. It was pitch black. Stella crept across the carpet, warily feeling her way toward the crack of light seeping through from the window. When her outstretched hand touched the thick, hanging damask fabric, she flung open the drawn curtains, revealing the green, broad-leaved woodland that encroached right up to the stone wall encircling Pilley Manor. Some of the trees, although not yet changing in color, had shed dried leaves into the backyard. A tiny, long-tailed, brown and white bird captivated her attention as it spiraled up a thick tree trunk, picking at the bark with its delicate, downturned bill. When it flitted away, startled by the cry of a more aggressive bird approaching, Stella turned her back on the view and faced the bedroom.

It was a man's room with dark green and eggplant striped walls, a towering Eastlake mahogany bed with matching nightstand, and writing desk. There wasn't a hint of a flower anywhere: not woven as a pattern in the rug, not painted on the walls, not carved into the bedstand, not wilting in a crystal vase. Instead, books were everywhere: on the nightstand, stacked beside the desk, packed into the trunk pushed against the footboard. With rare exceptions, they were accounting ledgers, studbooks, and books about husbandry and horses. On the desk, slitted envelopes and letters of correspondence filled the shallow wooden tray. A pair of reading spectacles lay on a copy of the *Sporting Times Life*, open to an article describing Challacombe's win at Doncaster. An empty crystal ashtray sat side by side with the inkstand. Despite the servants' best efforts, the stale stench of cigar still lingered in the air. *As if Daddy might come through the door at any moment and reprimand me.* Stella's heart raced.

As a child, Stella hadn't been allowed in her father's bedroom. But being curious, Stella had snuck in anyway. She'd pour over the engraved wooden boxes and tidy dresser drawers filled with the oddities only found in a gentleman's wardrobe. She'd run her fingers lightly over cuff links and shirt studs, watch chains and fobs, black silk ties and white detachable collars, admiring how strange and wonderful they were.

But she wasn't a child anymore. And her father wasn't going to walk through the door. Yet she still gravitated toward the boxes of glittering gold cuff links and bejeweled shirt studs, knowing she'd learn nothing about his death there. But they'd belong to him, things he'd purchased and prized, and that was enough. When the moment for loss and nostalgia was over, she tackled the business of sorting through his business and private papers.

Most of what she found, not surprisingly, concerned the breeding and selling of his horses in Kentucky, correspondences, bills of sale, and the like. His time in England hadn't diminished his involvement in the farm. Among these, she discovered the marriage settlement agreement between him and Lord Atherly. The language read, with words such as *asset*, *trustee*, and *benefactors* sprinkled throughout, as a dry, cold testament to what she thought marriage should be. She couldn't read more than a few lines before tossing it back in the drawer.

After rummaging through the drawers and the piles of correspondence, she thumbed through his studbooks and accounting ledgers. She was starting to doubt she'd find anything of use when she discovered a studbook under the desk on the floor. Tucked between two seemingly random pages recording the birth of two foals more than a decade ago was a copy of her father's will. Why had he brought it to England? Perhaps Lord

Atherly had requested proof Stella was to inherit the fortune necessary to pay off his debts and fund his future fossil expeditions? If so, Lord Atherly would be pleased. Initially, her father had promised that Stella would be bestowed ten million dollars on her wedding day. But now that he was dead, her wedding gift wasn't the half of it. Assuming Stella agreed to marry Lyndy, and her father didn't live to attend the wedding, she was to be his sole beneficiary. She inherited everything: his vast monetary fortune, the house in New York, the cottage in Newport, the horse farm in Kentucky, the horses, his railroad stocks, his priceless books, his Daimler car, even the diamond cuff links she'd admired earlier. Everything.

Stella gasped, her throat tightening, overwhelmed by the generosity she hadn't expected. Was his will proof, not just for Lord Atherly that he'd provide for her upon her wedding but for Stella, that he'd loved her all along?

She continued to read, her gratitude dissipating with every word as she discovered her inheritance had been entirely contingent on her doing his bidding. He wanted her obedience, not her love. If she'd refused to agree to marry Lyndy, he would've cut her out completely. Upon his death, the entirety of his wealth would've gone to building and funding a racetrack in Lexington, one to rival Churchill Downs, to be named Kendrick Park. Without an allowance to live on, Stella would've been destitute. Her father's threats had been real, startling so. Luckily, she'd agreed to his terms, and now her fortune was secured.

Staring at her father's wishes, she wondered. Did she wish she'd never known, blissfully believing he'd given her his fortune out of love? *No*. She was glad to learn the truth, however painful. Then Stella noticed the date, April 21, 1905, typed into the top of the page. He'd made this new will days before they'd left for England. What had the old one said? Had the contents of the old one been drastically different? A sourness seeped up from the pit of her stomach. Stella dropped into her father's desk chair.

Did Uncle Jed or Aunt Ivy or any of the others know the contents of the previous will and, not knowing it had been changed, expected to inherit a fortune? Was that why Daddy was killed?

CHAPTER 18

Lyndy couldn't remember being on Fleet Street before. But then again, it was an unremarkable section of the city, block after block of grimy, soot-coated, multistoried gray and red stone buildings squashed together lining the street. Lyndy abhorred London. Luckily, he wouldn't be stopping for long. When the hansom cab rumbled to a halt, Lyndy squinted up at number 52, a towering, drab monstrosity that rose seven stories, with rows of windows that reflected the bleak buildings across the street and stretched half the block. *What a dreary place to have to spend one's day.*

Thank God, he'd never be compelled to.

"Tommy!" Lyndy cried when Tommy Griffiths-King, proprietor of the *Sporting Times* and Lyndy's classmate from Eton, swung open the cab door before the muck on the street settled beneath the horse's hooves.

"By God, Lyndy, is it true?" Tommy said by way of greeting, stepping aside as Lyndy ducked out of the cab.

Lyndy couldn't remember the last time he'd seen Tommy, but it had to be years. The man hadn't changed a bit: that patrician nose, custom-tailored Savile Row suit, those unfortunate protruding rounded ears that stuck out from under his straw boater, and an irrepressible curiosity that lead to his buying a newspaper.

"Is what true, Tommy?" Lyndy combed fingers through his hair as if to rid it of the stench that had settled on him.

"Did your future father-in-law get murdered yesterday? Wasn't the wedding set for tomorrow?"

Lyndy wasn't surprised news had already reached Tommy here in London. Stella's father was a prominent man in their world of horse racing. If anyone knew of his death, it would be the owner of the *Sporting Times*. But knowing how a "journalist" had infiltrated their engagement party, Lyndy didn't want to hazard a guess by what means his friend had come by the morbid news.

"You're right," Lyndy said, "on both accounts. But for obvious reasons, the wedding's been postponed. Didn't you get Mother's card?" Mother had been considerate to inform the guests of the delay, without giving too much detail into the reason.

"I didn't, but then again, I haven't been at home since this morning. How is your bride holding up?"

"That's why I'm here, Tommy. Shall we?" With Tommy close on his heels, Lyndy yanked the glass door open, not wanting to prolong the visit any longer than he had to.

Unquestionably, Tommy was an agreeable chap, and Lyndy would have loved to go to the club and catch up—the man published Lyndy's favorite racing paper, after all. But as Tommy had so succinctly pointed out, Stella's father had been murdered; Lyndy was a man on a mission. The sooner Lyndy returned with something that could find Mr. Kendrick's killer, the sooner Stella and he could be married and put this bloody mess behind them.

Besides, he already felt the need for a bath.

"You were cryptic when you telephoned," Tommy said,

matching Lyndy step for step as they strode through the open lobby toward the lift doors, the tap of their boot heels echoing on the marble floor. "What are you expecting to find?"

"A connection between Miss Kendrick's father and an American jockey who was trampled on the Southampton docks a few days ago."

"Jesse Prescott," Tommy said, shaking his head. "Bad business that. And highly ironic. Man spends his whole life riding horses only to die beneath their hooves."

"Yes, I've come to learn about the dead jockey. If you recall, Prescott was involved in the Woodhaven Downs scandal a few months back. I'm hoping to read more about it."

"Well, you've come to the right place. If something was printed about the turf, you'll find it here. And this, my friend, is the man to help."

As if he'd been waiting for his cue, a middle-aged fellow wearing spectacles, suspenders, and no jacket approached them.

"Lord Lyndhurst," Tommy said formally, "this is Hoyle, my paper's archivist."

"I appreciate you helping me in this, Mr. Hoyle."

"Happy to be of service, Your Lordship."

"This is when I leave you, old chum," Tommy said, slapping Lyndy consolingly on the shoulder, "but I'll toast you at the wedding, whenever it happens."

"Thank you, Tommy," Lyndy said. With a jolly tip of his hat, his old friend strolled back toward the doors that lead out to the street.

"If you'll follow me," Mr. Hoyle said, leading Lyndy into the lift and instructing the attendant to bring them to the fourth floor, "I'll take you to our newspaper's morgue."

Morgue? Lyndy balked at the sound of that. *What kind of macabre sensibilities do these newspaper men have? How could Tommy not have warned me?* But Lyndy, having come this far, followed the archivist nevertheless when the lift door opened

to the *click-click-click* of a distance typewriter onto an unadorned, white-washed, empty hallway that resembled a servants' domain more than a place of reputable business. Lyndy
was pleasantly surprised when the newspaperman led him into
a well-lit room, furnished with a walnut table as long as the
dining room at Morrington Hall and several ladder-backed
chairs. Wooden filing cabinets, rising several feet above Lyndy's
head, lined the length of two walls. A few framed news clippings, the paper's distinctive pinkish salmon color faded to pale
peach, hung on the wall. The frame closest to Lyndy preserved
the paper's first issue dated: 11 February 1865. A clerk, in
waistcoat and shirtsleeves, pored over newspapers spread out
across half the table, not even lifting his head when they entered. The whole place smelled of ink and decaying paper.

"Every article we've ever printed, every photograph we've
ever taken is here," Mr. Hoyle said proudly, and understand-
ably so. "What was it you were looking for?"

"Anything on the Woodhaven Downs scandal or a jockey
called Jesse James 'Pistol' Prescott."

"Do you have a time frame?" The man approached a cata-
loging system and started to flip through the cards.

"The scandal would've been a few months ago, March or
April, maybe?" Lyndy remembered it was before he'd met
Stella, but not by much. "I don't know how long Prescott was
a jockey."

Mr. Hoyle combed through the cards, wrote down a few
notes, and then proceeded to a cabinet on the far end of the
room. He pulled open a drawer near the top and plucked out a
file folder. Then he located another drawer and then another,
pulling folders as he went.

"If it pleases Your Lordship," Mr. Hoyle said, indicating the
nearest chair at the table.

At the other end, the clerk's head sprung up, making Lyndy
wonder if he'd been correct in assuming few gentlemen fre-

quented the place. After a remonstrative scowl from Mr. Hoyle, the clerk quickly returned his attention to his collection of files.

When Lyndy settled in, the archivist laid four folders, three slim and one bulging full of newspaper clippings, on the table in front of him.

"Please, let me know if you require further assistance," Mr. Hoyle said, before tackling a stack of folders in a crate, waiting to be refiled.

Lyndy flipped opened the first folder. Each clipping made some mention of Prescott, chronicling races he rode, first in Kentucky and then all over America. Except for the jockey's penchant for toting Jesse James's gun, it was an unremarkable career of an unremarkable man. The second file was much like the first. Only the third had any mention of the Woodhaven Downs scandal, and that was no more than Lyndy already knew. He'd found nothing to connect Prescott to Elijah Kendrick.

Frustrated, Lyndy slapped the third file closed and swatted at a fly buzzing around his head. He slid the bulging file toward him across the table. The article on top was the one he remembered reading. It was dated April 22, 1905. Lyndy skimmed it, finding nothing more than he'd remembered, and put it aside.

Am I wasting my time? Lyndy swatted at the annoying fly again.

He read through several more clippings until he found something useful—a list of names including de Graat, Sallow, and Loughty, all well-known trainers, as well as those of men with whom Lyndy was unacquainted. Like Prescott, every one of them had been banned from ever riding, training, or owning racehorses in America again. Was that why Prescott was in England? Having lost his livelihood in America, had he found work here? Both Inspector Brown and Stella worried Jesse Prescott hadn't acted alone. Could one of the other Woodhaven Downs miscreants have joined Prescott in search of employment in England? Could one of these men have carried out Prescott's plan to kill Stella's father? If so, Lyndy wasn't any closer to working out why.

Lyndy made a mental note to tell the inspector to investigate this list of men further and kept reading.

What is this? Lyndy sat up straighter when he got to the end of the article. It insinuated, quite blatantly, that the list of wrongdoers was incomplete, that others had escaped the scandal unscathed. Was it supposition on the journalist's part, or did he know something he couldn't put in print? Lyndy noted the journalist's name in case he needed to contact him, put the article aside, and picked up the next. After skimming several more clippings, Lyndy found no other such speculation and chalked it up to idle conjecture on one reporter's part. Then he found what he was hoping for.

Lyndy shuffled the articles back into the folder, grimly satisfied he hadn't wasted a trip after all. And truth be told, immensely relieved neither his father's nor his own safety had ever been in jeopardy.

"Find what you were searching for, Lord Lyndhurst?" the newspaperman asked, turning from his filing work.

"That and more. Thank you, Mr. Hoyle."

Stella had been right. Jesse Prescott had every reason to want her father dead. He'd ruined the jockey's career. And, as she'd assumed, Prescott had indeed made the same mistake her uncle had. The fourth paragraph of the last clipping Lyndy read included a partial transcript from the ensuing court case. Listed were the name and residence of the man who broke the Woodhaven Downs scandal—Mr. Elijah Kendrick, who "is currently residing at Morrington Hall, the ancestral home of the Earl of Atherly, in Hampshire, England."

If Stella had reservations about searching through her father's things, his will, and the questions it sparked, had eased her conscience about combing through the other bedrooms.

Stella tackled the room Mrs. Robertson had put Aunt Ivy in first, the gold room, or so Stella called it, named for the color of the curtains, the accent pillows, the carpet, the piping on the otherwise snowy white bedcovers. It was bright and airy. Mindful of her aunt's potential return, she swiftly sorted through the wardrobe, the dress drawers, Aunt Ivy's hat boxes, and travel trunks. She found nothing out of the ordinary until she came across a stack of letters with the same return address, tied with a yellow satin ribbon, tucked into the nightstand drawer. Whom did her aunt know in Southampton? Could it be a coincidence these letters came from the same place where Pistol Prescott died? The address, for a hotel, was of no use. She'd have to read one to know more. Humming in the hall stilled Stella's hand as she tugged at the corner of an envelope. She dropped the stack of letters back where she found them and swiftly closed the drawer.

When it was safe to cross the hall, Stella tiptoed into the Swensons' bedroom. Rummaging through Mr. and Mrs. Swenson's things and then through Penny's, Stella discovered nothing suspicious or surprising. She hadn't expected to find anything troubling but wanted to be thorough. Finally, she entered her uncle's guest room.

He'd been given the purple room, the smallest in the house. A narrow but comfortable walnut bed, embellished with embroidered violets on the coverlet, a night table, and matching violet embroidered doilies, a wardrobe, and a spindly platform rocking chair were all it could hold. The children's makeshift nursery, converted from what was once the dowager's morning room, was more substantial. Not very welcoming of her father to put his brother in this tiny, feminine room. But then again, it was comfortably warm, despite only glowing embers in the grate, and if Uncle Jed had killed her father, this room would seem palatial compared to a jail cell.

Stella sifted through his clothes, clean but threadbare, hanging in the wardrobe and peeked into his one spare pair of shoes laid neatly out by the bed. Nothing was amiss. The nightstand drawer was empty. Next to a colorful five-cent cigar box on top of the nightstand (with two cigars left inside) was a framed picture of Stella's Aunt Martha and Uncle Jed on their wedding day. How handsome they both were. Stella remembered Aunt Martha as a quiet woman with long, pretty fingers. She'd died giving birth to Gertie. Both widowed with young children, the brothers should've had more in common than most. But they'd veered in different social and economic directions. Had it been her father's prosperity that drove a wedge between them? Stella suspected the truth was more complicated than that.

Not giving up, she slid her hand under the pillows, crouched down to peer under the bed, hoisted up the mattress. Nothing. That left his steamer trunk shoved into a corner. Stella slipped off the loose padlock and lifted the lid. Inside was an old, crushed red velvet photo album with a silver clasp and a sack of what looked like dirty laundry. Stella lifted the bag out and emptied it into a pile on the floor: men's white shirts that smelled of sweat, boy's stockings that needed darning, a little girl's stained pinafore.

Had Stella been wrong to suspect Uncle Jed? He wasn't the man she remembered from her childhood. But did that mean he killed her father?

Stella scooped up the dirty clothes, shoving them back into the sack, and dumped the bag back into the trunk. She retrieved the photo album and parked herself on the circular area rug. The album bulged with photographs, each framed in a cardboard page. She opened the padded lid. The top picture was a copy of Uncle Jed's wedding picture. Stella flipped to the next photograph: Aunt Martha holding Sammy in his christening gown. Touched by the serene expression on the new mother's face, Stella yearned for her mother again. After Stella's mother had died, her father had all the photographs of Katherine

Kendrick burned. If it weren't for Aunt Ivy, Stella would've been left with the vague recollection of an eight-year-old to rely on. But instead, a cherished photograph, given to her by Aunt Ivy on her tenth birthday, sat propped up on Stella's nightstand. Another reason Aunt Ivy's deception pained her.

Stella turned the page.

Oh, look at them. This one was of her father and uncle as boys, caps pushed back from their foreheads, each proudly holding the reins of a pony. For sons of a coachman, this was rare. In a time when photographs were less common, such children wouldn't have the opportunity or means to be captured on film. Despite their differences, it made sense Uncle Jed would cherish such a treasure. Stella flipped to the next page.

"No!" She was mortified.

Scooped out of the middle of the album was a large, secret compartment hidden beneath the authentic photo pages in the front. Inside lay a pearl-handled pocket revolver and a man's wallet. Stella, repelled by the weapon, reached for the wallet. It was a simple leather billfold, worn along the crease, containing a second-class ticket for passage on the American Line's *SS New York*, scheduled to sail two days ago, and a half dozen plain white calling cards. If the billfold ever held any money, it was gone.

Oh, Uncle Jed.

How he'd gotten them and why were all that concerned Stella, for there was no mistaking whom the things belonged to. The name on the ticket and the calling cards both read *Jesse James Prescott*.

CHAPTER 19

Inspector Brown immediately regretted his second helping of kidney pie when the smell of formaldehyde accosted him. He patted his jacket and trousers pockets but came up empty. No handkerchief. He must've left it in his overcoat, doing him no good hanging on the back of his office door. He shivered. "Must you keep it so cold in here?"

Hovering over the body, Dr. Lipscombe didn't answer Brown, but said instead, "Are you ready to proceed, Inspector?" Covered up to his chin with a white cotton sheet, Mr. Elijah Kendrick lay waiting, with the patience only afforded the dead. Poor sod.

Brown wrinkled his nose at the smell and nodded perfunctorily. He preferred not to linger here any longer than needs must. He had two investigations to get back to. Brown plodded toward the examination table in the middle of the starkly bright, whitewashed room, careful to watch where he stepped. Last time he'd been here, he'd ruined his shoes. The elderly medical examiner, his white hair and mustache matching his lab coat, all in need of a good bluing, wordlessly handed Brown a linen handkerchief doused in lavender essence. Brown gratefully held it up to his nose.

Studying the pale, eerily peaceful face of Miss Kendrick's combative father, he inquired, "What can you tell me, Doctor? Do we have a case for manslaughter, or was it a tragic accident after all?"

The words echoed, reminding Brown of the last time he'd had to consult with Lyndhurst's medical examiner over the body of a murdered man. That death hadn't been what it appeared to be either.

"As you suspected, there is evidence of strangulation."

"So, someone did precipitate the fall that broke our man's neck?"

"Yes."

Oddly, Brown had hoped to be wrong. Can't anything be straightforward?

"And no."

The doctor's contradictory announcement stopped Brown in midstep as he turned to go, believing the examination to be over. "Care to explain yourself, Doctor?"

"If you'd be so kind as to stay long enough to hear my full report, I'll do just that," Dr. Lipscombe chastised.

Fair enough.

Brown was impatient to carry on with things, but that didn't excuse his being less than thorough. "Pray, continue."

"Thank you. Now, I did locate several fractured cervical vertebrae. See here." The doctor pointed to the bones at the base of the victim's skull. "But that was caused by his descent down the stone stairs."

"I thought we'd already established that?"

"Yes, but his broken vertebrae aren't the cause of death."

"Didn't you just say our man died of a broken neck?"

"Indeed."

Brown pinched the bridge of his nose. What was Dr. Lipscombe rattling on about? As a rule, the doctor was a congenial man. Was the surgeon purposely testing his patience, or was the formaldehyde pickling his brain? Brown glanced around, expecting to spot a half-empty bottle of whiskey beside the porcelain sink among the trays filled with Brown didn't want to know what.

"You're not making sense," Brown said, unsuccessfully suppressing his exasperation. "How could he die of a broken neck, and yet the broken neck not be the cause of his death?"

Dr. Lipscombe scowled, his white, bushy eyebrows meeting in the middle. "What I said was that the broken vertebrae didn't cause his death. He also suffered from a fractured hyoid bone." He pointed to a bone near the victim's Adam's apple.

"His neck was broken in two different places, front and back?"

"Exactly. And each was caused by two different actions." Dr. Lipscombe directed Brown's attention to the back of the victim's neck again. "This injury resulted from the fall, and this"—he then pointed to the front of the dead man's neck—"is from strangulation, the direct cause of death. Your victim, Inspector, was dead before he hit the stairs."

But that can't be. A castle full of witnesses said otherwise.

"And there's more," Dr. Lipscombe carried on, frustrating Brown's desire to dispute the surgeon's findings. "Do you recall the black flecks you found on the victim's skin?" With a slow and measured gait, the medical examiner strolled to a small table neatly lined with shiny metal instruments and retrieved a small, shallow, glass dish.

"Was it coal dust?"

"No, see for yourself."

Brown took the proffered hand lens and studied the sparkle of the dark flakes, holding the glass closer to the low-hanging lamp. "They're metal?"

"Wrought iron to be precise." Dr. Lipscombe gently seized

the glass dish away from Brown, setting it carefully on the table beside the body's right arm. "Do you recall any such thing at Keyhaven Castle?"

"It was a medieval fortress, Doctor. Have you never been? The use of wrought iron at Keyhaven Castle was compulsory. They made everything with it: pots, poles, lances, lanterns, hooks, gates, cannons, coal storage doors, window casings, stairwell railings . . ."

"We're looking for something circular that might've made these." Dr. Lipscombe indicated the marks on Mr. Kendrick's neck, which Brown had assumed were strangulation marks.

"Not finger bruises, then?"

"Indeed not. I found additional flecks of wrought iron in the folds of the neck, on the palm of the right hand, and under three fingernails, two on the right hand and one on the left. And no evidence of blood on the victim, either."

"But what does that tell us?"

"That the killer didn't use his or her hands to strangle the victim. From the location of the marks, I believe whatever caused these marks is also what broke the victim's hyoid bone."

But that would broaden Brown's scope of suspects. (Without a motive, Sir Owen Rountree was the least likely of them.) If a weapon was used, even a woman might've been able to subjugate a bigger, stronger man.

"And it tells us he struggled against it." With his fingers curled, the medical examiner illustrated how someone would get the metal under his nails when he attempted to put space between his windpipe and the thing that was choking him.

"There are quite a few rings built into the walls for securing cannons, horses, and the like, but nothing . . ." Suddenly Brown remembered the purpose of the room at the top of the tower stairs.

"Inspector?"

"The drawbridge chains. The pulleys are housed at the top of the stairs from where the victim lay. From there, the chains are easily accessible and surprisingly pliable. You believe our killer wrapped the medieval chain around Mr. Kendrick's neck to throttle him?"

"That would indeed fit the pattern."

"And our killer then shoved the body down the stairs?"

"Yes, that would be my conclusion." Dr. Lipscombe lifted the cotton sheet over Mr. Kendrick's face. "I know you are a busy man, Inspector. If you are satisfied, I think we're done here."

"I have but one question."

"And what would that be?"

"If our man was dead before he hit the stairs, how could he scream as he fell?"

Stella stared at the drab, unadorned wall where the cracks of a break in the plaster resembled a whitewashed spiderweb. Inspector Brown was out on another call but should be back shortly, or so she'd been told. She could wait or come back. The room smelled of burnt coffee. The policeman at the desk, with sticky brown bits of the drink still clinging to his blond mustache, ignored her as he typed up a report, one key at a time. *Click.* Pause. *Clack.* Pause. *Click.* She rubbed her hand against the pile of the red velvet on the photo album, distorting the color and shine, then smoothed the fabric again. How long was she going to have to wait? *Click.* Pause. *Clack.* She sprang up, as if the hidden gun was burning a hole in her lap, and approached the desk again.

"May I speak to Sir Owen Rountree while I wait for Inspector Brown?"

"I don't think—" the officer behind the typewriter began.

"It's all right, Betts," Constable Waterman reassured his colleague when he rounded the corner. He acknowledged Stella with a respectful tip of his head. "I know Miss Kendrick."

The other shrugged, his attention focused a moment longer than was polite on Stella's forehead. "If you say so, sir."

Stella self-consciously tugged the brim of her short top riding hat lower, hoping to hide the cut there.

Constable Waterman waved for her to follow him to the end of the long, stark hallway to a row of painted metal doors. When the constable slid back the plate of the small opening set at eye level in the first door, Stella caught a glimpse of the man incarcerated inside. Seated on the wooden plank attached to the cell's back wall, his elbows resting on his knees, Sir Owen cradled his head in his hands, his tie dangling toward the floor. He wore the same brown suit he'd been wearing for the picnic yesterday.

At the sound of the constable wrangling an impressive set of keys, he glanced up. Stella flinched. Stubble dotted his cheeks, dark rings shadowed his eyes, and the gash on his face had scabbed over, a greenish yellow bruise spread beyond it. The family resemblance to Lyndy unnerved her.

The constable swung open the door. "Someone to see you, Sir Owen."

Sir Owen leaped to his feet. "Oh, Miss Kendrick. Am I to be released?"

Stella, stepping forward into the bleak, gray cell with more confidence than she felt, answered, "No, I'm here to ask you a few questions." She glanced over her shoulder at the constable. "In private, if that's possible."

"Of course. I'll be through there if you need me." The constable wagged his thumb in the direction of the offices they'd passed.

As if in silent agreement, neither spoke until the policeman's footfalls were no longer audible in the cell. Sir Owen spoke first.

"I didn't hurt your father, Miss Kendrick. I didn't even see him after we all parted ways in the courtyard. I swear to you on the honor of my family, our family." He motioned back and forth between them. "You have my sincerest condolences."

He was right. When Stella married Lyndy, this man would be her cousin too. She so wanted to believe him.

"Then what happened to your face?"

He touched his cheek as if he'd forgotten about the wound. "I'm ashamed to say."

"This is not the time for coyness, Sir Owen. You owe me an explanation."

"Will you promise not to repeat what I say? I shan't be party to damaging the young lady's reputation. It could cause quite the scandal."

"Scandal? You could hang." His face turned pale as if he hadn't considered that. "Is this about Penny? You claim she'd been with you."

"Because it's the truth." He plunked back down on the wooden bench. "Why won't Miss Swenson admit to it?"

"Probably for the reason you said. Penny's worried about tarnishing her reputation."

"But simply admitting she was with me wouldn't do that."

There was more to this story. Why else would Penny lie? She wasn't that cruel.

"You still haven't told me about your wound."

"That was her doing," He searched Stella's face as if trying to read whether she believed him or not. When she frowned, he rested his head against the wall. "Not that I didn't deserve it."

Why wasn't Stella surprised? Penny had been a bully of a child. It didn't take much imagination to picture her translating that into tantrums when she didn't get her way with men.

"If I'm going to help you . . ." What made her say that? Did she believe him? Sir Owen hadn't argued with her father, nor had he any reason to kill him. They hadn't known each other long enough.

"You will help me?" Sir Owen's head perked up; his face brightened. "Will you secure my release?"

"Maybe." Stella joined him on the plank bench, clutching the photo album to her chest. "But you must tell me everything. And I want the truth."

So, he did. Sir Owen jumped to his feet and paced the tiny bare cell, again reminding her of Lyndy, and admitted to flirting with Penny during the dinner party Stella had missed and to stealing off together at the castle.

"We were stealing kisses in a room off the tower when Miss Swenson asked when we were to be wed." He paused, staring at the concrete floor as if reliving the moment. Luckily, he couldn't see Stella's ears redden when she remembered her own intimate moment in the castle. "When I informed her I was soon to be engaged to another, she slapped me."

Stella was skeptical. He wasn't telling her the whole truth.

"One thing I don't understand is why, after a little flirting and kissing, Penny would expect you to marry her."

Sir Owen tugged on his lapels, a gesture she'd seen Lyndy do hundreds of times, reminding her again of their family ties. He shot a nervous glance at the open cell door, knowing the constable was close at hand. He approached and leaned slightly toward her to whisper. "We might've arranged an assignation after the dinner party."

"And?"

"And we . . . huh . . . were . . . uhmm . . . we . . ." He began pacing again.

"You didn't!" Stella was mortified. No wonder Penny was upset. Stella resisted the urge to slap Sir Owen on Penny's behalf. "And you call yourself a gentleman?"

"No, no," Sir Owen stammered, waving his hands in denial. "Steady on. I would never go so far as that."

Stella was relieved to hear it, but a suspicion flashed in her mind, and her question stopped him, midpace.

"That's why you were at Pilley Manor that night. You were in the library canoodling with Penny, weren't you?"

Sir Owen grew pink in the face and nodded sheepishly.

Oh, Penny. What was she thinking, being alone with a man in the middle of the night? No wonder Sir Owen worried about Penny's reputation. No wonder they worried about getting caught. If this had gotten out, it would've ruined her. "Go on. Tell me what happened at the castle."

"As I said, I didn't touch your father. Miss Swenson's outburst caused the gash."

"But Penny was wearing gloves, Sir Owen. No slap could've caused that." She pointed to his wound.

"No, you're right, of course. And do call me Owen. But Miss Swenson and I were in a dark recess and hadn't noticed how close we were to the wrought iron hooks on the wall. That bit was true enough."

Stella had noticed the hooks throughout the castle. Mounted in pairs, at about Sir Owen's height, according to Lyndy, they were used to store long musket rifles along the walls. She'd also noticed how rough and pointed the ends were. Smashing his cheek into one of them could've caused an ugly cut.

"Right after she stormed away is when I heard the shout. Concerned, I sought her out, despite our row, and ended up spotting you and your father at the bottom of the stairwell instead."

If he was telling the truth, then Penny could've killed her father. But despite Penny's capacity for lashing out, Stella couldn't think of a motive for Penny any more than she could Sir Owen. From what she'd discovered in her uncle's room, Uncle Jed had a perfect reason to want his brother dead.

But Uncle Jed had been nowhere near the castle, and Daddy was strangled, not shot. Stella hugged the photo album tighter.

"Do you believe me?" Sir Owen's pleading pulled Stella out of her reverie.

"I do."

The muscles in his face, his shoulders, his back relaxed as relief visibly washed over him.

"Miss Kendrick?" Constable Waterman approached, the echo of his footfalls preceding him. "The inspector is back and can see you now."

Stella followed the constable out of the cell, noting the fresh muddy boot prints that ran down the middle of the hall, and stopped at the inspector's office door. She turned back to Owen. "I'll do what I can to get you released. And to keep your secret."

Stella ignored the raised eyebrow on the constable's face when he grasped the metal door handle and tugged it to get the heavy door moving.

As the open space between them shrank, Sir Owen called, "My God, Lyndy is a lucky man. He told me you were cracking, but now I know he wasn't exaggerating."

"You're not a free man yet," she reminded him when the door shut with a loud clang.

No, he wasn't free, but she was convinced of his innocence. Her father's killer was still out there.

CHAPTER 20

Inspector Brown couldn't believe what he was hearing. They'd combed every inch of the Southampton docks, conducted thorough witness interviews, and had spoken to every resident and landowner within a half mile from the spot where Jesse Prescott died. They'd found not a trace of the dead man's billfold or revolver. Yet here was Miss Kendrick offering up the evidence he and the entirety of the Southampton County Borough Police couldn't track down.

How does she do it?

"And you found this, where?"

"In the steam trunk that belongs to my uncle," she said, pulling the long, pearl-tipped pin from her hair and setting her hat on his desk.

Brown wondered but said nothing of the cut that stretched across her brow.

"I had my suspicions, so I searched all the guest rooms."

Upon Brown returning from Dr. Lipscombe's, Miss Kendrick had arrived, thrusting the photo album at him as if it were a lump of hot coal, insisting he inspect it. He'd been dubious.

But having learned to trust her instincts, despite her tactics being highly irregular, he'd flipped through the photographs and been rewarded. In a hollowed-out middle of the album lay the dead jockey's missing wallet and pocket revolver. An ingenious hiding place. But not clever enough for the inquisitive Miss Kendrick. If the implications weren't so dire, Brown would've offered her a congratulatory handshake. Instead, he was to add to the poor young woman's misery.

"You know what this means, don't you, Miss Kendrick?" Brown said, setting aside the near-empty wallet to inspect the gun more closely. "Considering what you told me of the contents of your father's will?"

She nodded. "At best, Uncle Jed is lying about how he came to have these in his possession. At worst, he killed my father."

"Either way, I'm obliged to arrest your uncle, if only for obstructing the investigation into Mr. Prescott's death."

"But that's the least of it, Inspector."

Miss Kendrick eased herself onto the edge of his desk; Brown, much to his chagrin, was seated in the sole chair in the room. She looked askew at the bookshelf mounted on the wall and bit her lip in concentration. "Somehow, all three men are connected: Uncle Jed, my father, and Jesse Prescott." She wrinkled her nose. "You repainted the walls."

She was referring to the smell of paint and Brown's penchant to give his walls a fresh coat each time he started a new murder case. For years, his office had been pale blue, the color of a cuckoo's egg. Since this spring, his walls had been gray, yellow, and now olive.

"I did. You were saying?"

"All three men are connected. Before he died, Jesse Prescott wanted to kill someone. I think that someone was my father."

She explained the confusion over her father's place of residence. Brown, having to agree it made sense, leaned back in his chair, and patiently listened as she puzzled out the whole business out loud.

"Why the jockey hated my father so much, I don't know yet. But Uncle Jed had an obvious reason to want him dead—to make sure he, or more specifically Sammy, inherits. That gives us two men who wanted Daddy dead, neither of whom could've killed him." She held up one finger on her gloved right hand. "One because he was killed on the wharf the day before." She lifted a second finger. "And the other because he was supposedly out on the spit at the time of the murder."

She shook her head in disbelief and slipped from the desk. Brown straightened the pile of papers she'd inadvertently sat upon.

"And yet, my father was killed."

"That is the unfortunate truth." Brown sympathized, not only with the young woman's loss but with the difficulty this case presented for both of them.

"And then there's Uncle Jed's connection with Jesse Prescott." She continued as if she hadn't heard, staring into the corner of the ceiling, thinking.

Brown followed her gaze and spotted a large, dried paint drip partway down the wall.

"Did Uncle Jed know the jockey from Kentucky?" she continued her musing. "Or did he happen to pick up Pistol Prescott's gun and wallet from the street? No," she said, answering her own question. "If he'd come by the jockey's possessions honestly, he wouldn't have hidden them; he wouldn't have lied."

"Quite!" Brown agreed.

"But how did he get them?" she wondered aloud. "No matter what he's done, I can't imagine my uncle stealing them off a dead man's body."

"From what I know of the witness statements, no one would've been able to. There were too many people about."

"And what does Uncle Jed possessing Pistol Prescott's wallet and gun have to do with my father's death? Daddy wasn't shot. He broke his neck."

Brown warmed in admiration. She was a clever one, this one. *Too bad she's a woman.* Miss Kendrick would've made a good detective.

"For now, you leave this with me," he said, rising from his chair. "We'll get to the bottom of it. Waterman!"

The constable responded posthaste to Brown's shout, arriving readily equipped with pencil and paper. He hastily stuffed them into his breast pocket when Brown held the photo album out to him.

"See this is locked in the safe."

"Yes, sir."

When Brown turned back to her, Miss Kendrick was gazing out the bar-covered window behind him. A motley gray pigeon was perched on the window ledge, cooing. "If you'll oblige me, Miss Kendrick, I still need to ask you a few questions. Just routine, mind you. Please have a seat." Brown wheeled his chair from behind his desk, and the pigeon fluttered away.

"First off, since we are discussing Jesse Prescott's case, I'd like your opinion on something."

"Of course." She lowered herself into the chair, regarding him expectantly.

"We found articles of interest among Mr. Prescott's belongings: a wager receipt for the St. Leger Stakes and a ferry ticket to the Island. It's not surprising Mr. Prescott would wager on the horses in Doncaster. But after making inquiries, we are at a loss as to what would take him to the Island." Constable Waterman had visited the ferry station and made the crossing but had returned with nothing more than a damp uniform. "I wonder. Does that mean anything to you?"

If asked, Brown couldn't have explained why he presumed Miss Kendrick would think of something he hadn't considered. But then again, she was the one who unearthed the gun, not him.

"Maybe Lord Lyndhurst would know. I haven't been to the Isle of Wight yet. So, I wouldn't know. . . ." She paused. "Wait. Do you know who Pistol Prescott bet on to win the St. Leger Stakes?"

In answer to her question (he couldn't fathom what the dead man's visit to the Island had to do with his pick at the races), Brown slid open a drawer and retrieved the case file. A reminder to contact the ship's steward's office to confirm they'd located all of Mr. Prescott's luggage was clipped to the outside. Brown plucked the small notepad from among the loose papers and flipped it open to find Waterman's scribble. The pad crackled when Brown pried two of the crinkled pages apart.

"If I'm reading this correctly, our man bet on Challacombe to win."

"Then, Inspector"—Miss Kendrick smiled and slapped the edge of the desk in triumph, the glass inkwell clinking in response—"you should be talking to the baron, Baron Branson-Hill. He lives on the Isle of Wight, and he's the new owner of Challacombe. That has to be your connection."

"Yes, well done, Miss Kendrick." Brown dropped the notepad into the file and shoved the whole thing back into the drawer. He'd arrange to interview the baron as soon as he finished up here. "Now, to the questions I have regarding your father's death."

Her wide smile faded, her whole body deflating before him like a popped balloon.

"I do apologize, but—"

"No, it's okay. I want to help, Inspector," she reassured him. "Please ask me anything."

"Very well. Let's begin with where you were when the man cried out."

It had been his standard inquiry asked of all the witnesses. But when he posed it to Miss Kendrick, having said, "the man" and not "your father," he grasped the extent of his mistake. His assumption that the victim had cried out, which according to

Dr. Lipscombe was a medical impossibility, not only raised the question of who actually did and why but also required Brown to reestablish everyone's alibi; the time of death was no longer conclusive.

"I was alone . . . with Lord Lyndhurst." To her credit, Miss Kendrick blushed. "We were touring the castle together. He never left my sight."

Or her side, no doubt. "And when you arrived in the courtyard, you saw, what?"

She described the picnic scene, including the arrival of the others, precisely as Lord Lyndhurst had. So, unless they were in collusion and had made up their story, they were both in the clear.

"From what you told about your father's will, you are to inherit an immense fortune. And thus, a suspect. I would be remiss in my duties if I didn't ask. Miss Kendrick, did you kill your father or have him killed on your behalf?"

Her hesitation startled Brown. If this young lady was capable of such an act of violence, then Brown had investigated his last case. He stared at her in breathless anticipation.

Finally, she solemnly shook her head. With her focus on fishing a handkerchief from her handbag, Brown released his breath in one long puff.

"No, of course, I didn't kill him," she said, scrunching the handkerchief into a ball and patting it against her cheekbones. "I loved my father. I'm angry, and I'm sad this happened to him."

Brown perceived a slight hesitation. "But?"

"But, I'm ashamed to admit I'm not sure I'm going to miss him." There wasn't a more honest woman in all the world. To admit such a thing must've cost her. "I also don't believe Sir Owen killed him either," she added, before relaying what Sir Owen had confided.

Brown wasn't surprised; he'd never been wholly convinced Sir Owen had been his man. He knew the noble to be more the type to ruin a lady's reputation than one to murder someone. Besides, the man had no motive. But Brown didn't regret his arrest. Served the bounder right to spend the night in a cell; Sir Owen could've saved them all a great deal of trouble if he'd divulged the truth sooner.

"What about your aunt?" Brown asked, recalling the contents of the telegram she sent.

Miss Kendrick laughed. "Aunt Rachel? She's nearly eighty, Inspector, and doesn't have a mean bone in her body. Plus, she wasn't even there."

"No, the young one, Mrs. Mitchell."

"Oh, you mean Aunt Ivy," Miss Kendrick said, growing serious again and fiddling with a loose string on the hem of her glove.

Ah, Brown was onto something there then. Miss Kendrick, too, had her suspicions. But he knew better than to press. He'd try a more roundabout approach.

"Do you know a Mrs. Eugene Smith, staying at the Star Hotel in Southampton?"

Brown had made inquiries and, with the help of his colleagues in the port city, had tracked down Mrs. Smith, the recipient of Mrs. Mitchell's telegram. Unfortunately, the woman in question had been out when the Southampton policeman had visited. Brown was waiting on a follow-up.

Miss Kendrick shook her head. "No, but I did find a stack of letters in Aunt Ivy's room with Southampton as a return address. I don't know who wrote them. But why do you ask? Who is Mrs. Eugene Smith? Does she have a connection with the deaths of Jesse Prescott or my father?"

"We're making inquiries," was his tepid reply.

"You think Aunt Ivy's a suspect?"

Miss Kendrick studied Brown's face, searching no doubt for a chink in his armor. But she wasn't getting any answers from him. Not yet.

"Do you think she should be?"

"No, she's not capable of killing anyone."

"Not even *your father*?"

Miss Kendrick winced, and Brown immediately regretted his inflection, his choice of words. No one deserved being murdered, not even the overbearing Mr. Kendrick.

"You have a point," she said. "I don't want to believe it, but I did catch them arguing before we left for the castle." She rose unexpectedly, shoving the handkerchief back into her bag as she rounded the desk. "If you'll excuse me, Inspector," she mumbled as she passed him on her way toward the door.

Her sudden need to depart unsettled him. "Are you all right, Miss Kendrick?"

She turned to him. Her failed attempt at a smile pained him more than any frown would have. "Thank you, Inspector. I'm fine. It's just that a few days ago I'd been so happy. Now, instead of enjoying marital bliss, I've been secretly ransacking my guests' bedrooms and wondering who in my family killed my father."

Brown started to say something reassuring but found he didn't have the words. Miss Kendrick was right, and it fell to him to prove it.

Mrs. Robertson, neatly adding the cost of her recent purchase of five yards of black crape into her accounts, glanced up at the sound of the side door slamming shut. When Robbie, his arms stacked with kindling, passed her study, she rose to confront him in the scullery. His face was as pale as bleached cotton sheets.

"What is it, lad?"

After Mr. Kendrick's death, the local boy, who came every morning to clean the boots, haul the coal, and clean the servants' fire grates, refused to enter the house, as if it now be fey. But neither death nor spirits stopped the chores needing doing. Mr. Tims, of course, couldn't be expected to do such menial tasks. With Ethel now up at Morrington Hall and so many guests to attend, Mrs. Robertson had been at her wit's end until Robbie offered to stay on an extra day or two and help.

"Nothing, Auntie."

He knelt at his task, filling the kindling box, avoiding showing his face. But perspiration dripped down his temple toward his ear. Such a finely built young man didn't sweat like that from chopping a bit of kindling. Was his injury giving him trouble? It seemed to be healing nicely. He rose, lifting the last of his load, hoping to pass by unmolested on his way toward the library; the two aunts had let the library fire go out. But Mrs. Robertson would know what was wrong. She blocked his escape, her arms sternly crossed.

"Don't tell me it's nothing. Do I need to send round for the doctor?"

"I'm fine, Auntie. I don't need a doctor."

"But, Robbie, you look like you saw a ghost."

Robbie resigned to her meddling, jostled the wood in his arms to settle the smaller pieces, and stared straight at her. There was more than a little unease in his expression.

"Not a ghost, very much a living man."

"That doesn't narrow it down, lad. Men have been in and out all day, leaving condolence cards, including the likes of Sir Alfred or Baron Branson-Hill, come with his wife, the baroness. Was it one of the villagers or local merchants, maybe?" Mrs. Robertson suggested. "Been lots of them. Unlike those up at Morrington Hall, Mr. Kendrick spent his money, and he wasn't one to shun the local shops. But what did this man do to rattle you so? Shall I inform His Lordship? I'm certain he could take the man in hand."

"No, Auntie, it's nothing like that. He gave me a turn, all right, but because I'd seen him before, on the docks when that wee fella died under the horses' hooves and hoped never to cross paths with him again."

"Why? What did this man do?"

"They were arguing, the wee fella and the man. I didn't tell the police for I wasn't certain of it until I saw him again outside."

"Good heavens, Robbie, the police?" She thought the lad was done with all that. "What did you not tell them?"

"That it mightn't have been an accident."

"Why do you say that?" The scullery was suddenly as hot as Mrs. Downie's oven. Mrs. Robertson laid the back of her hand against her forehead to steady herself. "Tell me. What did you see, lad?"

"I think I saw the man push the wee fella, Auntie. Like he meant for him to die."

CHAPTER 21

Brown slipped into the Knightwood Oak unnoticed, behind two farmhands who smelled of sweat and soil. The pub was filled with locals, hoping for a good chinwag over Mr. Kendrick's death, no doubt. Tom Heppenstall, the publican, slapped the towel over his shoulder and shoved the till drawer. When it closed with a hard *click*, he was already reaching for another glass to fill. Scandal must be good for business.

Brown surveyed the room. Silas, the broad-shouldered caretaker of the vicarage, sipped a half-pint by the fireplace, his old hound at his feet. In the corner, a rowdy cluster of men passed around bawdy postcards one of them must've picked up in Paris. Brown fancied the scantily dressed, wide-hipped brunette he caught a glimpse of. Reminded him of Mrs. Brown when he married her. Moving on, he noted two tables occupied by men drinking ale and eating greasy chips. The lad who worked for the publican busily cleared the third table of its dirty glasses and a platter of what must've been shepherd's pie, considering the smell coming from the kitchen. The man Brown had come for shared the far end of the long, polished, wooden bar with the old fellow Brown had come to know as Old Joe. Broadsheets lay spread out before the old man who was bent over them reading. Jed Kendrick, downcast and staring over at the sleeping hound, nursed a half-finished pint. Brown took a few steps and halted at the sound of china clattering to the floor. At the table beside him, a sopping wet rag dripped water onto the floor as the lad stood over an overturned platter that had slipped from his tray.

"Oi! Clean that up," Mr. Heppenstall called.

The lad lowered the tray to the table and dropped to the floor. With the stack of dirty plates in his hands, he scrambled to his feet, knocking into Brown as the inspector attempted to step around him. Locking eyes with Brown, the publican scowled before yanking the towel free of his shoulder and attacking an invisible stain on the bar in front of him. As Brown continued his approach, Old Joe's high-pitched muttering grew louder, like a midge buzzing in your ear. It seems Mr. Kendrick didn't get the message that Old Joe preferred not to share his end of the bar with grockles. Or perhaps it was Brown the old chap objected to.

"Evening," Brown said, stepping up to the bar.

"What brings you here, Inspector?" Silas, the vicar's caretaker, had left his sleeping dog to lean his elbows on the bar close by. Even Brown knew the man's penchant for gossip. The vicar, no, the whole village, would learn what was said by suppertime. "Ain't the Red Stag but a block from the police station?"

Brown ignored him and addressed the man on the stool beside Old Joe. "Mr. Kendrick? I need to speak to you."

"What do ya want now?"

Old Joe turned a wary eye on Brown, as he and Jed Kendrick spoke over the old man's head, but he didn't budge.

"I think you should come with me to the police station."

The American's response was to motion for the publican to

bring another ale. "Unless you're arresting me, ya can ask me the questions here."

Brown glanced around him. The men with the Paris post-cards had grown suspiciously still; the lads he'd followed in sipped their pints in a silence that was broken only by the crackling of the small fire in the grate. Silas wasn't the only curious one about. "I don't think you'll want everyone to hear what I have to say."

"You don't think everyone will know anyway?"

He had a point. Despite stretching out over more than two hundred square miles, the New Forest was a tight-knit place. News regarding the posh Americans, whether it was the flavor of Miss Kendrick's wedding cake or that her father was found dead at Keyhaven Castle, spread fast.

"Very well," Brown conceded, moving around Old Joe to take up the stool on Jed Kendrick's other side. He didn't miss how the old man cocked his head to one side, and Silas leaned in. When Mr. Heppenstall asked him if he wanted anything, Brown shook his head (though he sure could use a pint about now) and set his hat on the bar. "Did you or did you not speak with Jesse Prescott on the morning he died?"

"Ya came here to ask me that?" the American scoffed, his breath reeking of beer. He insistently held up his empty glass, trying to catch the publican's eye.

Mr. Heppenstall busied himself with wiping out pint glasses and kept his head down.

"That'll be a yes, then. What did you talk about, Mr. Kendrick? How you both wanted your brother dead? How you were going to shoot him with Mr. Prescott's gun?"

Mr. Kendrick rolled his eyes, and fishing about in his pockets procured a cheap cigar. When he said nothing, Brown went on.

"And then it all went wrong, didn't it? The two of you had a row, and seizing the opportunity, you pushed Mr. Prescott into the oncoming carriage."

"What?"

The American lurched to his feet, his stool clattering to the floor. Old Joe instinctually threw himself over the stack of newspapers in front of him, and Silas's hound, awoken by the noise, howled.

"You're talking out your hat, Inspector." Mr. Kendrick bit off the tip of his cigar and spat it on the floor.

"Oi!" Mr. Heppenstall objected.

"I have a credible witness," Brown pressed, "that places a man beside the victim moments before Prescott died."

When the second person in so many hours, this time Robbie McEwan, nephew to Miss Kendrick's housekeeper, strolled into his office, offering up evidence in the Prescott case, Brown had to wonder why he bothered leaving his desk at all.

Because Jed Kendrick isn't going to arrest himself now, is he?

Kendrick stuck the unlit cigar between his teeth. "So?"

"That same witness believes the same man pushed Jesse Prescott to his death. I think that man was you, Mr. Kendrick."

Jed Kendrick's crooked smile, like he'd thought of a private joke, revealed a broken front tooth. "But I wasn't anywhere near that jockey when he died."

"Says you."

"Ask my Sammy and little Gertie too, if ya don't believe me."

"Then explain to me how you came to have Jesse Prescott's gun and wallet in your possession?"

The American's lip curled, his eyes narrowing to slivers, and for the first time, Brown thought he might make trouble. Luckily, a whistle from him would bring Constable Waterman running from his post at the door outside.

"I don't know what you're talking about."

"They were hidden," the inspector continued, keeping his attention on the man's face, and not at the man's tightening fists. "Quite cleverly, I might add, in a hollowed-out photo album in your travel trunk."

"You'd no right to rifle through my stuff."

"It was your niece who gave them to us. And before you say they belong to you, we've been able to verify the gun is the same as that which Jesse Prescott was known to carry."

"So, what if it is? Maybe he gave it to me."

"Or maybe you stole them?"

"You'll never know, will ya?" Jed Kendrick straightened up his stool and inquired if anyone had a match. Heads shook despite the visible matchbox on the mantelpiece.

"Oh, I know, Mr. Kendrick. I've put a call in to Scotland Yard, who'll, in turn, contact the authorities in Kentucky. But I don't have to wait to hear what they say. You're a thief, Mr. Kendrick. There's no use in pretending. But what I'm not certain of is whether you're a murderer too."

Brown had never seen scrawny Old Joe move so fast. When he slipped down from his stool, he collided with Silas backing away from the bar. The two men wrangled with each other, trying to beat the other to a safe distance.

"I didn't kill my brother," Jed Kendrick insisted, swiping the unlit cigar from his mouth. "I reckon whoever did had good reason, though. Lord knows I've thought about it, but ya can't pin this on me; I wasn't anywhere near that tower."

"Right!" Brown declared, snatching up his hat and standing. "I can't prove it yet, so for now, Jedidiah Kendrick, I'm arresting you for theft."

"What about my kids?" the American demanded when Brown grabbed his arm and deftly handcuffed the man's wrists together. "What will happen to Sammy and Gertrude?"

"You should've thought about them when you were stealing some else's property."

Jed Kendrick laughed mirthlessly. "Why do ya think I steal in the first place? Elijah's a heartless bastard, that's why. All my life he's been stingy with his money. But I came all this way, and still, he wouldn't give me a red cent, even when I begged for the sake of my kids."

The inspector pushed the cuffed man in front of him with difficulty. The drunken American lurched forward, tripping over his own feet. As they navigated the tables, customers scraped back their chairs to avoid the pair.

"Waterman!" Brown called when he reached the front door. His burly constable was quick to relieve Brown of the staggering criminal. "Who's going to provide for your children now, Mr. Kendrick? With you in prison? Did you not think of that?"

"Don't you worry about it. My brother's death did us all a favor. I've seen his will. He's left my boy a small fortune."

He thinks he's to inherit. *Quite the motive, I'd say.*

All Brown had to do now was prove Jed Kendrick was in the castle, and not out on the spit as he claimed, and he could peg him for that murder too.

"Didn't you know, Mr. Kendrick?" Brown said when he escorted him toward the police wagon. Brown unwrapped Matilda's reins from the post and climbed up onto the box seat as Waterman wrangled the American into the back. "Your brother made a new will in April. He cut out your Sammy completely. Miss Kendrick inherits the lot."

"Augh!" Jed Kendrick cried, kicking the boards so hard the wagon rocked to the side. Waterman pulled out his billy club, the gold paint of the royal crest flashing in the setting sun, and threatened to give the suspect a good wallop. That stopped the kicking.

"Which means," Brown called over his shoulder, as he snapped the reins and the wagon lurched forward, "if you did kill your brother, you did it for nothing."

On her way back from the stables, large drops of rain splattered around Stella. The sky had darkened since she left Lyndhurst. She dodged the garden fountain, cut across the lawn, and ran for the front door, missing the worst of the downpour. Shaking off her hat, she handed it to James, the first footman, and asked after Lyndy. He was in the music room, she was told. An odd choice, given it was only used when Lord and Lady Atherly hosted a large party, which was rare these days, considering their recent financial problems. Perhaps that's why Lyndy chose it.

Stella lingered in the open doorway, watching Lyndy pace, like a wildcat in a cage, from the grand piano to the window overlooking the pond and back, each time tapping different, discordant piano keys. When he caught sight of her in the doorway, he bounded toward her with an expression of concern, mingled with anger and frustration, subtle though it was.

"There you are! Almost called in the bloodhounds to track you down." His voice was stern and scolding, but the lightness to his step belied his anger. He took her in his arms, his skin smelling of soap and shaving cream. He was dressed for dinner. Stella expected him to pull back when he realized she was wet, but he didn't. Instead, the muscles in his back and shoulders relaxed in her embrace. "Come, sit. I know you'd like to change, but I have news that can't wait." Lyndy rang the bell. "I'll have someone bring you a cup of tea."

"I have news too," she said, settling beside him on the settee set closest to the piano. Like most everything else in the room, the jacquard fabric was a light shade of blue. From there, Stella had a perfect view of the tan, white-spotted deer at the water's edge, taking a drink as the splattering rain created circular ripples across the pond. She had to ask. "But why were you waiting in here?"

"To avoid Mother and the Swensons."

Stella nodded in appreciation. She was in no mood to cross any of their paths either. "They're still here?"

"They left to change, but their return is imminent. Seems

Mother invited them to dinner, given their host is dead. Speaking of, how are you holding up?"

She smiled but, overwhelmed with emotion, didn't want to talk about it. "But why hide in here?"

"This being a highly neglected room, I thought it our best bet."

"Unless, of course, Mrs. Swenson insists on showing off Penny's musical talents," Stella teased. How often had she'd listened to Penny complain about having to practice? "She's an accomplished pianist."

Lyndy groaned. "I hadn't thought of that."

"Never mind. Did you learn anything in London?"

Lyndy, turning to face her, took her hand and kissed it. "I did indeed. I learned a great deal about Mr. Jesse James Prescott today."

"Was there a connection with Daddy?"

He leaned toward her as if about to reveal a secret. "You were right. It was none other than your father who informed the authorities about the criminal actions of Mr. Prescott and his cohorts."

Stella leaned back against the wooden scrollwork of the settee. She knew it. She knew there had to be a connection between the two men. "A good reason to want to kill my father, don't you think?"

Lyndy nodded. "And considering the jockey wasn't the only one implicated or who had his life ruined, one might easily assume Prescott wasn't here in this country alone. An accomplice, you might say. Perhaps that's who killed your father, or perhaps who has the jockey's gun."

It was Stella's turn to relay her news.

"What?" Lyndy exclaimed when she'd told him where she found the gun. "How did your uncle get them? Do you think your uncle is Prescott's accomplice?"

Stella shook her head. "I don't know. But I do know Jesse

Prescott wasn't the only one with a motive to want Daddy dead." She told him about the will.

She thought Lyndy would be pleased (she knew Lady Atherly would be) considering her inheritance would soon be his. But as Stella laid out its details, Lyndy visibly reigned in his emotions: his admiration of her, the puzzlement over Uncle Jed's role in all this, the excitement in sharing his news. It had taken her months to be able to read his expressions, and one by one, they slipped from his face. He gently set her hand aside, though she reached for him, stood, and stepped over to stare out the rain-streaked window. The fallow deer was gone. The pond seemed bleak and lonely.

"Then you truly are free, to do as you like, to follow your heart's desire." His voice was flat and apathetic.

Like the first day I met him. She'd forgotten how open he'd become.

"Yes, I feel guilty about it, but relieved too. So relieved."

Lyndy turned back to her. His face was a blank, as flat as his voice. Had she said too much? Did he think less of her now?

"So, what will you do?"

"I'll follow my heart's desire, as you said. No matter what your mother and Reverend Paine say, we're going to marry, one way or another. It's what my father wanted. It's what I want."

He crossed the room with a few long strides, dropped to one knee, and took her face in his hands. He regarded her in silence as if committing her features to memory before leaning in. Stella hungered in anticipation of his kiss. But at the sound of approaching footsteps, Lyndy merely touched his forehead to hers and sighed. "I'd forgotten about the tea." He pushed himself back to his feet.

"Ah, finally back, are you, Miss Kendrick?" Lady Atherly said, entering the room, Lord Atherly, Lady Alice, and the Swensons right behind her. Lyndy immediately stepped back over to the window.

"What are you doing in here, Mother?" he asked, his arms folded across his chest.

Lady Atherly ignored him. "Whatever have you two been up to today? You didn't tell me you were going to miss tea. Shouldn't you get dressed, Miss Kendrick?" Stella still wore her damp riding clothes.

"Miss Swenson and I are going to play a duet on the piano." Lady Alice, setting her ever-present stack of American magazines on the piano, answered her brother's question. The top one had a bright red cover to match its name, *Redbook*. "When we'd exhausted reading my latest magazines, Mrs. Swenson suggested Miss Swenson and I entertain everyone before dinner."

Stella and Lyndy shared a smile at their earlier joke.

"And you, Miss Kendrick," Lady Atherly disapprovingly droned on, as if her daughter hadn't spoken, "are supposed to be in mourning."

"She couldn't have been out riding for this long," Penny muttered snidely, fluffing the pink ribbon roses sewn into the neckline of her dress.

"No, among other things, I had an illuminating discussion with Sir Owen."

Penny's jaw dropped. Then suddenly, the contents of her handbag seemed more compelling to Penny than learning more about Stella's day. But Lyndy and Lord Atherly were anxious to know more.

"How is Owen?" Lyndy asked.

"I do hope our young chap isn't buckling under the pressure down at the station," Lord Atherly said. "Sir Charles promised to have him out by tomorrow's supper."

"I think he'll be out before then," Stella reassured him. "Inspector Brown's decided Sir Owen didn't have anything to do with killing my father."

"Really?" Mr. Swenson said, voicing the question on Lyndy's face. Stella hadn't gotten a chance to tell Lyndy about that part of it yet.

Before Stella could explain further, Lord Atherly said, "That is jolly good news. I never did think he had it in him. Are you going to play something for us, Alice?"

When Lady Alice urged Penny to join her at the piano, Mrs. Swenson sat beside Stella on the settee, caressing the diamond chain around her neck with one hand, patting Stella on the knee with the other. "I thought you were going to change, Stella," she whispered from the side of her mouth while keeping her attention on Penny. "Lady Atherly's right. It's not decent for a young woman in mourning."

When Stella didn't reply, Mrs. Swenson continued.

"I've taken the liberty of ordering you more suitable attire from Jay's of Regent Street in London. They should arrive early tomorrow." Mrs. Swenson paused, waiting, no doubt, for a show of Stella's gratitude. It wasn't forthcoming.

As the young women arranged themselves on the piano bench, the others took a seat. Fulton arrived with a silver tray holding a small silver teapot, a delicate ivory teacup with bands of gold around the rim, and a stack of black-rimmed envelopes tucked beneath the saucer.

"Those arrived at Pilley Manor," Mrs. Swenson said, pointed to the envelopes. "Since Stella is staying here, I asked Mr. Tims to send them up. I left the wedding packages there. I hope I did the right thing, Lady Atherly."

"You did, Mrs. Swenson," Lady Atherly said, reassuring her guest. "Miss Kendrick needs to learn who remembers her in this trying time . . . and who doesn't."

Stella's ears burned in repressed irritation. Leave it to Lady Atherly to point out how people might still snub Stella, even now, after all this time.

"I dare say," Lady Atherly continued, "condolences and wedding presents arriving at the same time is unprecedented in my experience." As if such a thing happened all the time to Stella.

"The presents must've been sent before we learned of ... well, before the wedding was postponed," Lord Atherly offered. "Ladies?" He motioned for Lady Alice and Penny to play. "I do so love Schubert's *Fantasia*."

They obliged, with Mr. Swenson volunteering to turn the pages.

As the soft strains of the music filled the room, Stella sipped her tea and stared at the window, imagining the pond and the garden and the paddocks she could no longer see for the rain and darkened sky. Instead, it reflected the women at the piano, their fingers moving with agility and accuracy, Mr. Swenson beside them, periodically turning the score. The music was beautiful, and Stella appreciated the talent it took to play, but oh, how she wished she were somewhere else. Stella began sifting through the condolence cards. She recognized most of the names: those of Lord Atherly's neighbors, her neighbors in Rosehurst, acquaintances she'd met at dinners and balls across the Forest, merchants from the nearby towns. Even Mr. Heppenstall, the owner of the Knightwood Oak, had taken the time to send a note. But one envelope had no return address, though the handwriting was faintly familiar. Wasn't it the same as on the card enclosed with the thoughtful, though anonymous, souvenir spoon wedding gift? If so, she was eager to read their kind words.

Not waiting to find a letter opener, she ripped the fold of the envelope with her finger. Inside was a card of a beautifully embossed blue and green butterfly that appeared to lift off the ivory paper and flitter through the surrounding field of forget-me-nots. The caption read, *Sincere Regards*. Stella turned the card over, hoping it was signed. It wasn't. But in the same handwriting as the anonymous gift, the inscription read, *My dearest Stella, I thank God you are finally free of him.*

Stella flung the card as if it had burned her fingers. It soared past the piano, nearly clipping Penny in the ear, and landed short of the fireplace. The music stopped abruptly.

"What is it, Stella?"

Lyndy jumped from his chair, but Penny bolted off the piano bench, the first to retrieve the card. She read it out loud.

"That is awful," Penny said, in a rare show of agreeance after reading it. She handed the card to Lyndy, who tossed it onto the fire grate. It flared into flame and quickly dissolved into the ashes. "Who sent it?"

Stella shook her head. "It wasn't signed."

"How could anyone be so cruel?" Lady Alice said.

"And so cowardly," Lyndy added.

Everyone, even Lady Atherly, showed various heartfelt signs of agreement and disbelief. Yet guilt warred with Stella's initial anger and revulsion. Hadn't she had the same thoughts, the same relief to be free of her father's control? But who was this person, who refused to be known, to put into words such an ugly thing?

"Perhaps Tims saw who delivered it," Lyndy mused, thinking like Stella that they needed to know who this was.

"I would dismiss it altogether. Brush it completely from your mind," Lady Atherly said, with a sweep of her hand, as if that would do the job. "As you said, we have no idea who this person is. Therefore, they do not matter, and neither does what they say."

Mrs. Swenson nodded in hearty agreement, patting Stella's knee again. "You poor orphaned child, you shouldn't add to your troubles by giving it another thought."

"But the sender seems to have such perverse intentions," Penny said, ignoring the advice of the older women. "Besides the killer, who would possibly be happy Mr. Kendrick is dead?"

The crackle in the grate and the call of a far-off bird alone pierced the silence that ensued. The chime of the grandfather clock in the hall announced seven o'clock. And still, no one responded.

How could anyone answer a question like that?

Lord Atherly cleared his throat. "More Schubert, anyone?"

CHAPTER 22

Stella lifted her skirts, made of black crape to satisfy convention, and stepped off the gangplank unto the ferry's deck. She spied the upper promenade and, wanting a better view, made her way up. She gravitated toward the railing at the front, raised her face to the sun, and smiled.

Has it only been two days since I got the anonymous sympathy card? Two of the most miserable days of her life.

The rain and the mud had kept her from riding. Dark clouds had closed in on the Forest, shutting out the sun and all sense of color. The wind had whistled through tiny cracks in the window seams, slicing through every jacket and overcoat Stella had worn. But the weather hadn't been the half of it. The first day Stella had called at Pilley Manor. It had been stuffed to the rafters with bouquets of cut flowers sent by dignitaries, local merchants, and varied horse racing enthusiasts. She had appreciated the irony; her father had never been so well-liked. Stella loved fresh flowers, though not as much as Lady Atherly, and the color had been a welcome reprieve from the dreariness outside. But the fragrance of hundreds of them, set on every table-top, had been overpoweringly sweet. Among this circus of color and scent, Stella had sat through a tedious recount of all the ways Mrs. Swenson had helped with the funeral arrangements. She'd endured Penny's searching glare as Penny wondered how much Stella knew about her and Sir Owen. And worst of all, she'd had to face the short, tearful encounter with Sammy and Gertie when she'd told them their father might not be coming home. It had taken up much of her day, keeping her from doing much else. She'd hoped to hear news from Inspector Brown, but no word came, nothing further about Uncle Jed and the case against him, nothing about the inspector's interview with the baron, nothing. The highlight of that day had been Sir Owen's humble and abashed return to Morrington Hall after breakfast. Justice, for him at least, had been served.

Yesterday, taken up with her father's funeral, had been even worse. Stella painfully remembered listening to eulogies by people who barely knew her father who said kind words that didn't ring true as she searched their faces for a hint of who might've sent the anonymous gift and card. Only when Mr. Swenson had spoken—of her father's well-earned standing in the world of horse racing, his integrity on the turf (almost to a fault), his knack for knowing which foal was a champion, his love of winning, his tireless determination to get his own way—had Stella sensed any sincerity. Congregated beside the grave site, everyone dressed in black, their hats and umbrellas dripping with rain, Stella had heard Reverend Paine drone on but could no longer remember a word the vicar said. She couldn't picture how she'd gotten to the churchyard or how she got back. All she remembered were regrets: that her father wasn't being buried with his parents in the plot in Kentucky, that he'd never see her marry Lyndy and brag about it back home, that she wasn't crying or mourning him the way she should. She remembered only that, and Lyndy beside her, their shoulders touching, his hand clasped in hers. They should've been on their honeymoon.

So when Stella woke up this morning and learned of Baron Branson-Hill's invitation to join him for a "distraction from the recent unpleasantries," Stella wasn't about to let the rules of mourning stop her from going to the Isle of Wight with the rest of them.

If Inspector Brown isn't going to tell me whether the baron knew anything about Pistol Prescott or not, I will have to ask the baron myself.

Stella swiveled around and leaned against the railing. The full length of the promenade stretched before her. Dozens of fellow passengers milled about. She spotted Mr. Swenson, Penny, and Aunt Ivy emerge from the lower deck, the latter searching for Stella. Stella quickly turned her back, hoping to avoid detection. After so many social interactions these past two days, Stella craved to be alone, even for a few minutes.

Of those invited, Lady Alice and Penny had been the most enthusiastic. The others were less so. Lady Atherly had declined to join them, having no interest in the baron's horses (he'd promised to show off his most recent equine acquisition, the champion, Sceptre). However, she still insisted Stella, Lady Alice, and Penny be chaperoned. Aunt Rachel, having a proclivity to seasickness, had offered instead to care for the children. Mrs. Swenson was the obvious choice, but Mr. Swenson, eager to meet another famed racehorse, had graciously volunteered for the post. Lord Atherly had retired to his study, as usual. Sir Owen, still recovering from his time in the cell at the Lyndhurst police station, had begged off due to a terrible headache. Stella suspected he was fine but avoiding Penny. Aunt Ivy, who couldn't decide, caught up with them on Lymington Pier a few minutes ago when Stella and the others boarded the ferry, *P.S. Solent.*

Stella's heart pounded with excitement when the two giant paddle wheels on each side of the boat revolved, churning the blue-gray water of the Lymington River. A white cloud of smoke, from the steam engine, billowed from the ferry's smokestack, and they were off.

The ferry paddled slowly, imperceivably at first, passing several idle barges, anchored rowboats, and yachts. It glided by the open courtyard-like public slip where an unshaven man, who dangled his legs and a fishing rod over the edge of the landing wall, raised his hat in greeting. It passed the two-story white-washed warehouses and breweries of brick and stone lining the town quay. The ferry paddled by the squat wooden buildings and partially built yachts of a boatyard before finally breaking free of the town. Only once before had Stella been on a boat, the ship that had carried her across the ocean. On this low-lying ferry, the passage felt personal; she could sense the roll of the waves, taste the spray of the cold, salty water on her face. She loved it.

The paddle steamer slowly picked up speed, navigating between the sprawling thick brownish-green mats of floating marsh that marked the approaching mouth of the river. Stella breathed in their fresh, earthy, damp fragrance. Lyndy, restless as usual, complained of thirst and left with Lady Alice in search of refreshments. A loose flock of small, loudly honking, black-bellied geese flew overhead as Penny sidled up beside Stella at the railing. The geese landed on a nearby marsh bed, the little white patches on the bird's necks flashing in the sunlight.

"I hear I have you to thank for getting Sir Owen released." Penny stared out at the geese, her sarcasm as sharp as nails on slate. "I thought you'd outgrown your need to be little miss goody-two-shoes. I see I was wrong."

"And I see you haven't outgrown your propensity to lie when it suits you." Penny sniffed at the comment but didn't deny it. "Would you really have let Sir Owen take the blame for my daddy's murder because he took some liberties with you?"

"Took some liberties?" Penny snarled, turning on Stella. "The only reason I came to this cold, gloomy godforsaken country is to find myself a husband. What chances would I have if the truth got out?"

"So, it would've been better Sir Owen hanged than you be forced to find a husband back home?" It was Stella's turn to be sarcastic.

"You have no idea. You have your Lord Lyndhurst to fawn over you. You've always had everyone fawn all over you."

How could Penny have such a skewed view of reality? Penny was the one all the boys at home had adored.

"Who do you mean?"

"Your dad, for one. After your mama died, he gave you everything you wanted."

"Except for his attention and affection. At least your parents love you. My mother died, and my father left me to be raised by stable hands and housemaids, who thank goodness had more compassion on a little girl than he did."

"And you had Miss Ivy," Penny retorted. She clicked open her beaded handbag, the silver clasp reflecting the sun into a spot on the deck, and pulled out a handkerchief to dab at her watery eyes, "caused by the wind," or so Penny said.

Stella glanced toward her aunt, who was enjoying a laugh with Mr. Swenson farther down the promenade as a large gull, following the ferry, hovered with its outstretched wings not far above their heads.

"Yes, for a little while, I had Aunt Ivy. But when I was old enough to marry, Daddy sold me to the highest bidder. When I refused to do what he wanted me to, he crushed my hand until I thought my bones would break. Is that what you mean by fawning over me?"

Penny's lip curled as she shoved the handkerchief back into her handbag. "You're despicable, Stella. Do you know that? Your dad is dead, and here you are making up these horrendous stories about him. He can't even defend himself from your lies. He loved you. He found you a husband you'd never get, or deserve, on your own. He secured your future, and this is how you show your gratitude? By vilifying his memory? Mama was right about you."

Mrs. Swenson? What had she told Penny? Stella asked, but Penny continued as if Stella hadn't spoken.

"You know why I was never nice to you? Because I was jealous. I always wished I could be you. Now I can't even stand to be around you." Penny turned on her heels but called over her shoulder, "One day, you'll realize these British men are all the same. Sir Owen, Sir Alfred, Lord Lyndhurst. One day, you'll realize how I feel. Used and then tossed aside."

Stella was speechless. Penny, jealous of her? How could Penny have gotten it so wrong? And to accuse her of lying about her father's ill-treatment? Why would Stella do such a thing? The memories, the truth hurt. What tales had Mrs. Swenson been telling Penny? But something Penny said hit a nerve. Just as Sir Owen had taken advantage of Penny, endangering her reputation and prospects, Stella's father had manipulated her, changed the whole course of her life for his selfish purposes. But Lyndy wasn't like the others. He wasn't using Stella, being kind and affectionate to get her money. He wasn't going to throw her aside for someone else the moment they were married. No, Penny got everything else wrong. She was wrong about that too. Wasn't she?

Stella quickly aimed her face directly into the wind, letting it lash at her cheeks. It snatched at her hat, threatening to loosen it from the pins. Then she pushed off from the railing, marched across the promenade and down the metal stairs. She'd seek out Lyndy. She'd find all the reassurance she needed in his eyes. When Stella reached the lower deck, lying so close to the water that if she kneeled she could put her hand in, she aimed for the first-class saloon cabin. She was sure to find Lyndy there. But when she stepped into deep shadow, she paused to discover what caused it. A lifeboat dangled directly over her head, blocking both the sun and her view of the promenade above. She slowly closed her eyes, relishing the momentary solitude of the spot. Setting aside the doubts, the guilt, the sorrow, the unanswered questions, she listened to the rush of the waves, the hum of the engine, the cry of birds, the laughter from distant passengers. It was the first moment of absolute peace she'd had in days.

The sound of someone's approach marked the end of the moment. She regrettably opened her eyes and took a step forward, toward the saloon door. In the next instant, someone grabbed her shoulder. Before she could identify who it was, they slapped the brim of her hat over her face and shoved her off the edge of the boat. She frantically clutched for a hold that wasn't there, her scream drowned out by the whistling blast of steam from the ferry's engine. Airborne, like the gulls, squawking and cawing overhead, the skirts of her black mourning dress flapped and fluttered in the wind like a flag for an excruciatingly long second. Her breath caught in her throat, cutting off any chance of crying out again, when she crashed into the frigid water and was enveloped by the ferry's waves.

"Lord Lyndhurst! Lord Lyndhurst!"

Mrs. Mitchell, waving to get his attention, hurried toward Lyndy, the netting and rosettes swathed about her hat flopping as she moved. He and Alice met the aunt halfway on their way out of the saloon.

"Is Stella with you?" Stella's aunt breathlessly asked while searching the faces of the passengers seated nearby. A great many had decided to pass the journey out of the wind.

"No. She was enjoying the view on the promenade. Why?"

"I saw her against the railing in front of the boat earlier, but then she was gone. I've searched everywhere. It's as if she's vanished."

"How long ago was that?"

"Seven or eight minutes ago."

"Here!" Lyndy unceremoniously shoved the glasses of lemonade he'd purchased into his sister's hands, the liquid sloshing over the rims and onto Alice's gloves.

"What is it, Lyndy?" Alice asked.

Lyndy didn't stay to answer but ran, racing up the metal staircase to the promenade, dodging passengers who got in his way. He reached the stretch of railing where he'd left Stella, and spun around, searching the deck in all directions. Lyndy spied Mr. Swenson and his daughter, but nowhere did he see Stella. Lyndy did as Mrs. Mitchell must have. He strode the length of the promenade, descended the far stairs, and crossed the entire span of the ferry on the lower deck, peering into the windows of the second-class cabin, and then entered the saloon again before ascending the stairs on the other side. Where was she?

"Did you find her?" Alice asked when she and Mrs. Mitchell joined him.

"No."

"What's the problem, Lord Lyndhurst?" Mr. Swenson asked when he and Miss Swenson gathered around, searching Lyndy's face for answers. "What's happened?"

Lyndy shook his head. He could hardly breathe.

"Miss Kendrick's gone missing," Alice, still holding the glasses of lemonade, answered for him.

Miss Swenson forced a laugh. "Of course she has."

"I'm sure she's around somewhere," Mr. Swenson said, casting an admonishing glare at his daughter.

A lad, with the poor makings of a mustache, in a navy-blue seaman's cap, dashed by. Lyndy snatched him by the sleeve, swinging him around.

"Oi! Let me go."

"I'm unable to find my fiancée," Lyndy informed him.

"We've searched everywhere," Mrs. Mitchell added.

Grappling to keep his hat from flying off, the lad answered nervously, "Have you checked the ladies' toilet room?"

Lyndy glanced at Mrs. Mitchell, who was nodding her head. "I want her found."

"Of course you do, sir. I'm sure she's simply—"

Infuriated by the sailor's tone, Lyndy grabbed him by the lapels. "Do you know who I am? I said I want her found." Lyndy shook the lad as if the answer to Stella's whereabouts might fall from his pockets.

"Lord Lyndhurst," Mr. Swenson admonished. "There's no need for this."

Mr. Swenson be damned. Lyndy wasn't going to be persuaded to release this man until he agreed to help.

"I'm sure he'll help any way he can," the older American added as if reading Lyndy's mind.

"Of course, of course, milord. This isn't a large vessel. If she's onboard, we'll find her. I promise. Please let me go."

Dear God! He said, "if."

Lyndy released his grip, and the lad ducked away and sped down the wooden planks.

"Oh, Lyndy," Alice said. "Are you thinking what I'm thinking? Could she have . . . ?"

"Fallen overboard?" Lyndy said. He gripped the railing to steady himself and peered down. There was nothing but the roiling Solent beneath them.

Mrs. Mitchell's cheeks drained of color. "No. No, it can't be."

"Do you think it's possible . . ." Miss Swenson suggested, without a hint of petulance or pettiness, "that the death of her dad was too much? And with the wedding postponed and all, do you think maybe she . . . ?"

With his fists clenched at his sides, his heart pounding so hard it hurt, Lyndy rounded on the woman, who stumbled back, startled to be the object of his anger.

"Never, ever suggest such an un-Christian idea again," he quietly warned.

"I'm sorry. I didn't mean . . . I was simply suggesting that maybe . . ."

"I know what you were suggesting, Miss Swenson," Lyndy seethed. "If you knew Stella, as you claim, you'd never entertain such an absurd idea."

Mr. Swenson, whether to protect her daughter or assuage Lyndy's anger, stepped between them and gripped Lyndy's shoulder. "Now, now, this isn't helping, is it?"

Lyndy shrugged the man off and began to pace in a tight, clipped manner a few feet down the railing and back.

"I wouldn't worry so much, Lord Lyndhurst," Mr. Swenson said, smoothing a curl from his daughter's brow. "If Stella has gone overboard, the girl's a strong swimmer. Do you remember, Penelope, darling, how you and she once swam in the Kentucky River?"

Miss Swenson, too self-absorbed with her wounded pride, pouted and didn't reply.

How could the man be so nonchalant? Lyndy wanted to throttle him. Did Mr. Swenson not mark the churning water? The power of the paddle wheels? Did he not realize how cold it was?

"I doubt Miss Kendrick was wearing mourning attire on that occasion," Lyndy sneered.

Mr. Swenson stroked his beard and frowned as if he hadn't considered that. Suddenly the whistle blew, and the ferry picked up speed.

"What the bloody hell!"

Lyndy rocketed down the promenade and up to the ferry's wheelhouse. He threw open the door, sending it smashing against the inner wall. The captain, presumably, in his white cap and a double row of brass buttons on his jacket, stood rooted like a giant before the wooden steering wheel. The man must be six and a half feet tall.

"Steady on! You're not allowed in here," another man in a seaman's cap, consulting a clipboard, protested.

"Why are you continuing? If anything, we need to turn back," Lyndy demanded. "We haven't found her yet."

The captain calmly nodded to the sailor to take the helm and motioned to Lyndy to join him on the small platform beyond the wheelhouse door. "Lord Lyndhurst, is it not?"

"It is. And I demand you turn around this instant."

"I know of your request, my lord, and we are searching the ferry for your lady friend as we speak."

"But what if she's not on the ferry?"

"You think she's gone overboard?"

"It's possible. That's why I insist you go back."

"When was the last time she was seen?"

"Going on ten minutes, maybe a little more."

The captain solemnly removed his cap and tucked it under his arm, his carriage stiff and unwavering, as if bracing himself for what he was about to convey.

"If that is the tragic case, my lord, I regret the time has passed for any type of rescue mission. We should be almost two miles away by now. I am sorry."

"Is that it? Is that all you're willing to do?"

"I shall, of course, inform His Majesty's Coastguard, but I have an obligation to my other passengers. But let's not give up hope she'll be found onboard."

The ferry wasn't that big, and the captain knew it. If Stella were onboard, they would've found her by now. Lyndy pressed the heels of his hands against his temples, willing the pounding in his head to go away. She couldn't be dead. He wouldn't accept it.

"You have a lifeboat. I shall search for Miss Kendrick myself." Lyndy stepped forward to leave, but the captain's outstretched arm blocked his path.

"I can't let you do that, my lord. Your safety is my responsibility, and it is not safe out there right now."

"Which is exactly my point. Now, out of my way," Lyndy commanded, but the captain didn't budge.

"I understand your anger and frustration, my lord, but aboard this boat, I am in charge. You're more than welcome to

stay aboard when the others disembark in Yarmouth and return with us to Lymington straightaway, but I must insist you
calm down and return to your party. I, in turn, shall do my ut-
most to ensure a timely return."

Lyndy yanked on the bottom of his jacket but reluctantly
stepped aside. "Don't for one moment think this ends here,
Captain. I shall be taking this up with the Chief Coastguard.
My father, the Earl of Atherly, and he are personal friends."

"Do what you must, my lord," the captain said, tipping his
head before returning to the wheelhouse.

Of that, he could be certain.

Lyndy would comb every inch of this vessel, and the moment the ferry headed back to Lymington, he'd be searching
the waters for her. If he still couldn't find her, he'd borrow a
yacht if he had to. Lyndy would trace the length of the coast
from Hengistbury Head to Calshot Castle. He'd find her. He
had to. Her life, and his, depended on it.

CHAPTER 23

Brown hesitated to knock; black crape hung from the door. But why? Mr. Kendrick hadn't been a relative, nor was he much liked by the earl and his family. Perhaps it was done out of consideration for Miss Kendrick, considering she'd temporarily taken up residence here again.

That was the reason Brown had come. It had been a frustrating, fruitless two days. Jedidiah Kendrick, more comfortable in the cell than was natural, had persisted in declaring his innocence. The Southampton men had closed the case on Jesse Prescott's death in all but name. And with the weather such as it was, Brown hadn't a chance to interview Baron Branson-Hill. Brown had nothing more to convey to Miss Kendrick beyond the predicted outcome of the inquest, but she deserved to know he hadn't given up.

And he wouldn't until he'd found her father's murderer.

Brown lifted the brass knocker and rapped it strongly, hearing the echo in the hall on the other side.

Mr. Fulton, the butler, opened the door, a black band around his sleeve. "Inspector."

Brown asked after Miss Kendrick, expecting to be put off, as usual. The butler merely held the door and stepped aside. With such a somber air, if Brown didn't know the man better, he'd think Mr. Fulton had lost a loved one. The impression didn't stop there. The covered mirrors, the heavy silence as the butler escorted Brown toward the drawing room, their heels clicking on the highly polished parquet floor, all spoke of a house in mourning. All this for Miss Kendrick's sake? Knowing Miss Kendrick, as he'd come to do, it didn't sit right.

Brown entered the now all-too-familiar drawing room, filled with looming portraits of Lord Atherly's ancestors peering down on equally gloomy people. Mrs. Mitchell and Miss Luckett, Miss Kendrick's two aunts, huddling together apart from the others quietly weeping, struck him as particularly wretched.

"I'd like to speak to Miss Kendrick, if I may," Brown said, slipping off his hat.

"Oh, Lordy!" the elderly aunt wailed, seemingly unbidden.

"You may not," Lady Atherly said, with her typical civil disdain, carefully avoiding drawing any attention to the American women in the corner.

"I understand Miss Kendrick's in mourning, Lady Atherly, but—"

"She's dead."

Brown's chest tightened as if the words sucked every wisp of air from the room. Brown took a slight step back to steady himself. "She's what?"

"No, she's missing," Mrs. Mitchell insisted vehemently. "She's not dead."

"It is late September, Mrs. Mitchell," Lady Atherly explained, as if to a child. "Do you really suppose she could've survived?" The patronizing tone pierced Brown's distress.

"I do. Like Mr. Swenson said, Stella's an excellent swimmer."

"Then you have more faith than sense, I'm afraid, Mrs. Mitchell," Mrs. Swenson said, not unkindly. "Poor orphaned child. Now she's gone to meet her maker too."

"I think my wife's right. After all this time, I think we must accept the truth."

"How can you say that, Mr. Swenson?" Mrs. Mitchell bolted from her seat. She wagged a finger at him. "You're the one who said she'd be fine. You're the one who gave me hope."

Mr. Swenson held his hands up in surrender. "I'm as sorry as you are that I was wrong."

"Right!" Brown interrupted. "Would someone please explain what happened?" Brown stared at Sir Owen, leaning against the mantel, swirling a glass of whiskey.

Sir Owen took a sip and noted the direction of Brown's focus over the rim of the glass. "Steady on! I wasn't even there, Inspector."

"Baron Branson-Hill invited us for luncheon at his estate on the Island, Inspector," Lady Alice, a stack of magazines clutched to her chest, spoke up. "We were on the ferry when Miss Kendrick disappeared. After thoroughly searching the boat, we've assumed she fell overboard, and presumed drowned."

"Miss Kendrick was supposed to be in mourning," Lady Atherly said, her irritation and anger uncharacteristically seeping into her words. "Foolish girl. If she'd listened to me and done what was expected of her . . ."

"I told her as much," Mrs. Swenson said. "But she was stubborn. Reminded me of you, Penny. What was so important she'd ignore your wishes, Lady Atherly?"

"Stella always had to have her own way," Miss Swenson sulked, her resentment tinged with melancholy and regret. "Now, look what's happened."

Mr. Swenson noticed the subtle conflict behind his daughter's pout. "Are you okay, Penelope, darling?"

Miss Swenson, embarrassed by her father's attention, took out her enameled silver compact and began powdering her nose. "Stella had to come with us, didn't she? She just had to see the baron's new horse."

Brown knew otherwise. Miss Kendrick hadn't ignored convention to meet a horse, though it lent itself as the perfect excuse. She went to do what Brown hadn't done—interview the baron about Jesse Prescott.

Bloody hell! Brown cursed silently. "Where is Lord Lyndhurst?" The young viscount was conspicuously absent. Had something happened to him too?

"Poor boy has gone out to search for her," Lord Atherly said. "Refuses to accept she's gone." The earl sighed, absent-mindedly caressing what looked to be one of his fossil bones. "And with her all of our hopes for a brighter future."

Was Lord Atherly referring to the gaiety, the generosity, the warmth Miss Kendrick brought to this otherwise dour family or was he strictly speaking of her inheritance that, if rumors were true, they so desperately needed? Brown couldn't tell.

"I wouldn't worry too much on that account, Lord Atherly." Mrs. Swenson knowingly glanced toward her daughter. "I reckon there are many suitable heiresses more than willing to console your dear son's broken heart."

Lady Atherly visible stiffened. "Clearly, you don't know my son." The rebuke was unmistakable and surprising, perhaps even to the countess herself. Mrs. Swenson's cheeks reddened as if she'd been slapped.

"Frances is right," Lord Atherly said. "Miss Kendrick is irreplaceable. We shall miss her dearly."

"That's not what I said, William, but yes, Miss Kendrick will be missed."

"Mummy," Lady Alice said, astonished endearment in her tone.

Hardened policeman as he was, the sudden softening of Lady Atherly sought to undo him. *They aren't the only ones who will miss the young lady.* Brown couldn't excuse himself hastily enough.

"Ahem." Brown cleared his throat. "If you'll excuse me then, Your Ladyship, Your Lordship. I have a murder investigation to attend to. Please convey my deepest sympathies to Lord Lyndhurst."

Miss Luckett, the old lady, sobbed none-too-quietly at the mention of the young viscount, who was supposed to be on his honeymoon, not fruitlessly searching for the body of his drowned fiancée.

"Of course, Inspector," Lady Atherly said, her gaze on her lap as she smoothed her skirt.

Brown tipped his head briefly, slapped his hat on his head and, turning his back on the room, impatiently brushed a tear from his cheek.

Stella was so cold her weakened muscles ached, her heart was pounding, her breath was ragged, and she'd lost all sensation in her hands and feet. Her teeth chattered so hard her head and jaw hurt. But she did it. She'd gotten herself out of the water. *Barely.*

When she'd hit the surface of the river, the shock of it had struck her breathless. The temperature in the sun had been pleasant; the river was bitter cold. She'd began breathing too fast, gasping for air. Fighting against her rising panic, she'd struggled against the current to the surface, and spurted out what she could of the water she'd swallowed. She'd treaded in place for a few moments, getting her breath back. But the leaden weight of her clothes and the cold were already sapping her strength. She didn't have much time.

With the ferry too far away to help, she swam for the nearest floating mat of marsh less than fifty yards away. Stella had learned to swim as a child. Afternoon picnics on the beaches of Newport with her mother, and then with nannies, were a favorite childhood memory. But this was not the gentle, wave-lapped seashore in July. Every foot Stella gained was a fight. The waves splashed her face, blurring her vision and gagging her. Her mourning dress, floating around her like spilled ink, dragged her down, the stays of her corset pressing into her ribs with every breath. But she couldn't stop, even as her muscles weakened, her feet and hands grew numb, her lungs hurt with every inhale. When she'd reached the marsh bed, she hadn't considered it might not hold her weight when she clawed her way up on to it, digging into the soft, grassy mat with her elbows and dragging herself out of the water. But the roots of the brownish-green grasses twisted and intertwined so thick they created a flat floating island strong enough. She'd laid there a few moments, her cheek pressed against the coarse, earthy-scented grass, gasping, searching the horizon, with blurred vision, out across the endless gray water to the ferry, chugging out smoke and growing smaller and smaller by the moment. Surveying her immediate surroundings, she found only a precariously narrow strip about ten or so feet at its widest and nothing more stable than grass to hold on to.

Could she survive here long enough to wait for the ferry's return?

Suddenly, a head and pair of inquiring round eyes jutted up from the water on the opposite edge of her floating island. *Someone else has fallen off!* But she hadn't fallen, she corrected herself. Someone had deliberately pushed her overboard. But why? After their heated conversation, only Penny came to mind. But did Penny hate her that much? Or was she as mean and irresponsible in anger now as when they were children? Was this the stone-throwing incident all over again?

"Over here!" Stella shouted to the figure, but with her tongue thick, her face stinging from the cold, her voice was barely audible above the wind.

The figure swam toward her. When it got close, Stella began to laugh nervously. This was not a fellow passenger. It was a seal, a mottled gray creature, curious who this black lump of a human was. It slid its sleek belly onto the grass bed and flopped comically over to her. She lay mesmerized, her new companion inching closer, until the steady, rhythmic slapping of oars nearby penetrated Stella's rapt attention. A small dingy, rowed by two men, headed for one of the many yachts anchored in the mouth of the Lymington River.

"Help!"

Her call, enough to startle the seal back into the water, didn't carry to the boatmen. She twisted and turned, using all the strength she had left, pushed up on one elbow, and waved her hand above her head, calling out, again and again, hoping to catch their attention. But to no avail. When the wind drowned out the receding splash of the oars of the dinghy, she collapsed, flopping onto her back, her view a few wispy clouds until her vision dimmed and even the bright, blue sky went black.

CHAPTER 24

~

"You're a lucky one, you are, miss. If me brother, Dickie there, weren't such a fool for them seals, we never would've spotted you."

Stella, her hands wrapped around the hot ceramic cup, nodded in agreement. From hearing them tell it: finding her drenched, stone-cold, and unconscious, she didn't want to think about what might've happened if they hadn't doubled back when they did.

"Though I have to say, how you got yourself out of the water, it's just like one of them seals."

The man who spoke, who'd introduced himself as Fred Boothroyd, lit his wooden pipe. Puffing a ring of sweet-smelling smoke into the air, he eased into the second of a pair of worn, faded green wing-backed chairs; Stella huddled in nothing more than her underthings and two gray, woolen blankets in the other. Like his brother, Dickie, who fiddled with the fire, jabbing the coals vigorously with an iron poker, Fred Boothroyd wore a heavy wool sweater and kept his graying reddish hair cropped short. Stella would've mistaken them for twins, with their kind green eyes, thick droopy mustaches, and brown weathered faces, if Fred didn't exude the authority of an elder sibling.

"The seals, they be fey," Dickie said, in a deep baritone voice, ignoring the flashes of loose ember when they escaped the hearth and floated to the flagstone floor. He cast furtive sideways glances at Stella as if she too were supernatural. "Wouldn't be wise to ignore them."

Stella remembered the seal but only vaguely recalled the men's rough hands hauling her into the rowboat and nothing of the journey to their cottage on the coast. With their backs turned, the brothers had made sure she stripped out of her cold, soaked clothes and was comfortably wrapped up and ensconced in the chair before leaving her to doze off. They'd returned sometime later with a string of fish, which Dickie now cooked over the fire.

Through the steam rising from her cup, Stella took in the room: the hand-hewed mantelpiece, the fishing poles, nets, and tackle stacked in a corner, the pewter tankards on the table, one dented as if hit by an ax blade, the portrait of King Edward in a thin, silver-plated frame on the plain, white plaster walls. Each item raised a different question: were the brothers married, if so, where were their wives, were they fishermen, as their equipment suggested, how long had they lived here? Considering the men hadn't questioned Stella, not even to learn why she'd been floating on a marsh bed in mourning clothes, she suppressed her curiosity; Lady Atherly would've been proud.

But Stella, having stared at the tall, round wall blocking the view out the window for who knew how long now, couldn't help herself but ask, "What's that?"

"What's what?" Fred followed her gaze to the window. "You mean the light?"

"The light?" Stella didn't understand. The two men regarded her as if her senses were still muddled. Maybe they were right.

"The Keyhaven Light," Dickie explained slowly. "Don't you remember?"

The lighthouse!

Stella gathered the blankets more tightly around her, rose from the chair, and waddled over to the window. From the closer vantage point, she could peek straight up and see the whitewashed, tapered lighthouse stretch seventy or eighty feet into the sky. *If this is the Keyhaven lighthouse, then . . .* She crossed the room to the far window, ignoring the brothers' exchange of concerned glances, and pushed back the yellowing cotton curtain. In full view stood Keyhaven Castle, about three hundred yards away. Further on, a lone horseman guided his mount down the thin peninsula. Lyndy said the castle was popular with sightseers.

Would it be more so or less now that it was the site of a murder? She pulled the blanket up tighter around her chin.

"You have quite the view from here," she said with a mixture of pleasure and melancholy. "It must be wonderful from the top of the lighthouse."

"It is," Dickie said proudly, wrapping a towel around the handle of the wrought iron pan and lifting the cooked fish from the fire.

"Perhaps we can take you up there when you're more proper-like," Fred added, jabbing his pipe toward the tan, wool sack suit draped across the back of her chair.

Dickie, being the smaller of the two brothers, had offered Stella, whose clothes were ruined (even Ethel wouldn't be able to mend a waterlogged crape dress or the rents in her stockings), his Sunday best. It was unconventional but kind, like the brothers themselves.

"I'd like that."

She waddled back to the chair and snatched up the suit, the white shirt, a thick leather belt, and a borrowed pair of thin wool stockings. She found a spot in a back bedroom with enough privacy to change. Without a corset or fitted bodice, the baggy suit was as comfortable and as easy to dress herself in as a nightgown. She only had to roll up the pant legs to keep them from dragging on the ground. She stuffed her feet into her boots and winced; they were still damp.

When Stella presented herself, Fred, puffing on his pipe with the air of a man who saw women wearing trousers every day, said, "That'll do."

After the smoky, stuffy cottage, Stella welcomed the fresh air when they stepped outside. Rounding the vast base of the lighthouse, she caught sight of the castle again. The horse rider, the tails of his overcoat flying like pennants behind him, was getting closer.

"Living here, you must've heard about what happened at the castle," she said.

"Aye," Fred said. "Everyone knows what happened to the American chap. We gathered from the foreign lilt to your voice you might've known him."

"He was my father."

"Our condolences, miss," Dickie said.

"Thank you."

"Would it have been your uncle, then, who did it? At least that's the talk at the pub."

"My uncle was arrested, yes, but for stealing, not murder. Uncle Jed claims he wasn't even there when Daddy died, that he was out on the spit."

"Like that chap that's braving the wind out there right now," Fred said. The rider approached the castle and trotted across the drawing bridge boards.

"Wait!" Stella said. "If Uncle Jed had been out there, you might've seen him."

Fred was already shaking his head. "No, couldn't have. I was out fishing the marshes."

Stella let out a breath of frustration. She'd thought she'd found a way to prove whether Uncle Jed was lying or not.

"I saw someone," Dickie said, reaching for the heavy lighthouse door. "I was tending the light about that time. Watched him for a good bit of time, I did. The odd bloke was picking up stones and throwing them into the sea."

Fred jabbed his thumb toward his brother, as Dickie swung open the door, shedding light into the darkened, winding stairwell. "As I said, he's the curious one, him."

I have to tell Inspector Brown.

"I'm sorry." Stella stepped back from the open door. "Could one of you drive me, or do you have a horse I can borrow? I need to get to Lyndhurst immediately." When her pronouncement made the men hesitate, sharing another unspoken concern between them, she added, "I promise to return everything as soon as I get back to Morrington Hall."

At her mention of Lord Atherly's estate, Dickie spit into his palm and ran it over his hair.

"We knew you were posh," Fred said over the *clip-clop* of an approaching horse, "but Morrington Hall? Blimey. That must make you—"

"My fiancée," Lyndy declared, leaping down from Beau.

"Lyndy!" Stella rushed into his waiting arms.

"I thought I lost you." Lyndy's voice trembled when she slipped her hands into the warmth beneath his unbuttoned overcoat. He wrapped her in a tight embrace and buried his face in her hair, still damp and flowing loose around her shoulders, his breath hot on her neck.

Stella smiled, whispering into his ear, "You can't get rid of me that easily."

His hands reached for her face, and she shivered. The heat from his breath brushed her lips. His kisses, soft and tentative at first, as if unwilling to trust she was real, grew harder, more insistent as he pulled her closer, trying to meld his lips to hers as she clung to him as if he were an anchor in an angry sea.

"Ahem." A polite cough from behind her broke the spell.

Stella loosened her grip and glanced sheepishly at Fred, clutching his pipe in his teeth and contemplating the view of the famous Needles at the end of the Isle of Wight. Dickie studied the ground, kicking the gravel at his feet.

"These are the gentlemen who rescued me in their rowboat, the lighthouse attendants, the Brothers Boothroyd," Stella explained, remembering her manners. "Fred, Dickie, may I introduce Lord Lyndhurst."

"Your Lordship," the brothers mumbled.

Lyndy thrust out his hand, the one not still wrapped around Stella's waist, and the brothers shook it in turn. "We are forever in your debt. When she fell from the ferry, we'd assumed—"

Stella stopped him. "Lyndy, I didn't fall."

"What do you mean?"

"I was deliberately pushed. And what's more, Dickie saw Uncle Jed on the peninsula when Daddy died. Uncle Jed couldn't have done it."

Lyndy tightened his grip around her waist. "Which means whoever killed your father . . ."

"Tried to rid themselves of me too."

With one arm around Stella's tiny waist, Lyndy held her against his chest as they rode, his knees tapping the back of her thighs with every step Beau took. Throwing all convention to the wind, she straddled the horse in front of him, hatless and with trousers on. Free of all encumbrances, however fleeting, like the ponies that roamed the Forest at will, the pair cantered across the heath as one, Stella's lovely, broad smile never slipping from her precious face. What more could a man ask for? What did he care if it turned heads as they made their way back to Morrington Hall like this?

Morrington Hall. Lyndy breathed in the salty scent of the sea, fading from the air as they traveled inland but still lingering on Stella's skin and hair, and fancied never having to return to his family estate. At least not yet.

Beau naturally slowed to a walk when the Irish Hunter met with a swath of thick bracken lining the entry into a stand of ancient oaks. The stippled light through the thinning leaves danced across Stella's hair like flashes of gold.

"I think we should elope," Lyndy whispered in Stella's ear, stray tendrils of her hastily pinned bun tickling his nose.

He couldn't fathom the thought of another day, or night, without her. Her breath rose and fell beneath his hand; the taste of her was still on his lips. Why must they wait, yet again, to wed? If Stella's father hadn't been murdered, they'd already be husband and wife. How long would Mother insist they postpone the wedding for propriety's sake? A year? *Mourning etiquette be damned.* Lyndy wanted her to be his now.

He pulled her closer against him.

"Lyndy, relax your grip," Stella complained. "I may have fallen from the ferry, but I know how to keep my seat in a saddle." She was right, of course. Lyndy eased his hold, but only a bit.

"What do you say? Shall we ride on to Winchester and wed right now?"

"As if the bishop would marry us now with me in mourning, and wearing a borrowed sack suit."

"It is merely convention to wait."

"Merely convention? Your mother should hear you talk." She laughed.

A smile tugged at his lips at the sweet sound, but he hadn't been joking. "I mean to say there is no legal impediment. Everything is in place. We were to wed two days ago anyway. Besides, how could the bishop object to your request? You, who have lost a father and who nearly lost your life as well?"

"It's tempting," she said, sounding like a purring cat. "But I don't want to start our married life together with my father's ghost hovering over our heads."

Lyndy presumed she'd say such a thing, but it didn't make him any less discontented.

"And to be free of him, we have to find justice for him," she added, her smile waning.

What about justice for us? The words were on the tip of his tongue when an enormous pig trotted into their path. Grunting as it sought its acorn treasures, its belly inches from scraping the ground, the animal paid them no mind.

Instinctually sidestepping the creature, Beau snorted a warning at it, sending it squealing in the opposite direction.

"Atta boy, Beau," Stella said, patting the horse on the neck, but she quickly fell into reflective silence. They rode out of the wood and across a verdant grazing lawn, checkered with the shadows of passing clouds, before she said, "I can't stop thinking we're missing something."

"Like what?" Lyndy asked, though he'd rather return to the conversation about their wedding plans.

"Like why push me off the ferry?"

"Perhaps you are mistaken, and it was an accident after all?"

"No." Her tone had a dissonance to it Lyndy rarely heard. He didn't fancy it one bit. "It was deliberate, all right."

"Could it not have had anything to do with your father's murder?" he suggested. "Someone with a grudge against us, perhaps? Since Papa squandered my inheritance, the villagers haven't been as deferential as they should."

"Then why push me in? Why not you or Lady Alice?"

She had a point. The villagers, having overcome her American ways, adored Stella's kindness, her openness, and her practice of patronizing their shops.

"Jesse Prescott had a ferry ticket in his pocket," he said. "Perhaps the accomplice we suspected the jockey of having does exist and was aboard the ferry? And wanted to take his revenge out on you, being Elijah Kendrick's daughter?"

"But isn't it outlandish to think that person just happened to be on the ferry at the same time as we were?"

"You're right. It's too much of a coincidence."

"Let's think. Who knew I'd be on the ferry?"

"Mother and Papa, of course. Alice, your Aunt Ivy, the Swensons, and Owen. The servants from both houses, of course."

"No one else?"

"Yes, the baron's whole household knew as well. Mother had Fulton telephone that you were coming. She didn't want the baron to be unpleasantly surprised."

"That must be it," Stella said, with a determination so like her. "It must have to do with my inviting myself to the baron's luncheon."

"Someone didn't want you to reach the Island."

Her head began bobbing in agreement before he'd finished the thought. "And I think I know why. We have to talk to the baron."

Lyndy brought Beau to a sudden halt. A fluttering of wings rustled the dense gorse. Stella swiveled around to learn why they'd stopped, concern creasing her forehead.

"And risk you traveling on the ferry again?" he demanded. "No. Absolutely not. For all we know, it was one of the sailors who pushed you off."

"True. But that would mean getting the baron to come to Morrington Hall again. Do you think he will?"

"I suppose if Mother invites him. But whether she'll oblige me by doing so is another question."

Stella cupped his cheek in her palm and patted him like a good schoolboy, a playful grin on her lips. "Then, I guess that means you need to play nice with Lady Atherly when we get back." Then puckered her lips for a kiss.

He laughed, gladly obliging her, as he sensed he'd be doing for the rest of his days.

CHAPTER 25

In answer to Stella's knock, Fulton swung open the door. "Miss Kendrick?" His unflappable face went slack with astonishment. His typical steady upward gaze fell to studying her from head to toe. "Please forgive me for saying so, but you are indeed a sight to behold."

At any other time, it would've been the butler's way of telling her she looked ridiculous dressed up like a man, but Stella knew better. She smiled at the butler's unspoken relief in seeing her alive.

"I'm happy to see you too, Fulton," she said, stepping into the hall, and ignoring all she'd learned about the proper etiquette between the classes, planted a light kiss on the butler's cheek.

A few paces behind her, Lyndy cleared his throat in surprise.

Fulton raised an eyebrow at her impulsive gesture but nothing more, having already composed himself from the shock. A moment later, the butler strode over to the hall mirror, and with one decisive yank, tugged off the black crape draped over it.

"Everyone has gathered in the drawing room, milord," Fulton said, winding the black fabric into a ball before offering to take Lyndy's hat and overcoat.

"Telephone Inspector Brown, would you, Fulton," Lyndy instructed. "Tell him it's quite urgent he come round and to bring his photograph with him."

"And tell him Dickie Boothroyd can give my Uncle Jed an alibi for my father's murder," Stella threw in.

"Now, if only we could get the baron here as easily," Lyndy mused.

Rip! Fulton tore the strip of crape from his arm. "I beg your pardon, milord, but Baron Branson-Hill and his wife are with Lady Atherly in the drawing room."

What luck.

Stella, nervous but encouraged by the warm welcome by the butler, slipped her arm into Lyndy's when they approached the drawing room door. The room was crowded, as if for a dinner party, but a pall permeated the atmosphere. Lady Atherly, Mrs. Swenson, and their daughters, along with the Baroness Branson-Hill huddled around the low table set with a silver tea service. Most of the food on the plates had been left uneaten. Mr. Swenson, Sir Owen, and the baron, drinks in hand, were assembled near the fireplace, chatting softly while Aunt Rachel, chin on her chest, snored in the overstuffed chair. Aunt Ivy sat apart, staring out the window. Everyone spoke in hushed voices.

They all think I'm dead.

"Ready?" Lyndy whispered, tickling her ear.

She nodded, and, as one, they stepped over the threshold. Mr. Swenson, by the mantel, noticed her first.

"Good God, Almighty!" Theo Swenson swore.

"Miss Kendrick? By Jove, it is!" the baron, following Mr. Swenson's gaze, announced.

"Stella!" Aunt Ivy cried, leaping out of her chair and rushing to throw her arms around her. Stella relished her aunt's warm embrace but felt bereft when Lyndy slipped his arm away to grant her aunt space. "I knew it! I knew you weren't dead." Her aunt's tears damped Stella's cheek.

"Could it be?" someone exclaimed.

"Oh, my!"

Teacups clattered, and napkins were thrown down with abandon as the prim ladies by the tea table clambered to their feet and crowded around Stella. Aunt Rachel's snore cut off midsnort when she woke to the commotion.

"Hallelujah! It's a miracle!" Aunt Rachel cried, throwing her arms in the air when she spied Stella.

"I say! Well done, you," Sir Owen declared, beaming at both Stella and his cousin.

"Yes, thank you, Lord Lyndhurst," Aunt Ivy said, stepping back, clasping her hands to her chest. "Thank you for bringing Stella back to us."

"I had nothing to do with it," Lyndy said.

"Oh, you poor, dear child," Mrs. Swenson said, elbowing her way through the others.

Stella good-heartedly tolerated Mrs. Swenson's embrace. "What happened to your dress?" she whispered, quietly mortified. "The water ruined it so . . ."

Mrs. Swenson nodded sympathetically. "I'll make sure your maid pulls out the black bombazine dress I'd ordered you."

Stella couldn't bring herself to thank the woman. She'd never wanted to wear black to begin with.

"They said the water was freezing," Penny remarked over her mother's shoulder.

"Trust me," Baroness Branson-Hill said, brushing crumbs from her gray and silver tea gown. "Even on a pleasant day, such as this, the water is as cold as Her Late Majesty Queen Victoria's glower."

"Then how did you manage to survive?" Penny insisted.

"There will be time enough for that," Lady Atherly said,

pushing the button to summon the butler and calling at the same time, "Fulton!" When he arrived, she said, "Please inform Lord Atherly that Miss Kendrick has returned safely. Then arrange for a bath to be drawn, and fresh clothes set out."

"Very good, my lady," the butler said, and disappeared again.

Lady Atherly motioned to Stella to sit. "You must've had the most harrowing time of it."

Stella glanced at Lyndy, dumbfounded by Lady Atherly's concern. He shrugged, his puzzled face reflecting her own astonishment. She took the offered spot beside the countess on the settee, more grateful than she realized to be sitting down. Lyndy, who'd stayed close from the moment he'd found her outside the lighthouse, preempted Mrs. Swenson's attempt to take the seat on Stella's other side. Without a word, Sir Owen handed Lyndy a drink. It smelled like her father's bourbon. Lady Atherly poured Stella a cup of tea.

"You gave us all quite the fright, young lady," Baron Branson-Hill admonished, his face creased with worry. "And when someone said it was on account of your wanting to visit us, well, of course, we came immediately." His wife nodded vigorously in agreement.

"We were mortified, in fact," the baroness said. "Thank goodness the weather cooperated."

The couple's sincerity touched her. She glanced at the others. Each regarded her with varying degrees of wonder, concern, relief, and for some, even fondness. Stella took a sip of tea. It was extra sweet. For the first time, Lady Atherly had made it the way Stella liked it. Overwhelmed by the sudden intense sense of belonging, Stella reached for Lyndy's hand.

And all it took was for everyone to think I'd died. It was almost worth the ordeal. *Almost.*

"I do hope you'll allow me to make it up to you," the baron was saying.

"If you're willing, Baron, you might be able to help me,"

Stella said. "But we'll talk about that later." She gave him a re-assuring smile, and his face relaxed.

"Miss Kendrick," Lord Atherly said, strolling into the room, his arms outstretched, his right hand still clutching a hand lens. "I was pouring over Professor Gridley's latest finds when Fulton told me the good news." He leaned down and kissed the top of her head. "How lovely it is to see you in one piece."

"Thank you, my lord," Stella said, touched by his uncharacteristic display of affection.

So unlike Daddy.

Stella quickly brushed the unbidden thought aside. She didn't want to ruin the moment.

"Won't you tell us what happened?" Lady Alice asked, setting her ever-present magazines on her lap aside. A swimmer in bright orange startled by a misty mermaid illustrated the top magazine's cover. Even Lady Alice had thought enough of Stella to find a fitting issue to peruse.

"There isn't much to tell," Stella insisted. "After I tumbled overboard, I managed to swim to one of the marsh beds."

"See. I told you Stella was an excellent swimmer, Penelope, darling." Theo Swenson smiled at his daughter. Penny rewarded him with a nasty scowl.

"The Keyhaven lighthouse keepers were out in their row-boat and spotted me," Stella continued. She didn't tell them about her encounter with the seal, especially after Dickie Booth-royd's comment about it being supernatural. Even now, she wasn't sure if she had imagined it. "And from the top of the lighthouse, one of them spotted Uncle Jed out on the spit, right where he said he was when Daddy was killed."

"Well, I'll be a baked potato," Aunt Rachel declared, as relieved as Stella had been at the news. "He's a rascal that one, but I never did think Jed had it in him to hurt Elijah."

"But if Jed Kendrick didn't kill Elijah, Stella," Mr. Swenson asked, "then who did?"

A hush of anticipation descended on the room as if to speak or breathe too loudly might chase away the answer. Stella stared at the silver cross clutched in the hand of an ancestral portrait on the wall, listening to the crackle of the fire in the grate. Mack, the dog, barked off in the distance.

"I don't know," Stella admitted, breaking the silence.

"I still don't understand how you fell in," Aunt Ivy said, returning to the earlier topic of Stella's misadventure.

"Indeed. I've taken that ferry a hundred times and never heard of such negligence," the baron said after taking a sip of his sherry.

"I grant you I'll have the ship's captain up on charges for his handling of the situation," Lyndy said, "but it wasn't negligence that caused Miss Kendrick to fall overboard. She was pushed."

"What!" the exclamation echoed when several voices pronounced it at the same time.

"Are you certain?" Mr. Swenson asked.

"Why would anyone do that?" Aunt Ivy added.

"Who pushed you?" Lady Atherly demanded. For once, Lady Atherly wasn't angry at Stella, only adamant to learn who was to blame. "Who was it?"

"Pardon the interruption, Lady Atherly, Lord Atherly...." Inspector Brown, with Constable Waterman, strode through the doorway.

"Finally!" Lyndy slapped his thighs and rose from the settee. "What took you so long?"

"I do apologize, Lord Lyndhurst. I came as quick as I could. And may I say how pleased I was to learn of your safe return, Miss Kendrick."

"Thank you, Inspector."

"May we know the purpose of your visit, Inspector Brown?" Lady Atherly said tersely. "I do hope it's not to subject Miss Kendrick or my son to any more of your questioning. I think they've had enough to deal with for one day."

Did Lady Atherly just say that?

Stella and Lyndy exchanged bewildered glances for the second time. The countess's tone was typical, but her sentiment, the safeguarding of Stella, was unprecedented. Had Lady Atherly found a tenderness for Stella, after all? If so, Stella reevaluated her ordeal. It had been worth it, after all.

"Didn't Lord Lyndhurst and Miss Kendrick tell you?" Inspector Brown said. "I'm here at their request."

"And that being?" Lady Atherly insisted.

"I'm here to catch a killer."

"Would you mind showing the photograph to the baron, Inspector?" Stella said, soon after Lord Atherly excused himself to return to his study, and Lady Alice and the baroness decided to, as the baroness explained, "take a turn in the garden to capture the rare spot of sunshine."

For once, Stella wasn't envious of the ladies' escape outside. After experiencing too much fresh air earlier, she was grateful for the warmth and security of sitting shoulder to shoulder with Lyndy in the crowded drawing room. Besides, this was her chance to get answers.

And Baron Branson-Hill has them.

Uncle Jed's alibi had forced Stella to refocus her suspicions. On the ride back from the coast, her mind had been a muddle of *who* and *why*. Her father had made many enemies, but which one of them killed him? Who pushed her off the ferry, and why? Was it the same person? Was the crime connected to Jesse Prescott? Or was it two separate people, as Lyndy had suggested? Someone with a personal grudge? What with all she'd learned about the Woodhaven Downs scandal, the disgruntled, disreputable jockey, the Isle of Wight ferry, Challacombe, the same name popped up over and over. But Baron Branson-Hill hadn't even been at Keyhaven Castle that day. He couldn't have killed her father, but she was convinced he was the key to figuring out who did.

Inspector Brown retrieved the photograph of Jesse Prescott

from his waistcoat pocket. "Mind it was taken after death," the inspector said. "It's the man who was trampled on the Southampton docks."

"Should I know him?" the baron said, alarmed.

"He had a ticket for the Island ferry," the inspector said. "We think he may have called on someone at your estate."

Baron Branson-Hill solemnly took the photograph, found an empty seat by the French window, and pulled a pair of spectacles out of his inside breast pocket. Mrs. Swenson, not having seen the photo before, hovered nearby.

"I wouldn't if I were you," Aunt Rachel warned when Mrs. Swenson leaned closer to peer over the baron's shoulder. "Not if you don't want to see a fella who looks like the racetrack at the end of a rainy day."

Mrs. Swenson, whether duly warned or embarrassed to be caught peeking, Stella couldn't say, scuttled away like a frightened squirrel to the safety of the opposite settee. Lady Atherly frowned.

"Do you recognize the man, Baron?" Inspector Brown asked.

"I do," the baron said in astonishment. "It was he who delivered Challacombe. He was a nervous, curious little chap. Never got his name, though."

That's it!

Stella caught Lyndy's eye. It was the connection they'd been looking for.

"It was Jesse Prescott," Stella said, knowing the name would mean nothing to the baron. Anyone in the racing world would recognize the name of the disgraced jockey, but Baron Branson-Hill collected horses, he didn't race them. "Did he have anyone with him? Did he say or do anything unusual?"

"No. Rode up on Challacombe, alone. We barely exchanged a dozen words between us."

"And when was this?" Inspector Brown asked.

"About a week ago." The baron scowled in confusion. "I don't understand. What's this all about?"

"We think there's a connection between Mr. Prescott and the person who pushed Stella off the ferry," Lyndy said.

"Jesse Prescott may even have been connected to Daddy's death," Stella added. "Are you sure, Baron, that Mr. Prescott didn't do or say anything that might help us figure out if he was working with or for someone else?"

Before the baron could answer, Inspector Brown, a slight irritation to his voice, said, "Right! If you don't mind, Lord Lyndhurst, Miss Kendrick. I appreciate your aid in the matter, but I prefer to be the one asking the questions."

"Of course, Inspector," Stella said grudgingly.

"Thank you. Now, my lord, did you give this man the money for the horse, or was it your stablemaster?"

"Really, Inspector," Lady Atherly scoffed, perturbed anyone should think the baron so crass as to handle the money personally.

"Indeed," the baron agreed. "No money exchanged hands. That was taken care of through my bank. I had it wired as soon as I took possession of the racehorse."

"And the name of the bank?"

"The Phoenix National Bank of Lexington." The name meant nothing to Stella. From the frown on the inspector's face, it didn't ring any bells for him either.

"And to whom did you wire the money?"

"My bank has the account numbers, of course. Mr. Washington Singer was the animal's previous owner."

"You've undoubtedly been cheated, my good fellow," Sir Owen said to the baron. "I've met Mr. Washington Singer, on several occasions, and I'm afraid he doesn't hail from Kentucky any more than you do."

"But he's an American," the baron protested.

"Owen's right. Mr. Singer was born in New York but has

lived on the Devon coast since he was boy," Lyndy added. "He'd never use a bank in Kentucky."

"Have you spoken to this Mr. Singer?" Inspector Brown asked.

"Well, no. All our correspondences were through telegrams."

Sir Owen poured more sherry into the baron's half-empty glass. "I'm afraid the late Mr. Kendrick got it right, Baron."

"And what did the late Mr. Kendrick get right?" Inspector Brown asked, beating Stella to it.

"He claimed I'd been sold the wrong horse, an imposter if you will, and not the real champion."

The baron, flustered, glanced around for a sympathetic face. He settled on Stella.

She smiled at him warmheartedly, understanding the sting of duplicity, understanding that the baron was another victim of these sad circumstances.

"Don't feel bad, Baron," Sir Owen quipped. "I couldn't bloody well tell the difference."

Lyndy nodded in agreement. "I'll give Mr. Prescott that. He picked an exact look-alike."

"It does make sense," Inspector Brown mused. "Prescott had been convicted of horse switching schemes before. It's reasonable he'd do something like it again. And we have evidence Prescott had been to Doncaster for the races. So, he would've known what the winning horse looked like. But how did he get the look-alike?"

"He must've bought it," Mr. Swenson said.

"Surely, no one would sell a racehorse to a banned criminal?" Sir Owen asked.

"Perhaps they didn't know he was disreputable," Mr. Swenson said.

"And I'm a former beauty queen, Theo," Aunt Rachel said, scrunching her wrinkly nose to prove her point.

"Oh, I reckon anyone who is anyone would know better

than to deal with him," his wife suggested. "Don't you? No offense, Baron," she added when the baron sniffed at the insult.

Mr. Swenson stroked his beard and shrugged.

"Maybe he stole it," Aunt Ivy said.

"Maybe he brought it with him," Stella said when the memory of a Quarter Horse being raised into the hold of an ocean liner that day at Southampton flashed in her mind. "Isn't that something you could check, Inspector?"

Constable Waterman stopped scribbling and looked up from his notebook. "No need, Miss Kendrick. We received a list from the ship's steward's office. Mr. Prescott did ship a thoroughbred horse to England."

"But why would he do that? He couldn't have known Challacombe would win," Penny pointed out.

"You're right," Stella admitted. "He couldn't have. But I'm guessing it didn't matter. Such a remarkable horse would be valuable, win or no win."

"But that still doesn't explain how Prescott got such a horse," Inspector Brown said gruffly.

"In the newspaper accounts covering the Woodhaven Downs scandal, Lord Lyndhurst discovered insinuations that others were involved but were never named," Stella explained. "I think that's where Jesse Prescott got the baron's horse."

"Someone Prescott could still work with," Inspector Brown said, continuing Stella's reasoning. "Someone involved in the scandal but who hadn't been caught."

"Exactly," Stella said. "Someone who my father discovered was as willing to undermine the integrity of the sport as Pistol Prescott was."

"And you think that is why Mr. Kendrick was killed?" Inspector Brown said. "Because he discovered the duplicity of one of his colleagues and was going to expose them?"

"Why not. Isn't that why Jesse Prescott threatened to kill him?"

"Stella's right," Aunt Ivy chimed in. "Like Mr. Swenson so

eloquently said at the funeral, Elijah wholeheartedly believed in the integrity of the sport he owed his life and livelihood to. If he thought someone had done something to diminish the reputation of horse racing, and indirectly himself, I've no doubt he'd make sure the crook was punished."

"But what does any of this have to do with anything?" Penny whined, fiddling in her beaded handbag and pulling out her compact. She flipped it open. "Whoever gave the jockey the horse would be in Kentucky so they couldn't have killed Mr. Kendrick, let alone pushed Stella off the boat."

Penny was right. Everyone involved in the Woodhaven Downs scandal would still be in the States. Or were they?

"You forget the obvious, Miss Swenson," Inspector Brown said. "One highly disreputable chap did come from Kentucky to England before all this happened. Robbed the jockey of his valuables and then, according to Mrs. Robertson's nephew, pushed the jockey under the hooves of runaway horses, thus ridding himself of a liability."

"Uncle Jed?" Stella said, her heart pounding in distress. That's not the conclusion she'd come to.

"And to think I entertained him here at Morrington Hall," Lady Atherly said.

Stella wanted to remind the countess she'd entertained murderers before but, not wanting to upset the newly forged peace between them, held her tongue. But she had no compulsion with the policeman.

"You never said Robbie saw Uncle Jed push Prescott under the horses," Stella said, disappointed the inspector would've held back such a damning accusation. Despite everything, she still believed her uncle incapable of murder.

"Well, Mr. McEwan didn't accuse your uncle by name, but yes, he swore a man fitting Jed Kendrick's description he saw coming out of Pilley Manor was the same as the one who pushed Jesse Prescott. I came to tell you earlier, but you weren't in."

No, I was fighting for my life in the Lymington River, she wanted to say.

"But what about the lighthouse keeper?" Lyndy said. "Mr. Boothroyd told Miss Kendrick he saw her uncle out on the spit. He couldn't have killed his brother."

"But who else could it be?" Mrs. Swenson asked as if they'd already discussed the matter too much.

And then, Stella knew. "It wasn't Uncle Jed whom Robbie McEwan recognized at Pilley Manor. It wasn't Uncle Jed he saw on the wharf that day."

She caught Theo Swenson's eye over his wife's shoulder, resting his hand on the walnut carving on the back of the settee Mrs. Swenson sat on. "It was you."

CHAPTER 26

❧

"You were Jesse Prescott's accomplice. You killed him, and then you killed Daddy," Stella said, struck breathless with the weight of what she knew to be true.

"Well, shut the front door!" Aunt Rachel swore.

"Stella, darling," Mr. Swenson said, chuckling. "I think you're more shaken by that little swim of yours than you care to admit."

"You pushed Stella?" Lyndy flew from his seat with fists raised, bounding toward Mr. Swenson, preparing to lunge at him. He knocked into the table with his knee, rattling the teacups. "You bloody bastard!"

"Oi!" Inspector Brown blocked Lyndy's path with his whole body. "Let's not lose our heads now, Lord Lyndhurst." The inspector silently motioned for Constable Waterman, who had been inconspicuously scribbling down every word in his notebook, to step closer.

Lyndy backed off but began pacing the length of the Persian carpet in front of Stella, like a wolf protecting its den. He stopped once to point an accusing finger at Mr. Swenson, his hand shaking with rage. "I'll see you hang!"

Mrs. Swenson launched to her feet, the stiff silk of her skirt rustling as she confronted Stella. "I will not sit by and hear Theo accused of such horrible things."

With the tips of her ears burning, Stella turned away, noting how a ray of sun seeping through the window struck the whiskey decanter. The light sparkled off the crystal, spraying patches of rainbow colors across the floor. "Horrible but true," she said.

"How can you possibly think that, Stella, darling?" Mr. Swenson said. "You know I've always cared for you."

"Wish I could say the same," Penny muttered under her breath.

"It will be easy enough to have Robbie McEwan identify you," Inspector Brown said.

"I don't deny I was near the runaway horses, Inspector. I was trying to locate our luggage," Mr. Swenson said. "It was chaotic. I wouldn't blame the boy for what he thought he saw. But I didn't kill anybody."

"How do you respond to the charge you killed Mr. Kendrick?" Inspector Brown said.

"Well, that. I was nowhere near the castle tower's top room when Elijah fell. I was in the alley near the courtyard when he cried out. You, yourself, saw me, Stella, darling."

If he calls me darling one more time . . .

"Except it was not Mr. Kendrick who cried out," Inspector Brown said. "The victim was strangled with the drawbridge chains and already dead before he hit the stairs."

"Come again, old chap?" Sir Owen paused as he raised his glass to his lips. "Are you now saying someone else called out?"

"Dr. Lipscombe confirmed it, which means we're unable to use the time of the cry to establish the time of death," Inspector Brown explained.

"But if it wasn't Mr. Kendrick, who was it? And why would anyone do such a thing?" Sir Owen asked.

"To make Mr. Kendrick's death look like an accident?" Aunt Ivy offered. "It was what we all initially thought."

"Perhaps," Inspector Brown said. "More likely, the killer wanted to deceive us into believing Mr. Kendrick was alive long after he'd died."

"Thus, giving the killer an alibi," Stella said, staring at Mr. Swenson, bile rising in her throat. "You even used me as your witness."

"I'm telling you I didn't kill anyone. Think!" Mr. Swenson tapped the side of his head. His condescending tone sent chills through Stella. He sounded like her father. "I couldn't have done it. We all agree the cry came from the tower. I couldn't have gone from the top of the three-story tower to the bottom and then across the courtyard in the short time between the cry and when Stella saw me. It isn't humanly possible."

"You could if you shouted from the bottom of the tower," Penny said, her voice barely above a whisper. "From there it's a few yards to the courtyard."

"Penny?" Stella said. Penny glared at Stella, pure hatred in her eyes, her rouged lips curling into an animal-like snarl.

Maybe Penny had been the one to push me overboard, after all.

"If you know something that would help me in my investigation, Miss Swenson," Inspector Brown insisted, "you are obligated to inform me."

"What could my child have to do with this sordid affair?" Mrs. Swenson said.

"When does it ever have to do with me, Mama?" Penny sneered. "Owen was telling the truth. I was with him, and I did slap him. No one would blame me; he deserved it. Afterward, I went somewhere I could be alone. From the outside tower stairs, the second-story room looked empty. But it was dark, so I didn't notice Mr. Kendrick right away. He was lying there as though he'd flopped headfirst down the stairs. I was going to check on him when the cry echoed up from the ground floor below. I recognized the voice." Penny's gaze shifted, barely moving her head. "It was you, Dad."

"Penny!" Mrs. Swenson cried, shocked by her daughter's betrayal.

Inspector Brown called Constable Waterman into action. The broad-shouldered constable stuffed his notebook in his jacket pocket and marched forward, apprehending Theo Swenson by the arm.

"Theodore Swenson," Constable Waterman said, clamping the accused's wrists with handcuffs, "you are under arrest on suspicion of murdering Jesse James Prescott and Elijah Kendrick."

"Don't listen to my daughter, Inspector," Mrs. Swenson pleaded. "She doesn't know what she's saying."

"I know exactly what I'm saying."

"Why are you doing this?" Mr. Swenson said, scolding his child. "Your mother and I have given you everything. We even came to England to find you a husband."

"And you think murdering Mr. Kendrick helps my chances of finding a husband? Admit it, Dad. You've never done anything just for me in your life."

"You ungrateful child!" Mrs. Swenson exclaimed.

"Penny?" Stella said. "All this time you knew?" No wonder she was willing to let Sir Owen take the blame. Stella had assumed it was to avoid embarrassment over the indiscretion. She had no idea how much Penny was hiding.

"What was I supposed to do? Turn in my father?"

Stella was mortified. But then again, how many times had she covered for her father's multitude of misdeeds.

"Besides, crying out isn't a crime. It wasn't my fault y'all thought it was Mr. Kendrick who'd done it. I never thought it meant my dad killed yours."

"Aunt Ivy was right, wasn't she, Mr. Swenson?" Stella said,

facing her father's killer. "Daddy died because he caught you disgracing the one thing he believed in and threatened to expose you."

Mr. Swenson shook his head solemnly, like he couldn't believe what was happening. "The pigheaded son of a coachman wouldn't listen. He'd turned a blind eye to my involvement in the Woodhaven Downs scandal. He understood what it cost me when the race results were overturned after the scandal broke. So why couldn't he understand how much I needed the cash now? When he saw Charmer switched for Challacombe, he knew what I'd done, that I'd teamed up with Pistol Prescott. But this time, Elijah refused to ignore it. At the castle, he warned me he was going to inform the Jockey Club right after the wedding. I couldn't get him to see reason. What harm was I doing? The baron wasn't ever going to race the horse. But dang it! Turns out, your father valued the sport more than our friendship."

More than he valued me, Stella thought.

"And Jesse Prescott?" Stella asked.

"Our plan was simple. Challacombe was running the St. Leger Stakes, and I had the horse's dead ringer. As Challacombe, Charmer would bring in much needed cash, whether Challacombe won his race or not. It worked in Kentucky, so why not here? So, we shipped Charmer over and passed him off as Challacombe to some unsuspecting Brit." Theo Swenson shrugged at Baron Branson-Hill, who, pale and stricken with grief, slumped in his chair. "I was to meet Pistol at the fruit sellers by the wharf when I arrived from New York, pay him, and part ways. Like Elijah, if Pistol could've just kept from shooting his mouth off . . ."

"And Stella?" Lyndy said coldly, his hands clutching his jacket lapels. "You could've killed her!"

Stella held her breath, expecting Mr. Swenson to deny it, expecting Penny to fess up to an impulsive bout of anger and jealousy. But Penny, like everyone else, waited expectantly for the answer.

"Dad?"

"How was I supposed to know the water would be so cold? Besides, she was in mourning. Who knew she'd throw all convention to the wind and come with us?"

"Anyone who knows her," Lady Atherly scoffed.

"You must believe I never intended for you to drown, Stella, darling," Mr. Swenson pleaded. "I knew you were a good swimmer. I never planned for any of this to happen."

She'd assumed someone had pushed her overboard to prevent her from talking to the baron. That was her mistake. It hadn't been the baron Mr. Swenson hadn't wanted her to see.

"But you couldn't risk me seeing the baron's Challacombe," Stella said. Charmer, though rarely finishing in the money, had been a favorite of Stella's. He and Tully had been born on the same day. "At least not until you'd left the country. Like my father, I would've recognized Charmer the moment I saw him."

Theo Swenson didn't deny it.

"Take him away, will you, Waterman," Inspector Brown said. "If you'll excuse us then," Inspector Brown said, with a curt nod before slapping his hat on his head and following Mr. Swenson and the constable through the door.

As Mrs. Swenson gathered up all the dignity she could before following her husband, Penny turned on Stella. "This is all your fault, Stella Kendrick." She raised her handbag and whipped it at Stella's face.

As Stella dodged out of the way, Lyndy snatched it in midair, yanking it from Penny's grip. He flung it back at Penny's feet. With the compact inside, it hit with a loud clang.

"Fulton!" Lady Atherly snapped. The butler promptly appeared. "Mrs. Swenson and her daughter were just leaving. Be sure to show them the way out."

"Very good, my lady."

"Who would want to stay a moment longer in this dingy old place, anyway?" Mrs. Swenson scoffed.

Lady Atherly, her back as straight as a hat pin, ignored the fuming Mrs. Swenson and smoothed her skirts as if brushing the memory of the woman from her mind before she'd even left the room. Frustrated at not getting a bigger reaction, Mrs. Swenson grabbed her daughter's arm and jerked Penny along as the heels of their shoes marked their steady retreat.

Stella almost felt sorry for her childhood friend. Surrounding Stella were people who cared for her, even loved her. Even the ancestral portraits on the walls seemed to have circled the room in her defense. Penny faced a bleaker future.

Lyndy came to stand beside Stella, gently curling his arm protectively around her shoulder. "It's over now," he whispered in her ear when the room grew quiet. He eased them both down onto the settee opposite his mother. Stella sighed, relaxing into Lyndy's embrace, relieved. He was right. She'd found the answers and the justice she'd been seeking. They could finally get on with their lives.

As if reading her mind, Lyndy added, "What say you to marrying me, Miss Stella Kendrick? Tomorrow, if not sooner."

Stella turned to face him. He tried to feign boredom, fiddling with the silver cuff links on his sleeve, but a smile played on his lips.

"And throw convention to the wind?" she said teasingly, catching Lady Atherly's grimace and the expectant joy in her aunts' faces. "I don't mind if I do."

CHAPTER 27

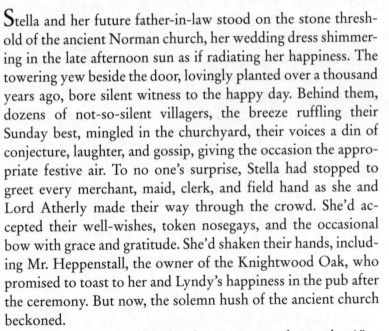

Stella and her future father-in-law stood on the stone threshold of the ancient Norman church, her wedding dress shimmering in the late afternoon sun as if radiating her happiness. The towering yew beside the door, lovingly planted over a thousand years ago, bore silent witness to the happy day. Behind them, dozens of not-so-silent villagers, the breeze ruffling their Sunday best, mingled in the churchyard, their voices a din of conjecture, laughter, and gossip, giving the occasion the appropriate festive air. To no one's surprise, Stella had stopped to greet every merchant, maid, clerk, and field hand as she and Lord Atherly made their way through the crowd. She'd accepted their well-wishes, token nosegays, and the occasional bow with grace and gratitude. She'd shaken their hands, including Mr. Heppenstall, the owner of the Knightwood Oak, who promised to toast to her and Lyndy's happiness in the pub after the ceremony. But now, the solemn hush of the ancient church beckoned.

Lord Atherly patted her hand. "Are you ready, my dear?"

Tully neighed as if to answer for Stella. Stella beamed back at her beloved horse, with Mr. Gates just beyond the stone wall. The mare wasn't allowed inside the church, but Stella had made it clear she wasn't going to get married without Tully present.

"I think that would be a yes," Stella laughed.

"As I said before, dear girl, I am honored to be giving you away, but I do wish your father could've been here to do it. He so wanted to see you wed."

Despite the mixed emotions Stella held about her father, she couldn't help being grateful he'd brought about this moment.

"Yes. Yes, he did."

With such short notice, and in acknowledgment of Stella's mourning status, they'd all agreed to the same small, quiet affair they'd first planned in June. Back then, she'd been blindsided by her father into an arranged engagement. *How things have changed.* When she and Lord Atherly stepped into the cool, almost chilly hollow of the vestibule, she remembered how these squat, gray, ancient stone walls once cast shadows of uncertainty over her future. Now, with her heart racing with the thrill, the anticipation of beginning her new life, she couldn't imagine marrying anywhere else.

The tiny church, fragrant with the fresh flowers arranged by Lady Atherly and matching the ones in Stella's hand: cream, pink and peach dahlias, deep green ivy, and delicate Queen Anne's lace, was more than half empty. Seated in the pews on the groom's side were Lady Atherly, Lady Alice, Sir Alfred, and the full staff from Morrington Hall. On the opposite side of the aisle, her father and Uncle Jed, still in jail for robbing Jesse Prescott, were conspicuously missing. But Aunt Ivy with Sammy, in a new suit, waited with eager faces from the front pew. Behind them, to Stella's delight, were the Baron and Baroness Branson-Hill. Despite the baron's humiliation at the hands of her father's friend, the baron's choice of pew signaled to everyone he'd forgiven Stella her association with the Swensons and that she retained his friendship. The news would spread through the Forest like a fire. Lady Atherly, when she'd learned of the baron's intention, had been visibly pleased.

Behind the Branson-Hills sat Inspector Brown and behind him, the staff of Pilley Manor: Mr. Tims, Mrs. Robertson, her nephew, Robbie McEwan—who had positively identified Theo Swenson—Mrs. Downie, and Ethel. It was right they should be there. Stella, in her way, had come to think of them too as family. She'd make sure they always had a place in her home if they wanted it. Gertie, her flower girl, squirming with excitement in green silk ribbons and a new lace pinafore, and Aunt Rachel, "tickled as pink as a pig" when Stella had asked her chaperone to be her maid of honor, waited with her in the vestibule.

On the altar, Reverend Paine, dour and taking his responsibility seriously, waited in his ceremonial robes. Before the vicar stood Lyndy, handsome in his long coattails, his face wearing the same stoic expression as the day they'd met. He was intently listening to something Sir Owen, his best man, was saying. Her throat tightened when a surge of adoration for her groom caught her off guard.

Suddenly, as if on cue, the stones hummed with the power of the organ as Dowland's "The King of Denmark's Gaillard" rang out. Aunt Rachel shooed Gertie ahead. She winked at Stella before hobbling down the aisle behind the flower girl, a small bouquet in one hand, her cane in the other.

The wedding guests rose, every pair of eyes following Stella as Lord Atherly escorted her down the center aisle. She glided toward the altar, never feeling so light or so merry. She stifled a giggle at Lyndy's sudden slack jaw when he first caught sight of her.

After Lord Atherly relinquished her into Lyndy's care, taking his seat beside Lady Atherly, Stella wholeheartedly beamed at her groom. For the first time since she'd known him, he couldn't keep that characteristically thin, crooked grin off his face. She longed to reach for him, kiss him, whisper to him but turned dutifully toward the vicar instead.

With the last strains of music still echoing in her ears, Reverend Paine announced, "We have come together in the sight of God for the joining in marriage of this man, Edwin Henry Searlwyn, the Right Honorable Viscount Lyndhurst, to this woman, Stella Eleanor Kendrick."

The service moved on, sweeping Stella away with it. Overwhelmed with emotion, Stella heard little of Reverend Paine's address to the congregation until he declared, "If anyone can show why they may not lawfully be joined in marriage, speak now, or hereafter remain in silence." She, like everyone else, turned when the outside door opened, and the rush of wind stirred up dried leaves that littered the churchyard.

A middle-aged woman in a high-necked gown of lavender silk and lace and a wide-brimmed hat, hesitated at the end of the aisle. Aunt Ivy, smiling, nodded to the woman in acknowledgment.

Beside Stella, Aunt Rachel exclaimed softly, "As I live and breathe."

Stella glanced at her aunt questioningly, but Aunt Rachel avoided her gaze. Who was this woman both her aunts seem to know?

Reverend Paine waited as if the stranger had come to prevent the wedding, but the woman, hiding her face with the tilt of her hat, said nothing, taking a seat alone near the back. The rustling of silk against the wooden pews, a few stifled coughs, and the congregation turned to face the altar again. The vicar continued with the service, and before Stella knew it, he announced the speaking of the vows. Lyndy, with calm authority, recited his. Stella, her heart nearly bursting, paused once or twice, as she said hers. That satisfactorily done, Lyndy took her hand and slipped the gold wedding band on her finger.

With a hint of a mischievous smirk at the corner of his mouth, he said, "With this ring, I thee wed, with my body, I thee worship, and with all my worldly goods I thee endow: In the name of the Father, the Son, and the Holy Ghost. Amen."

When the vicar pronounced them man and wife, Lyndy wrapped his arm around her waist and pulled her against him, several gasps, giggles, and claps encouraging him. He smelled of a new musky cologne when he kissed her, briefly but hard, his lips hinting of all the passion yet to come. They too quickly parted, leaving her slightly breathless and unbearably happy.

They turned to applause and passed down the aisle, arm in arm, husband and wife, accepting well-wishes as the organ pumped out Henry Purcell's "Trumpet Tune and Air." Lyndy shook every man's hand; Stella had a smile for everyone.

When they reached Aunt Ivy, she said excitedly, "There's someone I want you to meet, Stella." Waving the late arrival forward, she added, "Oh, how I've prayed this day would come."

The woman shyly approached, slowly lifting the rim of her hat back from her face. Stella gasped. Despite telltale signs of aging, Stella would know that lovely, heartbreaking face anywhere.

But it's impossible! Her mind was playing tricks on her again.

"Lord Lyndhurst, Lady Lyndhurst," Aunt Ivy said, the first to use Stella's new title, "may I introduce Mrs. Eugene Smith."

Mrs. Eugene Smith? Stella had heard the name once before, as someone Inspector Brown was making inquiries about. She couldn't be who Stella had mistaken her for.

Could she?

"Pleased to meet you, Mrs. Smith," Lyndy was saying. Stella couldn't bring herself to talk. "And how do you know Mrs. Mitchell?"

"I'm her sister."

"But that would mean you and my wife are also related."

Lyndy's quizzical expression nearly made Stella laugh as confusion, longing, and hope sought to overwhelm her.

"You are correct, Lord Lyndhurst," Mrs. Smith said, observing Stella's reaction with eyes that could be Stella's reflection staring back at her. Mrs. Smith smiled, with a joy intimately entangled with a sadness only Stella understood.

"So that would make you my wife's . . . ?" Lyndy said, his confusion written on his face.

With a weight on her chest making it hard to breathe, Stella forced out the word she never thought she'd utter to this woman again, "Mama."

Mrs. Smith, once known as Katherine Tully Kendrick, opened her arms and Stella, without hesitation, flew into them.

CHAPTER 28

⁓

Stella, seated at her dressing table, regarded Ethel's reflection remove the orange blossom tiara and veil from Stella's hair. The soft strains of music wafted up from the grand saloon below. The toasts had been made, the cakes had been cut, and Stella was soon to leave for her honeymoon. As Ethel attacked the buttons down the back of Stella's wedding dress, a quiet tap on the door preceded Aunt Ivy and Mama as they joined Stella and her maid in the bedroom. Stella beamed at her mother through the mirror. She still couldn't believe this wasn't a dream. And yet, a hint of melancholy tainted the sight of her mother standing there.

"Oh, how lovely you are," Mama said, smiling back but with a restraint in her posture that evoked the unspoken awkwardness still between them. "I still can't believe what a bright, vivacious, courageous, beautiful woman you've become." Sadness, perhaps at years lost, tinted her voice.

"We know you are heading off soon and wanted to say our good-byes in private," Aunt Ivy said, congenially, seemingly unaware of the war of emotions bouncing between mother and daughter.

During the reception, Stella had learned from Aunt Ivy how she'd kept in touch with her sister, even after she'd supposedly died. She explained that they'd traveled to England together (That had been Mama Stella saw in Southampton!) and had corresponded daily since arriving (hence Aunt Ivy's deception). From her mother, Stella had learned of her life in Montana with Eugene Smith, her second husband, and young son (Stella had a half brother.). Yet Stella was plagued by questions. She'd stifled them, not wanting to dispel the magic of her mother's return. But, knowing of her imminent departure, couldn't hold her tongue a moment longer.

With Ethel finished unbuttoning her, Stella slipped her arms out, stood, and stepped out of her dress. "Why didn't you tell me?"

"Tell you what, sugar?" Mama said, instinctually bending over to help Ethel pick up the dress. The term of endearment brought back a rush of tender memories.

"That you were still alive?"

"I couldn't. If I did, Elijah would've disinherited you, disowned you. I couldn't risk it. Besides, I'd remarried," Mama added. "If Elijah found out, he'd have me arrested for bigamy. I managed to tell Ivy though, without Elijah knowing, and made her promise to stay as close to you as she could."

"Then one day, Elijah found a letter I'd written to your mother, and he sent me away too," Aunt Ivy interjected, explaining why she had left Stella's life abruptly.

"Are you saying Daddy knew you were alive and purposely staying away?"

"Knew? He insisted on it."

Could this be true? Yet Stella knew her father. How could she doubt it? Look at the lengths he'd gone to force her into this marriage.

"But why? I thought he loved you."

"He did, once." Mama's face saddened, her voice dropping to a whisper. "But not enough to forgive what I did."

"What did you do, Mama?" Stella asked as Ethel helped her into her traveling dress.

"I'm not proud of it, but . . ." Her mother raised her chin, in an eerie imitation of Lady Atherly. "But your father was so difficult, so inattentive. . . . I fell in love with someone else—Eugene, my husband. Elijah found out. He wouldn't forgive me or divorce me or let me take you. Instead, I was dead to him, and you."

"You're back now."

"When I read the announcement of your wedding in the newspaper"—Stella's mother reached over and cupped Stella's cheek—"I had to come. I had to know you were marrying a man who would make you happy. And seeing you together, I know he does."

Stella suddenly remembered the thoughtful gift with no name. "It was you who sent me the souvenir spoon," Stella said, holding her mother's hand on her face.

"I did."

"And the unsigned sympathy card?"

Her mother nodded. "That one I regret, sugar. Elijah was your father, and you were mourning him. I shouldn't have let my feelings for him get the best of me."

"Thank you." She almost added that her mother was right. Stella was better off without him, but she wasn't prepared to say it out loud yet. If ever.

"I would've called on you myself, but I didn't know how you'd handle another shock. I came to the wedding instead."

Another knock on the door and Mrs. Nelson, the housekeeper, peeked in. "The train leaves at half past, my lady."

Will I ever get used to being called that? Stella acknowledged the need to leave with a nod, adjusted her hat in the mirror quickly, and turned to go.

"I've missed so much," her mother said, rushing to grab Stella's hand. "And now you're leaving so soon."

"My honeymoon won't last forever. And when you go back

to Montana, Lyndy and I can visit you," Stella reassured her, squeezing her hand. "We have our whole lives to get reacquainted."

"Oh, sugar," her mother said, a slight catch in her throat when she let go of Stella's hand.

Aunt Ivy and her mother accompanied Stella to the top of the stairs, but Stella descended alone. Lyndy was waiting for her at the bottom.

"Our carriage awaits. Shall we, Lady Lyndhurst?" He held out his hand.

Lifting her skirts, she floated down to him. "Oh, Lyndy, I do love the sound of that."

Not because it meant she'd achieved the social status her father so craved but because it meant she belonged to someone, to something bigger than herself. She wasn't born to the name, she didn't buy the name, but was granted it through love.

She took his hand, her gold wedding ring glimmering in the light of the stained-glass window above. The manor, her mother, the music faded away.

"And I love you, Lady Lyndhurst," Lyndy said, adoration shining on his face as he raised her hand to his lips. "And I shall . . . always."

ACKNOWLEDGMENTS

While in the New Forest researching this book, I was fortunate to encounter several people who went above and beyond to aid me in my pursuit of minute details. To these, I say thank you: the ever-helpful staff of the New Forest Heritage Museum and Christopher Tower Reference Library; the wonderful guides of New Forest Platinum Tours who cheerfully drove me everywhere I wanted to go, regardless of the strangeness of the request; and Ron Kirby, a particularly gracious and knowledgeable gentleman who, despite the pouring rain, gave me what became a private walking tour of Lymington. As always, it is my fault if I got the details wrong. Having written most of this book during a pandemic, I leaned more heavily than usual on my support network at home: my fellow Sleuths in Time writers; the ladies of my book club; my dear friend, Jacqueline Clark Fisher; and my family. All without whom. Thank you!

AUTHOR'S NOTE

Although the New Forest is famous for its sweeping heath-land and stands of ancient oaks, it also boasts miles of coastline. There you will find grassy coastal cliffs, sandy and shingle beaches, saltmarsh, mudflats, and lagoons. In addition to the city of Lymington, the coastline is dotted by villages like Barton on Sea, Milton on Sea, and Keyhaven. Flanking approximately either end of the New Forest coastline are the medieval castles of Calshot and Hurst. It was Hurst Castle, set out at the southern end of a coastal spit, that I primarily modeled my fictional Keyhaven Castle on. It was built by King Henry VIII between 1541 and 1544 using the stone from the nearby dissolved Beaulieu Abbey. England is dotted with such castles, many that were open to the curious eyes of Edwardian sightseers. Hurst Castle, however, was not one of them. From its onset, Hurst Castle was an important artillery fort used to defend England against foreign invasion until as recent as 1956. Luckily, it is now a museum. I spent a very fulfilling day wandering its narrow halls, climbing its spiraling stone stairs, and admiring the breathtaking views from the top.

One of the joys of writing historical fiction is the ability to weave historical facts into the fictional story I've created. And as always, I've tried very hard to get my factual details right. Southampton was (and still is) a bustling port (most famous as the origin port for the RMS Titanic) just a few miles outside the New Forest and if you were by the docks in the early part of the 20th century, you couldn't have missed the exotic banana display at Snook's Fruit Market. Likewise strolling the New Forest in 1905, it wouldn't have been unusual to walk beneath the spreading limbs of an oak tree (one bearing a name like Knightwood Oak and Eagle Oak) that was at least 500 years old. As to the practice of using horse "ringers," the switching of one racehorse for another was cause for scandal throughout the 19th and 20th centuries. But occasionally, to make the story work, I'm forced to take a few liberties with the truth. One example of this is the horse that placed in the St. Leger Stakes in 1905. Challacombe, the winner of the St. Leger Stakes, the oldest of the British classic horse races and the final leg of the British Triple Crown, was the real champion. In my story, the Kendricks' Thoroughbred Tupper takes second in the race. In reality, it was a three-year-old colt named Polymelus, owned by the Marquess of Crewe. Another example is the .38 revolver claimed to be owned by Jesse James. My research never uncovered such a gun. However, Jesse James's mother was notorious in crediting hundreds of guns as once belonging to her infamous deceased son. I modeled Jesse James Prescott's revolver after one supposedly belonging to Mrs. Zerelda Mimms James, the outlaw's widow.